ADA
THE
COSTER GIRL

Lynette Rees

© Lynette Rees 2021
Contact Lynette:
http://www.lynetterees.com
Blogs:
https://lynetterees.wordpress.com/
http://www.nettiesramblings.blogspot.com
email: craftyscribe@yahoo.com
Facebook author page for latest updates:
http://www.facebook.com/authorlynetterees/

Chapter One
Whitechapel, London
June 1888

Twelve-year-old, Ada Cooper, blinked in the semi darkness of the low beamed bedroom. It was almost midnight. Her older sister, Connie, was getting herself dressed by candlelight—the flickering flame throwing a dancing shadow on the wall behind her. Where on earth was she off to at this time of the night? Ada rubbed her weary eyes. It was only six months ago their parents had been taken with the consumption. Up until now, Connie had managed to scrape a pittance of a living together to take care of Ada and their younger brother, Sam, doing this by working long shifts at the match factory at Bow. They hardly got to see her of late, so for her to be going out at this time of the night when she needed to rise early the following morning made no sense whatsoever.

'Connie!' Ada hissed, 'where yer off to this time a night?'

'Sssh,' Connie soothed putting her index finger to her lips as she softly whispered, 'We just need a few things for breakfast for the morning, 'tis all. I will be back before you know it, by the time you wake up. Take care of Sam for me till I return.'

Ada glanced at the lifeless form beside her, her brother was usually dead to the world once he'd drifted off to sleep, there was no rousing him. Even when a mouse had scarpered over their shared bed, he'd not felt it nor heard it squeaking. But the scratches from rodents along the wooden skirting boards, disturbed Ada's sleep many a night in this rented place. It was only two rooms, a bedroom, and a living room with a small cooking range over the fire. The privy was shared between five other apartments in the tenement block and sometimes, like when it was summertime and the weather was hot, the place smelled rancid. Then she felt she'd rather pee behind a bush than in that horrible toilet outside. Then in winter if it were cold enough, the ice would need breaking on the toilet pan itself as it froze solid. A paraffin lamp was left in there, suspended on a hook from the cistern, in the hope it wouldn't freeze over too much, but often it did.

Connie leaned over the bed to peck Ada on the forehead, and as she did so, Ada inhaled the odour of sweet parma violets. Her sister was wearing her best perfume, but why? 'Go to sleep,' she whispered to Ada.

Ada had little choice but to nod at her. 'All right. Promise you'll come back though?'

'Of course, I'll return. I said so, didn't I? And if Sam gets up in the night keep an eye on him.'

'I will.' Though she knew he wouldn't rouse, sometimes she wished he would as if he got himself into a real deep slumber then he wet the bed and the sheets needed washing and drying the following day. It was a bloomin' nuisance and made more work for her whilst her sister was at the factory.

Ada heard the bedroom door click shut and then her sister's boots click-clacking on the tiled floor of the landing, clip-clopping down the wooden stairs, then the main outer door shut behind her. A shiver ran the length of Ada's spine now that her sister had left them all alone. In the daytime, it had been fine as she felt safe, the only one she and her brother feared then was Mr Winterbourne, the rent man. On more than one occasion, Connie had warned both children not to answer the door to him. It was really a question of borrowing from Peter to pay Paul sometimes. It was better than going starving at any rate. So, Connie would avoid the rent man for a few days and then cough up what they owed, a little behind time when they had the money. Sometimes Winterbourne became angry with her for doing so and threatened to turf the family out of the hovel. Ada had no idea what sort of arrangement Connie had with the man, but so far, she'd managed to keep both him and the wolf at the door at bay, but then again, Ada reminded herself that maybe Winterbourne was the very wolf himself.

Apart from hearing the couple from the apartment below coming in late and going to bed as they sang loudly off the top of the heads, no doubt after consuming several gins at the pub on the corner, Ada heard no more as she drifted off to a silent slumber.

***

Slivers of daylight filtered into the bedroom through the thin, moth eaten curtains when Ada awoke the following morning realising that something was very wrong. It was much lighter than it should be for when Connie rose to go to work at the match factory. Usually, it was still dark outside. Startled, she leapt out of bed to see her sister's bed hadn't been slept in, it was still neatly made, and her nightgown folded on top of it. Could she have arrived home and not wishing to disturb her brother and sister, left them asleep while she got ready for work? But no, Ada was always such a light sleeper, she would have heard her sister pouring water into the basin to wash her face and hands before starting work or she'd have heard other noises like the kettle boiling for tea. Connie liked to eat some breakfast before she got to the factory as they were forced to eat their food there at their workstations, and she'd said on more than one occasion, they were reprimanded for taking visits to the toilet and washroom, even their pay could be docked without warning for it. So, she liked to have a big breakfast when they could afford it of porridge and toast and a tin mug of tea before setting off. That way she'd go most of her shift with no food inside her at all, only a cup of tea at work as she felt it was safer to drink from a mug or cup than it was to lift a slice of bread and jam to her lips with powdery fingers.

Ada glanced at Sam who was still asleep beside her, thankfully, this was one occasion when he hadn't drenched the bed. Nudging him with her elbow, she said, 'Come on. It's later than I thought it was. I don't know where our Connie is this morning, but I think something might be up.'

Sam groaned and opened one eye and then another. 'Maybe sshhhe's in the yard getting water from the pumpsh,' he said sounding unintelligible, like the pair of drunks she'd heard staggering from the public house into their apartment below last night. Of course, she realised Sam was still half asleep.

'You go and use the privy before you 'ave an' accident with your bladder again,' she warned, 'I'll go and put the kettle on to boil and make us breakfast.'

He nodded and smiled and then rubbing his eyes with both fists, he let out a loud yawn. 'What then?' he asked.

'Then we go to look for our Connie,' she said solemnly. 'We need to find her.'

***

By the time Sam had returned, Ada had put the kettle on to boil on the fire and was in the midst of searching the cupboards to see what she could make them for breakfast. Usually there was some oatmeal around, but the small hessian sack was empty. Maybe that's why Connie had gone out late last night to try to buy some, but why hadn't she returned home as yet?

'We'll have to make do with some bread and scrape,' she said to her brother. There was only a large stale crust left that had seen better days but with some dripping in the tin spread over it, it would go down a treat on a cold day. There was no milk in the jug either so they'd have to have their tea without it but at least there would be something hot inside them to set them up for the day.

Following breakfast, they washed and dressed, Ada ensuring that Sam put his woollen socks on inside his boots as both had small holes in the soles from wear and tear. They were stuffed with newspaper and Connie had promised next time she got her pay that she'd take them to the cobbler's shop to be re-soled. They just couldn't afford to purchase new shoes at the moment. Ada also insisted he wore a second jumper over the first and then he put on his twill jacket which was getting too small for him as it was riding up well over his wrists. She donned her warmest dress, thick woollen stockings and took a second shawl with her. It was going to be a perishing walk over to the Bryant and May factory. Even though it was early summer it had done nothing but rain so far throughout the month of June. Her plan was to hang around the gates outside to ask if anyone had seen their Connie or if they could pass a message on to her. At this time of day, the outworkers often queued up to purchase the cardboard, glue and string to assemble the boxes at home. They were paid a pittance for their trouble but it was something that the whole family could help with and deemed safer than working on the factory floor with the white powder at any rate.

Ada worried about her big sister at times as she'd heard tales of how some of the girls and women lost their teeth after working at that place as some sort of disease ravaged their features, eating away at their jawbones. Not only that, but some lost their hair too and even their lives because of the white powder that was going into the matches. She'd heard her sister refer to the condition as "Phossy Jaw". It was a risky occupation for her sister, that was for certain.

It took Ada and Sam a good twenty minutes of walking through torrential rain to arrive at the factory gates. The rain was cold and hard as it hammered down in little darts on their frail bodies. Ada had the second shawl over her head to give her some protection, but it was sodden through. She looked at her brother as she saw the droplets of rain fall from his peaked cap and dribble down his face. He sniffed loudly and then began to cough. Maybe she should have left him back home but she feared Winterbourne might break down the door this time to get his rent money as it was the longest it had ever been due and Connie wouldn't have been there to sweet talk the man this time.

Ada's heart sank when she saw all the girls and women waiting in a line to pick up the materials they needed for a day's work. Her spirits lifted when she recognised one middle aged lady who lived in the same street. 'Excuse me, Mrs James,' she said looking up at the woman who appeared as drenched as she was.

The woman looked at her and smiled. 'Hello, Ada, me love. How are you?'

'I'm all right ta. I'm looking for our Connie. Have you seen her?'

'No dear.' The woman's dark grey eyes searched her own and then she frowned. 'Is there anything wrong then?'

'I don't know to be honest.' Ada swallowed a lump that had formed in her throat. 'She went out real late last night and hasn't come back home. I thought maybe she'd gone straight into work here and she might have passed you.'

Mrs James smiled and nodded in a kindly fashion. 'I understand, ducks. If I see her, I'll tell her you was looking, shall I?'

'Yes, please, if you will.'

Mrs James had a strange expression on her face at that point and Ada wasn't sure what she was thinking. Was it sympathy or concern in her eyes? Or maybe both? What would the woman be thinking about their Connie stopping out all night long?

A tall, spindly woman, with a shock of flaming red hair came striding towards the children. 'Did I 'ear you askin' about Connie Cooper?' she asked, her green eyes flashing.

Ada didn't like the look of her, she looked very brazen, and her manner was brash. 'Yes. Do you know where she might be?'

'Not now darlin' but she weren't half knocking the port and lemons back at The Duke of Wellington last night.'

Ada frowned. Surely the woman must be mistaken? Connie wouldn't have had the money to pay for one glass of port never mind several glasses. 'Are you sure?' Ada gave her a hard stare, surely the woman was lying?

'Course I'm sure, I was in there meself, weren't I. What's a girl to do on a cold evening when she could be warming the cockles of 'er own heart and somebody else's!' She tipped back her head and laughed uproariously. How dare this so-called lady make fun of her sister.

'Who was she with then?' Ada challenged.

'Can't say I knew him meself, he was a stranger to the pub, but looked well-dressed enough to me. Plenty of coppers in that gentleman's coffers!'

Ada scowled. 'Did you see where she went afterwards?'

The woman shrugged. 'Don't keep tabs on her, do I?' Then she frowned. 'Didn't she come home last night?' She drew in close with a look of concern in her eyes. Her earlier offhand manner now disappearing.

By now Ada was close to tears. 'No,' she sniffed.

'Aw, look at them poor kids!' an old lady commented loudly to the women around her. 'They're looking for their sister.'

There was a lot of mumbling, then someone shouted. 'Kids, go and see the foreman at the head of the queue and ask whether your sister showed up for work today. That's the best thing to do.'

There were murmurs of agreement as the woman with red hair, pushed Ada forward. 'Go on gal, go and ask him.'

Ada took her brother's hand and slowly, with many pairs of eyes on them, they walked to the head of the queue where the foreman was handing out cardboard boxes of matchmaking equipment.

'Sorry, I've got enough people for today!' The foreman said as he appraised Ada and Sam from outside the large red brick imposing building. The wrought iron gates were there to keep the workers in and the riff raff out, whilst a clock in the centre of the building was there to ensure the workers were all aware of what time of day it was, else they'd be docked a morning's wage for being late.

Ada cleared her throat. It was important they find Connie so she wasn't about to lose her chance. 'We're not seeking work, sir. We're looking for our sister who works here. She didn't come home last night.'

He stared hard at both children. 'What's her name?'

'Constance Cooper, Connie,' said Ada.

'I know that name.' He smiled as if he wanted to help them out. Then ran his hand over his black moustache as if in contemplation. Finally, he shouted to summon a young lad who was stood behind him to go and check whether Connie Cooper was at work or not today.

It seemed an age while Ada and Sam stood there watching the women paying the foreman for their matchmaking boxes of equipment. Then finally, the boy stood on his toes to whisper something in the foreman's ear behind his cupped hand. The man shook his head and then looking at the kids, gravely announced, 'Sorry, your sister didn't make it into work this morning. If she doesn't show up tomorrow, I won't be able to keep her job open for her. As you can see there's plenty of able and willing workers who would only too gladly take her place. If you do see her later, tell her that as a warning from me. There's many others who work here who wouldn't warn her mind, they'd immediately sack her on the spot!'

Ada nodded sadly. 'Thank you, sir. If she does turn up later today, please don't sack her.'

The foreman looked at her with compassion in his eyes. 'I'll do my best, but she will get her wages docked accordingly, mind you, and a severe ticking off from the management.'

Ada thanked him and both children made their way past the queue which appeared to have grown even longer than when they first arrived on the scene. She felt totally bereft as she heard the sighs and mutters of sympathy for them both as they walked away.

It seemed as if their big sister had vanished into thin air. And who was the gent she went to meet last night? That didn't make sense at all.

Chapter Two

Stunned that their sister hadn't shown up for work as yet, Ada and Sam trudged home along the shiny wet pavements, across cobbled streets, dodging puddles and the odd horse and cart before it split them in half on their way to Harlington House on Sycamore Street. Ada still clinging on to the faint hope that when she turned the key in the lock she'd find Connie there with a big beaming smile on her face, the fire roaring away in the grate and the smell of apple pie wafting towards them. But when she inserted the key in the door and turned it, the first thing she noticed was the fire in the grate had gone out. The room was dank, damp and perishing cold as her heart plummeted to her sodden boots. They needed that fire lit to get themselves warm again and to dry their drenched clothing.

'Take everything off, Sam!' Ada commanded, 'I'll fetch a blanket to wrap you in while I try to get this fire going again.' There were a couple of logs and a shovelful of coal beside the hearth that Connie had put there the previous evening, she'd use those for time being and then beg or borrow what she needed afterwards.

Sam nodded, and shivering, removed his sodden clothing and tossed them in a heap on the floor, which Ada immediately retrieved to string on the small rope line that her sister had constructed over the fireplace. It would have to suffice for now. She removed her own clothing and did the same thing, then she donned her old linsey wool dress that was a size too small for her and wrapped a blanket from her sister's bed around her shoulders while she went off in search of a box of matches. To her dismay, the matchbox on the mantel was empty. Could this day get any worse for her? Tears were near to the surface now, but she fought to keep them at bay. Could she borrow some matches from someone or get a spill to take a light from someone else's fire? Mrs Adler who lived across the landing was a nice sort, she'd knock on her door.

'I won't be long, Sam,' she said firmly trying to keep the boy's spirits up. 'We ain't got no matches for me to light this flippin' fire and our Connie working at a match factory and all!' She huffed out a breath of disbelief. 'I'm going to give Mrs Adler's door a knock.'

Her brother gazed at her, his chocolate brown eyes seemed huge this morning. Then he nodded and coughed harshly. That cough didn't seem to be getting any better. Why did life have to be so unfair?

She left the room with the door ajar as she didn't want Sam to get frightened, then she rapped her knuckles on Mrs Adler's door. The puce paint was peeling off it, the landlord never kept up with repairs in the building, yet he expected the rent paid on time each week from his tenants.

There was no answer and Ada feared Mrs Adler was out shopping at the marketplace, but then quite suddenly, the door swung open, and she was looking up into the kindly hazel eyes of the middle aged woman, who always looked nicely turned out. She had very dark hair with hardly a grey hair for a woman of her age, neatly coiffed into a bun, her gold rimmed round specs were perched on her nose and her dark blue dress seemed to speak of another age to Ada. The neckline was very high and with a white frill that reached the woman's chin. She did admire her so. Connie had said that the Adlers had arrived in this country from somewhere in Eastern Europe maybe it was Czechoslovakia or Hungary, she couldn't remember which. She barely recalled Mr Adler, who had passed away a couple of years since, all she remembered was a little wizened old man whose stature appeared small beside his elegant, tall wife. Mrs Adler had told Connie that her husband was a clockmaker and that's about all they really knew about him, except that he'd evidently been a hard worker as he'd toiled from dawn until dusk, often bringing work home with him.

'Hello, dear,' Mrs Adler said kindly. '*Vat* brings you to my door?'

'Hello, Mrs Adler. I was wondering if you have any spare matches so I can light a fire for me and my brother?'

'Of course, but *vere's* your Connie, is she in work today or is she at home *vith* you?'

It always amused Ada that Mrs Adler sounded her Ws as Vs, but not today as she was so concerned about her sister. She was about to tell an untruth as she didn't want the woman to think badly of Connie being out all night, when she decided instead to tell her what had occurred.

When Clara finished relating her tale to the woman, she frowned and shook her head before saying, 'That is very strange indeed. Bring your brother over here and you can both sit in front of my fire and have something to eat and drink. I'll send Jakob to light your fire for you.'

Ada smiled with relief. Jakob was the Adler's only son and a very nice young man he was too. He worked at the local tannery but was sometimes at home during the day if he worked a night shift. 'Thank you so much, Mrs Adler.'

Ada went to relate the good news to Sam, whose eyes lit up like a pair of beacons when his sister explained that not only would they get their fire lit for them, but Mrs Adler was going to feed them too. Quite soon they were seated around the hearth in Mrs Adler's apartment, which seemed so much cosier than their own as she had some nice furniture like a walnut dresser that housed her blue and white tea set and dinner service. At some time or another, the living room walls had been decorated with an embossed flock wallpaper. Ada guessed that maybe the woman's husband had wallpapered the room many years ago, although very pretty, it looked a little worn with age.

'You can toast your own crumpets by the fire,' she said, handing the children a toasting fork each and a plate of crumpets. Ada thanked the woman and Sam licked his lips; he was positively drooling. 'I made them fresh this morning. Then when you've done that I've got a nice bit of salted butter in the larder for you to spread on them.'

Ada smiled; she could think of nothing nicer at that moment. She watched as Mrs Adler went to brew up a pot of tea to warm the children.

At that point, Jakob entered the room, rubbing his hands. 'It's right cold out there,' he said, as if he'd been outdoors and he must have been as Ada watched as he removed his cap, jacket and muffler and smiled at them. 'What you pair doing here then, nippers?' he asked amicably. He did not have a strange accent like his mother, he sounded like a proper Eastender to Ada's ears.

She explained their predicament to him. 'Well, now, that does sound strange your Connie going missing like that.' He frowned. Ada realised long since that Jakob liked her sister and may have been sweet on her, so she did not mention the fact Connie had been spotted with a stranger in a pubic house last night for fear he'd think badly of her sister. She intended to protect her reputation at all costs.

Mrs Adler entered the room carrying a tea pot and several china cups on a tray. She smiled when she saw her son and he bowed down to kiss her rounded cheek. 'Can you go please light the fire for these poor *childen*,' she said. Ada noticing the woman always omitted the letter r in that word. 'They have the kindling but no match for it to set aflame,' she explained.

He smiled. 'Of course, Ma. I'll be two ticks and my tea will still be hot by the time I return.'

'There's a good son you are,' she said her eyes shining as she looked up at him. 'A son to be most proud of. Your Connie could do no *vorse* than to marry my Jakob. I've told her this on more than one occasion,' she said more to herself than anyone else as she tutted and shook her head.

Ada noticed that Jakob's face had flushed bright red, and he quickly exited the room to get the fire alight for them.

As the children sipped the hot tea and ate their crumpets with relish, Ada felt all warm and cosy inside and for a brief time, she almost forgot anything was amiss, until Jakob returned and lifting his teacup asked, 'How's your Connie, then?'

Ada watched his mother's face cloud over as she pulled him to one side and his eyes widened so that the whites were on show. Slowly, he made his way to the fireside and sat in the armchair with his mother seated opposite and both children kneeling comfortably on the rug with their blankets enveloped around them. 'So, you mentioned that Connie didn't come home last night?'

Ada shook her head. 'No, and there was no sign of her this morning either. We walked over to the factory to find her and the foreman asked about, but no one has seen her there either.' She bit her lower lip wondering whether she ought to risk Connie's reputation and tell him the truth about that stranger, but then thought better of it.

'That must be very worrying for you,' Jakob said soberly. 'I can help you look for her, if you like?' He swallowed hard as he took a long sip of his tea while he waited for Ada's answer. Of course, she realised he'd search high and low for their Connie as he thought so much of her.

'Thank you, Jakob,' she said, forcing a smile as her stomach flipped over with the uncertainty of it all.

'Has your sister ever gone missing before, dear?' Mrs Adler asked angling her head on one side.

Ada shook her head vehemently. 'No, never once. If she's promised to come back, then she always has.'

Jakob and his mother exchanged worried glances which unnerved Ada. Then Jakob smiled and said, 'When I've finished this I'll go and look for her. Any special places I could try?'

'What about your sleep?' his mother looked concerned.

'I can go to sleep later, Ma. The sooner I search the better.' He turned to look at Ada. 'Anywhere I can start looking?'

She thought for a moment. 'She sometimes goes to the library of an afternoon. Or shopping in the marketplace,' she said hopefully. 'But to be honest…' She chewed on her bottom lip with uncertainty.

Mrs Adler quirked a brow of puzzlement. 'What is it, Ada?'

'I can't really see our Connie going shopping or to choose a book from the library without never having returned home last night. She's just not like that.'

'You mean it is unlike your sister to not inform you of her plans?'

Ada felt a lump in her throat which indicated she might break down in tears. She swallowed hard and just nodded at the woman.

Jakob rubbed his chin as he stared into the flames of the fire.

'Are you thinking what I'm thinking?' his mother said as if the children were not present, which caused Sam to startle as his eyes grew large with fear.

Jakob gave his mother a stern glance. 'Please Mama, we don't wish to alarm them, but I do know what you are thinking.'

Such consternation caused Ada to rise to her feet. 'Please tell me what that is, I need to know!' she said firmly.

'Very well,' said Jakob looking into her eyes. 'There has been some sort of gang working in the area for a few weeks.' He swallowed hard. 'They have been kidnapping young women,' he paused as if to think carefully how to choose his words, 'with a view to…'

'To what?' Ada demanded to know.

'There is talk that they ship them overseas and sell them to various, er, houses of ill repute…'

'Brothels!' said Mrs Adler.

Ada's jaw dropped. 'But no one would dare to do that to our Connie, she'd fight them off!' she said proudly. 'Even if it was a man trying to take her.'

'I know she would,' said Jakob smiling. 'It doesn't mean that's what's happened to her. It might be something else.'

'I hope so,' Ada sniffed, fighting to hold back the tears that were threatening to form.

Jakob smiled at her and kindly laying a hand on her shoulder said, 'I promise you children I shall do my utmost to find your sister.'

'What's a brothel?' Sam asked innocently as if he were asking a question about a sort of food rather than something salacious.

'Nothing to concern you,' said Ada, draping a comforting arm around her brother and hugging him towards her. She thought she knew what a brothel was as she'd once heard someone in the street outside talking about one of those places. It was where men went for entertainment, she thought. Like the theatre, where the women dressed in gay, gaudy clothes. She couldn't imagine her sister would ever want to go to one of those places.

'What about contacting the police?' asked Mrs Adler, glancing at her son.

'No, police, not yet anyhow,' Jakob said with a worried frown as he held up the palms of his hands. 'From the experience many have had with those lot, I could well end up as a suspect and get thrown into a prison cell, then what help would I be?'

'*Vat* is true,' Mrs Adler said, shaking her head. 'I remember *ven* they took away one of our neighbours once, he was supposedly caught stealing from a market stall. I ask you!' She threw up her arms as if in despair. 'When did Mr Richmond ever steal from anybody? Anyhow, he was carted away like a common criminal and he never to return here. We not have seen him to this day and his family move out of here soon afterwards. We don't know where they go to, but I have my suspicions.' She rolled up her dress sleeves as if preparing for a fight which amused Ada greatly.

'What do you think happened to them all?' asked Ada innocently.

'I think the family ended up in the *verkhouse* as they had no money coming into the home to feed themselves because the head of the house was removed from it. Mr Richmond, himself, I do not know, but it was back in the days when people could be transported to Australia for little things like stealing a loaf of bread or some other little crime that shouldn't have involved them being sent half *vay* around the *vorld* far from the home they love.' She pursed her lips in disgust, and then, she murmured something to herself in a language that Ada couldn't understand as she made the sign of the cross as people did in church.

'That's a truly awful thing to happen though,' said Ada, shaking her head. 'I hope that won't 'ave happened to our Connie. I couldn't bear it if she was sent that far away from us.'

Jakob glanced at his mother then back at Ada. 'Now don't you be getting concerned about such things, I'm sure your sister hasn't ended up on a ship going all the way to Australia. Ma, tell Ada that happened a long time ago?'

'Ah...' Mrs Adler let out a long breath. 'Yes, it was many years ago before you *childen* were even born. So don't worry too much about it, I still get angry about it even now to this day.'

'In any case,' said Jakob, 'transportation stopped some time ago.'

Ada puzzled for a moment wondering why the woman got so upset by something that happened so long ago.

Noticing her confusion, Jakob explained, 'Ma was very friendly with Mrs Richmond, you see...'

Mrs Adler's face took on a dreamy expression. 'Freda, she was like a sister to me, we would see each other every single day and even help one another. I would look after her *childen* for her to go out shopping and she would do the same for me with Jakob. *The childen* all got along with one another too. So, for her to leave here so how do you say, without *varning*, and for us never to see the smiling faces on those little ones ever again and to *vonder* where the family disappeared to...' she turned to look away, and Ada noticed the woman rubbing her eyes as if she didn't want them to see how upset she was. She turned back to face them before saying, 'Anyhow, I still miss Freda and her family even to this day.'

Ada felt a surge of sympathy for the woman and figured it must be hard to lose a friend like that so suddenly, not just a friend but a whole family. 'We've taken up enough of your time,' she said firmly as she glanced at Sam, who looked perfectly happy where he was seated on the rug in front of the fire. 'We will go back to our place now and wait for Connie to come home. Thank you, both.' She stood and put out her hand for her brother to take. Sam took hold of it and reluctantly stood as if he wanted to remain in the comfort of the Adler's warm and cosy home forever.

'Any time, little *darlinks*,' Mrs Adler smiled.

'I meant what I said,' Jakob looked at the children, 'I'm going out to look for Connie. You both stay where you are in case she returns.'

Ada nodded with tears in her eyes. She couldn't believe the kindness of her neighbours and wondered how they'd both cope without them.

Chapter Three

For the next few hours, Ada and Sam sat huddled up beneath a blanket in the armchair in front of their own fire which had drawn nicely thanks to Jakob. It would be a couple more hours before their clothing fully dried out. Mrs Adler had sent them away with half a loaf of homemade sourdough bread and a small pot of strawberry jam she'd also made herself. Ada had thanked the woman profusely as she had no idea where they'd get their next meal from, and although Mrs Adler had told the children if they needed more food, they could go to her, Ada had too much pride for that. She planned on coping on her own. In any case, surely Connie would return soon and then the household could get back to normal with Connie going back to work at the match factory and shopping for odds and ends to eat on the market as she usually did.

But Ada was to be disappointed, as she watched the hands on the mantel clock turn the hour there was still no sign of their sister. It was now nine o'clock in the night and the dimly burning wick of the candle on the small table beside them, flickered half-heartedly in its holder, as if it had given up all hope of their Connie ever returning home.

Oh, Connie, where are you? She asked herself as a gnawing pain in the pit of her stomach told her that something was amiss.

A short, sharp knock on the door caused the children to startle and Ada put her index finger to her lips to warn her brother to keep quiet. She hoped he wouldn't start to cough just in case it was Winterbourne after his rent money, so she was relieved to hear Jakob's voice on the other side of the door.

'It's only me, kids,' Jakob said speaking softly as if he now realised he might have frightened the pair.

Ada clambered out of the armchair and went to pull the bolt on the door.

Jakob smiled at her. 'Ma says you can come over for your supper if you want, she guessed you'd still be awake worrying. Or she can send it over for you?' he said kindly.

'Thank you,' Ada said. 'I think it would be best if she could send it over, just in case our Connie returns home.'

He nodded at her. 'That's no problem. I'll bring a bowl each over for you.' Jakob's frame cast a large shadow against the wall as he stood in the candlelight. Any other man and the children would have been fearful, but Jakob they trusted with their lives.

Ada chewed on her bottom lip. 'Did you go to look for Connie afterwards?' she wanted to know.

'I did and I'm so sorry but even though I looked in all the places she might have been, and asked a few people who know her, no one has seen hide nor hair of her.' He shook his head.

'Not even in the library?' Ada asked hopefully.

'Not even there,' Jakob shook his head. 'I even asked the librarian. Look, don't give up hope, Ada. I'll be back now with that stew for the both of you and then we can plan what to do next. I have to go to work for my night shift in an hour or so, but I promise I'll never give up looking for your sister and will start again first thing in the morning after I return home.'

While Ada waited for Jakob's return, she sat back in the armchair with Sam and wrapped the blanket closely around them.

'Are you all right?' she asked the boy.

He nodded but then he coughed again. A deep hacking cough now which troubled Ada so. It just wasn't getting any better.

'What's all this?' Mrs Adler was at the door, smiling, but then a look of concern swept over her face. 'I'll be back in a moment with some cough mixture for you, young man!' She wagged a finger at him, and she turned to return to her apartment just as Jakob appeared with a tray of food for the both of them. Whispering something in her son's ear, she scurried off to deal with the task in hand.

'Here's Mama's stew!' Jakob announced. 'Get it down inside you while it's good and hot.' He turned towards the fireplace, 'How's that fire coming on?'

'It's warming us up nicely,' Ada said. 'Our clothes will be dry soon.'

Jakob nodded and placed the tray containing the two bowls of the delicious smelling stew down on the small low table beside the children. The steam arising from their tattered and torn clothing was evidence of how well they were drying out. 'Watch that clothing don't get too close to those flames, mind,' he warned.

'I will,' said Ada gratefully. Usually, Connie would take care of things like that but now without her sister here, she was aware as eldest child she'd have to step into her sister's shoes for time being.

Mrs Adler returned just as her son was leaving. She had a silver spoon in one hand and a brown medicine bottle with a cork stopper in the other. 'Now take a spoonful of this, young Sam,' she said kindly. 'I always swear by the stuff.' Sam opened his mouth ready for it but scowled as he swallowed it. 'I should have *varned* you. It's bitter stuff but my tasty stew will take the taste away for you.' Then turning to Ada, she said. 'Give him one spoonful three times a day until his cough improves.'

Ada nodded. 'Thank you, Mrs Adler.'

When the woman had departed, the children got down to eating the stew which was a delicious concoction of mutton, carrots, onion and dumplings. Ada had never felt so full in all her life, but Sam found it hard to eat all of his. 'Don't worry, Sam,' she said, 'you just eat what you can and I'll warm the rest up in a saucepan on the fire later, if you like?'

He nodded gratefully.

She'd seen Connie warm things through in that saucepan often enough, so she knew what to do.

The children both drifted off to sleep, Sam in Ada's arms as the daylight continued to fade and the room almost in darkness except for the small candle which was just about holding on. Several sharp knocks on the door disturbed them.

'Mrs Adler?' Sam muttered drowsily, but Ada knew it wasn't her, she'd know that knock anywhere—it was Winterbourne's! He always knocked the door in a rhythmic fashion, exactly five times. She'd forgotten it was Thursday today, the day when he came to collect his rent money and Connie wasn't here to pay him. Drat!

She put a finger to her lips to warn Sam not to say anything. There was another series of five sharp raps. Then she heard Winterbourne's voice. 'I know you're in there, Miss Cooper. I'm not prepared to wait for my rent again. For the past month I've had to wait a few days to get it. If it's not paid in full by tonight, you lot will be out on the street and won't be welcome to my benevolence ever again, especially after what happened last night!' He shouted, which caused both children to tremble with fear.

What had happened last night for Winterbourne to be making these sort of threats to them?

Sam began to sniffle and was doing his best to hold back his choking sounding sobs, when Ada heard the doorknob rattle. The man was trying to open the door. Then he suddenly stopped before yelling, 'I'll be back in one hour and if you don't have the money for me then after I've done my rounds for this evening, you're all out on your ear!'

Silence. Then retreating footsteps. Now Sam could cry freely he was letting rip. Huge shuddering sobs engulfed his frail little body.

'Don't worry, Sam, we'll think of something,' Ada said, hugging her brother tightly to her. But it was no use, she could think of nothing. She didn't want to keep asking Mrs Adler for help. In any case, she and her son weren't flush themselves, it was unlikely they could afford to pay the rent for them as Ada knew that Connie had said it wasn't just one week's rent owing, it had now gone up to two. Winterbourne also added on a bit of interest if payment was late and all, so maybe instead of six shillings for the fortnight, it would now be seven. Where on earth could she get that sort of money from?

There was another knock on the door which startled both children, but Ada realised it wasn't Winterbourne's knock. 'It's me, Ada!' Thankfully, it was Jakob's voice and not the landlord's she recognised.

Ada scrambled out of the armchair and unbolted the door to allow Jakob inside.

'I heard Winterbourne shouting out there!' he said. 'He'd just arrived to take our rent money from us. If I'd thought I ought to have made it appear we were out and then left our rent money with you so you could pay him when he returns.'

Ada's eyes began to glaze with tears. 'It's no use,' she sobbed. 'Our Connie had let the payments mount up, we owe two weeks now and the interest he keeps adding on to it. She kept it back so she could feed us this week.'

Jakob laid a kindly hand on her shoulder. 'Look, don't worry if he tries to put you out, I'll take you in with us.'

'You'd better not do that,' said Ada. 'I remember someone else doing that here and they lost their home as well. He'll see you and your Ma out on the streets too. He doesn't care about anyone 'cept himself.'

'I'm really concerned for you kids,' Jakob said with a worried frown. 'Look, pack all your belongings and come to hide over in our place, at least until we figure something out. That way Winterbourne will think you've all done a moonlight flit. 'Go and get all your clothes and anything of value together, then come over.'

Ada nodded; she could see the sense of that. Jakob left them to it closing the door behind himself as she helped Sam into his clothing, which thankfully was now only slightly damp. Her own thick linsey wool dress wasn't quite dry, so she borrowed an old one of her sister's which, although a little long, wasn't too bad with a piece of string tied around the middle. It was either that or wear the one that was too small for her. Then she packed a carpet bag of as much of their clothing as she could manage, though she had nothing she could put Connie's in, so she thought she'd ask Jakob if he had something suitable. She'd just filled the carpet bag when the door burst violently open.

***

Ada grabbed hold of her brother and pushed him behind her as she stood to face the raging beast before her. 'Out now!' ordered Winterbourne. The whites of his eyes seemed enlarged, almost as though his eyes were bulging out of his head and a line of spittle had formed at the sides of his mouth. He looked like an ogre by candlelight.

'B...but you said we had one hour to leave!' Ada protested.

'Ah! So you were here then and heard me?' he shouted. 'You could have opened the door to speak to me. I always believe in surprising the enemy, I catch a lot out that way!'

'I...I could have opened the door for you, but my sister said we aren't allowed to open it when she's not here.'

'Where is she then?' he snarled as his eyes roved the small apartment. 'She's a sly one and make no mistake!'

Not wanting to tell the man the truth, Ada said, 'She's taken some stuff to the pawn shop to get the rent money for you.'

'I don't believe a word of it!' said Winterbourne, stepping forward and grabbing Ada by the collar of her dress and shaking her roughly. 'Rent money now or you leave here this instant!' He shook her so hard that Ada felt her teeth chatter inside her head. And then Sam was trying to kick the man's shins, but with little effect, as although he now had his boots on, Winterbourne was easily keeping him at bay with his other hand and laughing at the plight the pair were now in.

Suddenly, he released Ada so that she toppled on the floor and Sam went to her aid to help her onto her feet.

'You should leave her where she is!' Winterbourne scoffed. 'Pair of trollops yer sisters are! In any case, as yer sister can't cough up what's owed each week, you two oughta be in the work'ouse by rights. I know someone working there. I'll take you with me right now. Be doing you a favour I will an' all!'

Ada couldn't believe her ears. After all their Connie had done this past few months to keep them from such a place—that horrible man was threatening to march them there— right now at this very moment.

'We won't go! Never!' she yelled at him as Winterbourne threw back his head and laughed.

'Oh, yes you will! You little scroat!' He began to shake Ada roughly, so much so that Sam burst into tears and she began to scream which caught Winterbourne off guard.

Hearing the children's distress, Jakob came rushing towards them through the open door. The way his hair was tousled, and the fact he had no shoes or socks on his feet, made Ada realise the young man must have been asleep as he had another night shift ahead of him.

'Leave those children be at once, man!' Jakob yelled and he stooped to lift an iron poker from the fire grate and held it over Winterbourne's head.

Winterbourne gulped as if he realised Jakob was stronger and fitter than him and could do him some serious damage. Roughly, he released Ada from his grasp, pushing her to one side. She immediately grabbed hold of Sam and held him to her to silence his sobs.

'Look, I'm a reasonable man,' said Winterbourne holding up the palms of his hands as if in self-defence. 'I've given this family weeks of good grace…'

Sadly, Ada realised he was telling the truth about that as she had previously heard Connie pleading with him to allow her extra time, she'd been soft soaping him to keep him sweet up until now as he'd seemed a bit taken with her. Connie was a good-looking girl, Ada realised that and she wished her sister was here right now to sort things out.

'Then you can give them a bit longer, surely?' Jakob said firmly dropping the poker with a clatter back in the fire grate. 'They've really had to struggle since their parents' death. Have you no compassion, man?'

Winterbourne relaxed and shook his head. 'I can't. It's gone on long enough as it is.'

'Then let them stay at our place for a while at least?'

Winterbourne appeared to be mulling things over in his mind. Then finally he said, 'It's not in the terms of our agreement but if I allow it, it will cost you, mind! Yer'll have to pay double the amount!'

It was at that point that Ada noticed Jakob's mouth fall open with shock. She realised that he and his mother were struggling themselves and she had no wish to condemn them to further hardship.

'It's all right,' she said softly. 'Mr Winterbourne says he can arrange for us to go into the workhouse for a while and maybe when Connie returns, she'll get us out of there.'

'Yes,' nodded Winterbourne. 'It'll only be until your circumstances change and that sister of yours can pay her way,' he said smiling, now seeming a lot nicer than the brutal beast he'd been a couple of minutes hence, but she guessed it was all for Jakob's benefit. He was a good actor—she'd give him that. But she had no intention of going into any workhouse or for causing the Adlers any problems either, it was a question of pride for her.

Jakob stood there open mouthed. 'I don't know what to say…'

'Just tell our Connie where we are when you find her,' Ada said.

'Look, can't the kids stop with us for a couple of nights at least?' Jakob pleaded.

'No, certainly not. The parish need to take care of this pair if their sister can't. Where is she anyhow?' His beady eyes searched the room as if she was in hiding somewhere.

'Sorry, kids,' Jakob said, laying a hand of comfort on Ada's shoulder. He turned to Winterbourne, 'Which workhouse are you taking them to?'

'The Whitechapel and Spitalfields Union Workhouse,' he answered abruptly.

Jakob narrowed his eyes. 'And what do you get out of it? Someone paying you to round up all the waifs and strays in the area?'

Winterbourne gulped as he swallowed hard. 'Er, no. I does what I does out of the goodness of me 'eart. Honest.'

'A right benevolent sort, ain't ya?' Jakob sneered.

Winterbourne smiled nervously. 'You could say that.'

'Then I'll tell you what, I'll take the kids there myself as they know and trust me…'

Winterbourne frowned. 'Then you might not get them in there. I have a special contact what works there who does me a favour from time to time. In any case, if you want to keep a roof over both your and your mother's heads then I suggest you leave me to it.'

Jakob scowled at the man and Ada could see he wasn't comfortable with the idea at all but what choice did he have if he didn't want to lose his own apartment? This area was so overcrowded, and rooms were hard to come by. Besides, why would the pair wish to move now when they were so well settled here?

'It's all right, Jakob,' Ada reassured. 'We'll go with Mr Winterbourne for now, just keep an eye out for our Connie and tell her where we are.'

Jakob nodded. 'Will do, Ada love.' Then turning to Sam, he said, 'Don't worry. You have to be a big boy now, understand?' Sam nodded and then Jakob ruffled his hair.

If Ma and Pa were still here all would be well, but they were both lying beneath that cold, damp earth right now and it fair near broke Ada's heart.

'Come along then,' said Winterbourne as he forced a smile at the children in front of Jakob. 'Pack yer bags and let's get out of here!'

Ada had already packed them. 'I've just one or two more things to put into them,' she said firmly.

Winterbourne quirked a brow. 'Was planning on doing a moonlight flit, was yer?'

Jakob glared at the man. 'I'll just go and get me Ma to say farewell to them,' he said.

Winterbourne shook his head, 'Please don't make this any harder than needs be, it might upset the children.'

Jakob nodded and Ada guessed they'd cry even more if they saw Mrs Adler's kindly face brimming with tears before they left here.

Jakob looked on with pity in his eyes as Ada collected a carpet bag of their clothing to take with her. She'd had to leave her sister's belongings there, but Jakob promised he'd collect everything else of theirs and take them to his apartment with a firm promise to Mr Winterbourne that he'd secure the door behind himself when he left. 'Please don't worry, kids,' he reassured as Ada glanced over her shoulder as she left. 'I'll still keep looking for your Connie and I'll try to visit you at the big house!'

That thought comforted Ada a little, but she had no intention of going to the workhouse anyway. As soon as they got the chance, she and Sam were going to flee from that big bully. Else who knew what might happen to them otherwise, maybe he had plans to sell them on to someone for cheap labour. She didn't trust the man an inch. But the main reason she'd left with Winterbourne was not to concern Jakob and his mother in their affairs, they had enough problems of their own without dragging the pair into it. In any case, if she'd put up a protest which involved Jakob and his mother wading in, then she had a terrible feeling Winterbourne would turf them out of their apartment too. Apparently, it was in the terms of agreement that tenants could be evicted if they caused a 'ruckus'. Connie had read that out to her just last week when she was checking up on what it said about late payment of the rent money. It had read, *'Tenants are expected to pay the weekly rent money on time. If more than three consecutive payments are missed and a warning issued, the landlord then has the right to evict the tenant and others living at the property from the premises forthwith.'*

She had remembered that as she prided herself on her memory. Even her schoolteacher had once told her she had the best memory of any pupil in the school that she'd ever known. It was true as when she'd once had to learn three bible verses and a poem off by heart for a competition, she was the only one who managed it word perfect. But these days, she and Sam no longer went to school as her sister couldn't afford to pay the fee. There was a local board school close by which they wouldn't have to pay to attend, but that was full up and the classes large. When her mother and father were alive, they could afford to send them to a small school that was held in a church hall. It was a church school really where she went to Sunday school and the fee wasn't all that high she supposed as some of it was met by church funding from the benevolence of several wealthy parishioners. Even that small sum they could no longer afford to part with anymore, and as a consequence, had no schooling since the death of their parents.

Ada stifled a tear as they tramped along the corridor in front of Mr Winterbourne, she was just wondering when to make a run for it when she felt a sharp prod in the small of her back. The man was pushing her along with his walking cane as if she were part of a cattle run off to market. Now Jakob was out of view, the man changed his demeanour once again. 'Hurry up, you pair of scroats!' he snarled. 'I've got better things to be doing with me time. The sooner I offload you bleedin' varmints the better! It'll be stale bread, gruel and hard labour where you pair are off to!' A shiver coursed Ada's spine as she took Sam by the hand, urging herself to walk as quickly as possible so the man could no longer prod her in her back. If he did anything to her brother, she was going to scream to bring attention to him, but thankfully, he left him well alone. It was evident that it was she who he had it in for.

Outside on the street, Ada gazed up at the building she had once called home with its red brick work and dilapidated window frames, the panes of glass stuffed with old newspapers. It did look run down and dreary, but she had never known any other home. Ma and Pa had made it a welcome place, there'd always been a fire lit when necessary and their tummies had been full most of the time. It was only now in recent months that things had got so dismal. On the opposite side of the road, she noticed their playmates Polly and Arthur playing hopscotch on the pavement outside their front door, blissfully unaware of their predicament. Their parents left them out at all hours of the day and night, Ma and Pa would never have allowed such a thing if they were here. Would they ever get to see their friends again if they were admitted to the workhouse?

Her plan had to work and she was about to yank on Sam's arm to warn him to run off with her, she knew of an alleyway around the corner where they could hide whilst Winterbourne's attention was taken by a black shiny coach that had just pulled up. He suddenly turned and started speaking to a lady through the open window. It seemed evident that he already knew her and maybe even have been expecting her.

Beneath the street gas lamp, he smiled at the children, but Ada noticed the smile didn't quite reach his eyes. 'This is Mrs Darlington,' he introduced. Then glancing at Ada, he announced, 'Your brother will be going to stay with her for a while!'

'Never!' Ada stamped her foot as her chin jutted out. 'I will not stand for it. He's to stay with me!'

'N...now come on,' said Winterbourne as he removed his bowler hat as if to make himself seem less intimidating. 'It's all arranged. You wouldn't want your brother to suffer in the workhouse, would you?'

Ada could hardly believe her ears. So, it sounded as if the man had arranged this all along, the way the carriage was waiting in the street ready to whisk her brother away. 'Can't I go with him then?'

She stared hard at Winterbourne whose face flushed bright red as he appeared to stammer.

'I…I'm sorry. No can do, young lady. Mrs Darlington can only take one child and she wants a young 'un she can mould and make her own, like your brother.'

Ada tried to appeal to the man's better nature. 'But I don't have to live there as a guest, I can work in the kitchen or something. Please sir, do not part me from me little brother. He's all I have left in this world.'

As if having second thoughts, Winterbourne turned and walked back to the coach where he spoke with Mrs Darlington. Ada could only catch the odd word here and there like "Workhouse", "brother" and "destitute". She held her breath as if that might cause the lady to change her mind, but she could tell as Winterbourne approached it was to be bad news as she let out a steadying breath to prepare herself for the worse.

He shook his head. 'Sorry, Mrs Darlington ain't taking on any new staff right now. Yer'll have to come wiv me, darlin',' he said.

Ada glanced at her brother and grabbed him by the arm. 'Come on, Sam! Run!'

Both children ran at a pace down the wet cobbled street, narrowly missing the splatters of manure here and there left by cart horses. By now, Sam was snivelling, but Ada had no time for that as Winterbourne was hot on their heels. Gasping for breath, Ada was aware it would be their only chance to scarper, she just could not bear to be parted from her brother, as she realised that once he was taken to that house, she might never see him again. At least with the workhouse there was a chance they might someday leave there, but who knew what might happen to her brother once he'd gone off with that posh lady in her carriage.

'Come back 'ere, you pair of rascals!' Winterbourne shouted after them.

Ada changed her mind about hiding in the alleyway, if she could get as far as an area dubbed by the locals as "No Man's Land" they would be safe from his clutches there as it was inhabited with all sorts of undesirables like beggars and drunks who would keep him at bay, she figured they'd be safer there than with the likes of Winterbourne. The area was a place that many feared because of its undesirable populace. It was reputed that the police would only patrol there in twos or more. No copper would consider going there alone for fear of being mugged or worse as the police were the enemy of the people there. The area divided the rich from the poor because on the other side of it, from Adam and Eve Court onwards, there was a more respectable tree-lined street. Although the houses were a little run down, it was evident for all to see it had once been a posh place. From that street onwards, the houses became more upmarket and were three and four storeys high. It was a world away from the one she and her brother had inhabited in Sycamore Street. That street was full of doss houses and apartments, peppered with the odd family home here and there. There was a pub on either end of the street which could get quite rowdy at times.

She figured if she could just get Sam through No Man's Land and out the other side, they'd be safe for time being. Then she'd figure out what to do next. What a pity that lady wouldn't take them both. They might have had the opportunity to live a life of luxury for once, that was until they found Connie.

Winterbourne was gaining upon them as he puffed out between heavy breaths. 'I'll have you pair of varmints, if it's the last thing I ever do!'

Then she felt it. A sharp whack across the head with his walking cane, which caused her to momentarily release her brother's hand, leaving him within an arm's reach of Winterbourne.

'Ada!' Sam shouted as she suddenly stumbled backwards. His terror apparent as she could see the whites of his eyes as they enlarged. 'Our Ada, save me!'

But being momentarily stunned, she was powerless to get to her feet to run after Winterbourne, who was now dragging Sam away by the scruff of his neck, it all felt like a bad dream. And then she was in a heap crying her heart out as her brother's cries became more distant as he and Winterbourne disappeared from view.

'Are you all right, dearie?' She heard a kindly voice beside her. She looked up to see a middle-aged woman bending over her. The woman appeared to be wearing layers of ragged clothes that had seen better days, and she had her shawl wrapped around her head as well as her shoulders. She had the most wrinkled, weather-beaten face Ada'd ever seen on anyone, but her eyes were a bright cerulean blue. Those were wise eyes, Ada thought.

'I'm all right, thank you,' she said through shuddering breaths as she pulled herself unsteadily onto her feet. 'It's me brother I'm worried about, Winterbourne snatched him away from me!'

'And who is this Winterbourne?'

'He's our rent man, he said 'cause we can't pay the rent as our sister, Connie, has gone missing that he was going to take us to the workhouse. But once we got outside our building, he had plans to separate us and send me brother off to live with some posh lady. So, I grabbed hold of Sam's hand and we ran like hell!' She paused to get her breath, before finishing, 'But he caught up on us, whacked me across me head with his walking cane and has taken my brother away!'

The old woman nodded with grave concern in her eyes, then inserting a thumb and forefinger in her mouth, she let out an ear piercing, shrill whistle, which caused two well-built young men to bound towards them.

'What's up, Ma?' asked the bearded one.

'It's this young lady here, her brother's been abducted by a man named Winterbourne, he's taken him off to some posh lady, can you run after them?'

'We'll try, Ma,' said the younger looking of the two.

'Which direction did they go?' Asked the bearded one.

Ada pointed. 'He's taking him back to the lady's coach on Sycamore Street. But please, you'll have to be quick about it!'

He nodded. Then he slapped his younger brother on the forearm, 'Come on!'

'Don't worry, darlin',' said the woman. 'Come and 'ave a warm with me. My name's Maggie Donovan, what's yers?'

'Ada.'

'That's a lovely name. Now don't concern yerself, Billy and Davy will see if they can get your brother back for you. There'll be no messin' with those two. Good pair of boxers they are an' all!' She beckoned with her hand. 'Come over 'ere and warm yerself, there ain't nothing of yer, is there? All skin and bone you is.'

Ada's legs felt boneless as Maggie led her to a metal brazier that was glowing red hot as several down and out sorts were warming their hands around it as it billowed out grey smoke. The shadowy figures scared her at first but as she approached, she noticed a middle-aged man, wearing black woollen fingerless gloves, who was taking a swig out of what appeared to be a whiskey bottle and handing it on to someone else.

'Now don't you be fearful of this crowd,' Maggie joked. 'There's none what would 'arm an air on yer 'ead, it's people like that rent man of yours and some of those posh nobs what might want to hurt you. These are decent, honest folk 'ere what 'ave just hit on hard times. Understood?'

Ada nodded, she thought she did understand all too well as her family had hit hard times themselves lately.

Maggie whispered to her. 'Alfie, he's the one passing the whiskey bottle around, you'd never believe he was a wages clerk until a few months ago. His missus ran off with another fella and then he hit the bottle hard and got his marching orders from his boss at work. He lost his wife, his baby son, his job and his home all within the matter of weeks. And see 'er over there?' Maggie pointed in the direction of woman, who in Ada's opinion, wore some garish looking garments and whose appearance had probably seen better days. Ada could well imagine that she would have been a beauty in her youth. ''Er name is Breda, comes from Ireland she does. She works the streets at night as she can't get money doing anything else. Used to work at the match factory…'

Hearing that, Ada's ears pricked up. 'What happened?'

'Well, she was struggling to make ends meet, weren't she? So, she took a job at night supposedly being a companion for wealthy men up West, but then…' she tapped the side of her nose with her index finger. 'But then…she suddenly disappeared. She told me she got abducted by a couple of gentlemen and sent to a place in Belgium. She remembers little of it, mind you. Turns out she was locked up in some kind of whore house and put out to work for her keep.'

Ada frowned. She didn't quite understand, and she was far too worried about Sam to take it all in as her attention was diverted towards the side street where the brothers had disappeared to. Surely if they'd found Sam they'd be back by now? Her heart was slowly starting to submerge into her boots.

Aware of her distress, Maggie patted her on the top of her head. 'If anyone can find your brother and bring him back here to you, my boys can!' she said, smiling to reveal a couple of rotted stumps in her mouth and rubbing her roughened chin with her fingertips as if in contemplation. Ada noticed a couple of white whiskers sprouting from the woman's chin which she hadn't noticed before. As if on cue, Ada hearing a commotion, whipped her head around to see Billy and Davy striding triumphantly towards them. The bearded one, which she was later to discover was Billy, was cradling a petrified looking Sam in his arms.

'It was a tough fight to get this one back!' he beamed, settling the boy down next to his sister. Ada immediately hugged him to her, feeling his thin and wiry body next to hers as his body convulsed with tears as they both wept with relief.

'What happened then?' she heard Maggie ask.

'We caught up with the coach all right, just as the geezer was pushing the boy into it,' Davy explained. 'We were lucky as it looked as if your brother was refusing to get into the carriage and creating something of a palaver about it, so I managed to grab ahold of him! But we were too quick for the man to hang on to him as we surprised him. Billy knocked him out of the way onto the pavement, the old geezer didn't know what had hit him! Then we threatened him if he was to ever come near you kids again, he'd have us to deal with—we'd kick him from here into kingdom come! Don't think he'll be bothering you pair ever again!' He smiled at the children as Ada nodded with glazed eyes and muttered her appreciation at them.

'Now then,' said Maggie kindly. 'I think we'll have a brew, shall we?'

Maggie and Sam nodded as Davy said, 'We'll leave you to it, Ma. Glad the kids are safe, we're off to *The Bull's Head* for a jar or two.'

''orright,' she said, waving them off. 'You deserve it!' She turned to another woman who was warming her hands by the brazier. 'Can you brew up, Sally?'

The old woman nodded.

After the children had supped the tea which was surprisingly good, Ada was wondering what to do next when Maggie said, 'Yer'll be wanting a bed for the night then, I'll be bound if youse been kicked out of your digs?'

'Yes, but we ain't got no money, see,' Ada said sadly.

'Don't be worrying about that for tonight, you can bed down beneath the arches with us and then tomorrow, my youngest son, Danny, will take you to market with him.'

Ada screwed up her eyes. What was the old biddy on about? Going to market?

'Aw, you don't know what I mean, do you?' Maggie threw back her head and laughed. 'Danny takes his barrow to Spitalfields market very early in the morning and buys what he can to sell on the streets. He's a coster boy.'

'What's a coster boy?' asked Sam, now seeming to have bounced back from his earlier shocked state as if he'd risen like Lazarus from the dead, appearing none the worst for his unpleasant ordeal.

'A coster boy,' said Maggie bending down to speak to him and now in a gentle tone, 'is someone what sells produce to members of the public.'

'What sort of produce?' Ada wanted to know.

'Fruit and veg that kind of thing. When he can find a good pitch, he sells well. He finds during the daytime that housewives like to buy cauliflowers, cabbages and the like but at night he stands outside the theatre and sells those toffs oranges and bags of nuts—they love that kind of stuff do the nobs.'

Ada felt surprised by this. 'How old is Danny?' she wanted to know.

'Thirteen years old!' Maggie announced proudly.

Ada thought she looked too old to have a son of that age as her elder sons seemed very grown up, but then again, maybe a life on the streets had aged the woman badly.

Maggie went on to explain to Ada, 'There are many big street markets in London where coster families live cheek to jowl, their houses practically on top of one another...'

'But I thought you were living on the streets?' Ada frowned.

Maggie smiled. 'I were many years ago before I met me Arthur. He's dead now, gawd bless 'im. But he rescued me and we brought up a family together. He were a costermonger, see. Had a donkey an' all what pulled a cart. Must have felt sorry for me I suppose—a young girl down on her luck.' She sniffed loudly. 'Anyhow, he never made what you'd term an honest woman out of me until a few years back, and we lived over the brush for many a year and brought up a family together until then. That's how I know all about the costering way of life. Davy and Billy still work the carts and visit marketplaces, but Danny like I said, takes to the streets with his barrow.' 'So, you don't live in No Man's Land then?' Ada quirked a curious brow.

'Well, I do and I don't. See those arches what I told you about?' She nodded. 'When I mentioned about sleeping under them tonight I meant in that little house there!' She pointed to a ramshackle looking building with a small garden and a wooden gate. 'It can get noisy mind you living beneath the railway arches.' Ada didn't much care about the noise as long as she and Sam had a bed for the night.

'So, you and the young 'un can sleep on a pallet on the floor, got plenty of blankets as well as I go around selling rags and what nots me self.'

'Why do you stand here then with all sorts of people?' Ada wanted to know.

'I do it from the goodness of me heart as I knows what it's like not to have a roof over your head. I get the brazier going to help keep 'em warm in cold weather and there's always a cuppa or a bite to eat for those that want it. Gets lots of left over veg from the lads at the end of the day so I make a nice stew for the down and outs with some bones from the butcher shop. Bakes some fresh bread and all to go with it.'

'That's truly kind of you,' said Ada.

'Come along with me, you pair,' Maggie said. 'I'll take you to my abode where you can use the convenience and I'll see if I can kit you out with some clothes from the rag cart what I takes to the marketplace.'

**

They followed the Maggie along the way as she turned and shouted at the woman who had given them tea, 'Won't be too long, Sally. Just take over for a bit, darlin'!'

Sally nodded at her.

The whiff of horse manure and something rotten permeated Ada's nostrils as she and Sam trailed in Maggie's shadow. Ada shivered, this was a scary place to be, she gently squeezed her brother's little hand as a mark of reassurance, and he looked up at her and smiled. She knew in that moment she had done the right thing in preventing him from going off with that posh lady.

Beneath the arches, Ada heard a train rattling overhead and to the right was a small crooked wooden gate which Maggie opened for them. 'Welcome to my humble home,' she said. She led them in through the door which looked as though it had seen better days from its peeling paint, and walked them down a dark corridor into the living room. The room was lit by an oil lantern on the mantelpiece. A pair of identical pottery dogs stood either side of it, and above that a cracked mirror adorned the wall. Pictures of saints were plastered on the wall above the fireplace. In the corner, was a brass bedstead covered by a patchwork quilt and in the opposite corner of the room was a pinewood dresser adorned with a mismatch of cups and blue plates. Ada turned and noticed a pot of stew bubbling on the fire.

'That's for the boys for later,' Maggie said, 'but you can have some as well.'

Ada nodded eagerly, even though it was only an hour or so since Mrs Adler had fed them, the whole ordeal had thoroughly exhausted her, so she gratefully took a seat at the table with her brother, who was also as keen as mustard to tuck into the rabbit stew as he hadn't managed to eat much of Mrs Adler's.

'I rent out rooms to a few other costers,' Maggie explained. 'Five people live in the next room up. I sleeps in this one with Danny and the other two lads sleep upstairs. Ada had noticed a barrow parked outside the window on her way in and she wondered if that belonged to the two brothers who had helped her or to Danny himself. The rusty railway bridge rattled so loudly that she noticed Maggie stopped talking until the train had passed by as the cups vibrated in their saucers. A black cat appeared weaving in and out of the woman's legs and then settled itself in front of the hearth, purring softly. 'Sheba keeps the rodents at bay,' said Maggie, 'she's a good 'un.'

Ada smiled. The cat did look very regal indeed, she had coal black fur which was shiny and sleek and her eyes gleamed like two emeralds. She was a mysterious looking cat indeed. 'She's lovely,' said Ada.

Maggie nodded. 'Us costers live most of their lives on the streets so it's nice to have Sheba to come home to of an evening.'

'What do you do all day then?' asked Ada, and then she wondered if that was an impertinent question to ask the woman, but Maggie just beamed at her as if only too pleased to relate the details of her day.

'Breakfast might be bread and butter at a coffee stall in the marketplace and maybe a pie at lunchtime, but I have to watch the boys or otherwise they'd spend half the day in the pub away from the stall. Beer shops are a big pull for coster folk, unfortunately. It's not just the rigours of ale either what's the pull but the gambling what goes along with it…' she paused, 'I've known some men spend half their earnings on gambling and other vices.' She sniffed loudly as if in disgust. 'It's the dog fights I don't much care for, mind.' She crossed one hand over the other and pursed her lips. 'And they're illegal and all…'

Ada could sense the woman was going a little off track. 'You were saying about your working day?' she prompted.

'Ah yes,' she held up her index finger. 'While me elder boys are on the fruit and veg stall, I got me barrow of old clothes…' she pointed to the barrow Ada'd seen outside the window. 'I goes around buying them from folk then selling on me own stall at the marketplace. Sometimes I take in clothes repairs and all to make a little extra brass when times get hard. Danny though, like I told you, has his own barrow, he wheels along the streets then he's orf to theatreland at night to sell those oranges and nuts. In fact,' she said and by the gleam in her eyes, Ada could tell she had an idea, 'If I put together some small flower sprays you could go along and sell them outside the theatres tomorrow evening. Make a few bob for yerself. Danny'll show you the ropes. How's that suit?'

That suited very well indeed. 'Oh, thank you, Maggie,' Ada said getting out of her seat and wrapping her arms around the woman's voluminous waist.

Chapter Four

Ada startled as she heard someone enter the front door of the property. Noticing her distress, Maggie smiled. 'Now don't you be worrying none, darlin',' she said, ''tis only our Danny arriving home. He's finished selling at the theatres for tonight.'

Ada let out a breath of relief, for a moment there she had feared it was Winterbourne back again to try to snatch Sam away from her.

The living room door opened and there stood a boy who looked not much older than herself, dressed in a tweed waistcoat and long trousers, with his grubby white shirt sleeves rolled up above the elbow. On his head he sported a flat cloth cap and around his neck was tied a red and white spotted handkerchief. He blinked when he saw Ada and Sam seated at the table and appeared to open his mouth to say something but closed it again.

'This is Ada Cooper and her brother, Sam,' said his mother. 'I've taken them in as lodgers for time being as their landlord turfed them out.'

'Oh,' said Danny. Then he went over to the fireplace and warmed his hands as if wondering what he could say to that.

'We're sorry to impose on your family like this,' said Ada, 'but we really have nowhere else to go, 'cept the workhouse.'

Danny turned to face her and he smiled broadly at her, showing off a set of white even teeth. It was then she noticed the smattering of freckles across his face and his bright blue eyes, just like his mother's. Maybe he was wise too.

'It's 'orright, honest,' he said. 'We're used to our ma taking in folk here. Wouldn't know any different, anyways.'

'Now sit down by the table, son,' Maggie commanded. 'Your stew is ready for you. Ada here is going to join you outside the theatres tomorrow night…' For a moment he frowned as if fearful she would be taking over his pitch but then his mother went on to explain, 'It's 'orright, she'll be selling some little corsages for the ladies to attach to their gowns or cloaks and maybe some gents' buttonholes too.' She turned towards Ada. 'I used to sell them meself afore the boys were born. I've got some nice pink peonies growing in the garden and some sprigs of lavender they'll go nicely with—the posh ladies love the scent of those. It's a bit early for the violets as yet, they won't be ready until September. Tomorrow, you could get over to the marketplace and buy some blooms to sell and even purchase some fruit and veg.'

'But I don't have any money,' Ada protested.

'That's not a problem,' said Maggie. 'I'll loan you some and you can pay me back out of your earnings for time being.'

Ada nodded and thanked the woman, hardly believing that in the space of one day she'd gone from being a young girl living with her brother and sister to becoming a fully-fledged coster girl.

Maggie turned to Danny. 'Perhaps you can take Ada to the market place with you in the morning, to get her set up?'

He nodded. 'Sure thing, Ma. He turned towards Ada. 'You come with me then but it will be very early in the morning just before first light. You can buy some stuff to sell from a basket. Or if you like, there's an old barrow you could use? Yes, that would be easier for yer back. I'll take you to a couple of pitches I've used in the past to settle you in then I'll leave yer alone to go about your business when I can see you are coping well.'

'Thank you,' she said, disbelieving of how kind both Danny and Mrs Donovan were being towards her and Sam.

***

Considering that Maggie's mattress pallet was a little lumpy in places, Ada slept pretty well until Danny roused her to get ready for the marketplace. She had forgotten to mention Sam's bed wetting to Maggie last night. There was no sign though that her brother had wet the pallet when she touched it beneath his blanket when no one was paying attention. Sam still dozed as if in a deep slumber after last night's aggravation with Winterbourne and Maggie said she'd wake him later and keep an eye on him when Ada was away.

After Ada and Danny had washed and dressed, Maggie placed two bowls of steaming porridge down in front of them on the table and a tin mug each of tea which had been sugared. 'For energy for you both today!' She declared. 'Yer going to need it being on the streets for hours on end but as you're not that far away, you can always wheel yer barrow back here for a break, Ada, me love!'

Ada smiled, determined that she would remain on her feet for as long as she could as she wasn't expecting a free ride from the woman, she did intend earning her keep and paying her way if she possibly could.

As they set out for the market with Danny wheeling his large barrow, Ada fought to keep her rather smaller one going in a straight direction.

'Yer'll get used to it!' Danny laughed. 'It is a little temperamental at times, it's got a mind of its own. Best thing is to try to steer it slightly to yer right and that way it will keep in a straight direction.'

She nodded, grateful for the helpful advice. As they pushed their barrows through No Man's Land, Ada was shocked at the bodies lying on the ground, some on top of one another, almost in a heap, but then she realised they'd been doing that to keep warm as one of them stirred. A couple of braziers were still aflame, and one elderly gent with a blanket wrapped around his shoulders, stood before it with his palms turned towards the flames to get some warmth in his old bones.

'Morning, Wilf!' Danny greeted, tipping his flat cap to the man. 'I'll see if I can pick up some cheap fruit for you at the marketplace.'

'Aye, I'll be grateful for it an' all,' Wilf said. Then his old rheumy eyes fell on Ada. 'And who do we have 'ere then?'

'This 'ere is Ada. She's staying at our house with her brother, Sam.'

'Hello, Ada!' Wilf greeted.

Ada smiled at him. 'Hello.' She immediately liked the look of Wilf, he seemed warm and friendly. She would never have thought in a million years that the folk living rough in these parts could be so welcoming.

'Me ma will be along soon to brew up for you all!' Danny said as Wilf nodded, and they walked away from him.

'Does your mother do that every day then?' Ada asked incredulously.

'She sure does. Me ma is the type who even if she had very little would give her last away to those most in need.'

'Just like the story of "The Widow's Mite" in the bible,' Ada marvelled.

'Er, what's that?'

'It's a story about a woman whose husband had died. She didn't have much to live off but what she did have, she gave away. Jesus said that the woman had given the most out of poverty out of everyone as she had so little whereas the others were wealthy and could afford to give. Something like that, anyhow. I don't remember the exact words but it's one of my favourite bible stories. You don't go to church or chapel, Danny?'

He nodded. 'Sometimes if I'm not working on a Sunday. Trouble is Sundays are usually the best trading days for me as housewives make a big dinner then. Me ma goes though. I suppose I only goes for special occasions, like.'

Ada's cartwheels hit a rut in the road, so she carefully steered over it, proud she was now getting the hang of things. She suddenly noticed a gang of young women walking on the cobbled street ahead of them, making a racket as their clogs hit the road and pavements as they gossiped to one another. Some wore headscarves and all had woollen shawls adorning their shoulders. 'Matchgirls,' Ada thought to herself and she pushed ahead to see if Connie was amongst them.

One she recognised as Rose was in deep conversation with the girl beside her. 'Rose!' Ada called. 'Rose!' It seemed an age until the girl stopped in her tracks and whipped her head around to look at Ada.

'Ada!' she said as she smiled broadly. 'But what are you doing up at the crack of dawn?'

'I'm off to the market with my new friend, Danny.'

Rose narrowed her gaze. 'New friend? What's going on?'

'It's our Connie, she's missing. I hung around the factory gates with Sam yesterday, but she wasn't in work. The foreman asked about for me. One of the women in the queue said they'd seen her drinking in a pub the previous night, the night she never returned home to us.'

Rose drew nearer to Ada and lifting her chin with her thumb and forefinger said, 'I don't know what's happened to your Connie. But if she turns up today, I'll be sure to let you know, all right?'

Ada nodded gratefully. 'I'm staying at Danny's house as we've been thrown out of our rooms.'

'That's dreadful,' said Rose with sympathy in her eyes. 'Where yer living Danny in case I need to call with news for Ada?'

'Just the other side of No Man's Land, in the house on the right beneath the railway arches.'

Rose nodded. 'I know it. Think I know your mother and all.'

'Rose, hurry up!' Another young woman that Ada didn't recognise called out. 'We'll be late if we don't get a move on and they'll dock us pay!'

Rose shot Ada one more long, lingering look, before saying, 'I have to go as I can't afford to lose me flamin' job, but I promise I'll keep a look out for yer sister, poppet.' She patted Ada amicably on the head before running off after her friend, most of the other group of girls having now disappeared around the corner of the street. Soon the factory hooter would sound and woe betide if anyone were discovered outside the building after that time as the powers that be at Bryant and May, were renowned as hard taskmasters.

***

'Come on, we better get a move on us selves or we'll miss the pick of the crop as the other barra boys will get first pickings!' Danny grinned.

Ada struggled to keep pace with him as they rushed towards the market as their cartwheels rattled along the cobbles. By now daylight had almost broken through and as she studied the large market building with its dome shaped central conservatory window and it's grand terraces either side, she gasped in awe. A wagon packed with cabbages trundled past them as they entered and porters balanced baskets of fruit and vegetables on top of their heads. It was like another world here as already vendors were hard at it selling their wares and shouting out to all and sundry. 'Get yer ripe fruit 'ere, folks!', 'Fresh strawberries a ha'penny a punnet!', 'Tasty taters!' and so on it went. Some traders were even selling eels and there were stalls displaying fine materials too. Everywhere Ada looked it seemed awash with vibrant colours. Some of the smells she loved like the citrus fruit, but she found the fish quite strong for her nostrils and stomach. The slippery looking fish were laid out on slabs of crushed ice for folk to peruse to see if they liked the look of that early morning's catch.

People jostled each other as if seeking the sensations of taste, sight, and smell. 'Yer get all sorts 'ere,' declared Danny. 'From the fashionable lady to the poor lady, they all rub shoulders with one another at some time of the day.' He sniffed loudly.

Ada nodded and holding the palm of her hand to her chest declared, 'I've never seen such a colourful scene in all me life!' She was totally transfixed by it all before her but realised that being mesmerised wasn't of any help as now they needed to be quick and thrifty and to hit those streets as the competition would be fierce.

'There's a guy over there,' said Danny, 'he's the cheapest I knows. He won't be 'ere too long neither. Come on!' He grabbed her hand and pulled her through the crowd where they found an elderly guy seated beside a wooden stall. 'He's a market gardener, see. Now we might have to barter with him to get the best prices.'

Barter? What on earth did that mean? But she watched in awe as Danny drove the prices of the selected goods down and finally came away with a cartful of turnips, potatoes, cabbages and carrots while he'd secured Ada some shiny red and green apples and a selection of juicy looking pears.

'I managed to knock some money off as some of them is what is known in the trade as "windfall apples". What that means is that they have fallen naturally from the apple trees so might be a little bruised. Some of them housewives likes to purchase them though as they're cheap, though might in some cases be a little unripe. They boil them to a mush to make a jam or chutney from them. But don't worry, I've got some good eating apples for you to sell as well.'

After dipping into his pocket to pay the man, Danny loaded his own barrow up and helped Ada sort out hers and they walked together out of the market and out onto the streets which had now livened up a little as more folk were about their daily business. 'Now you take this street 'ere,' he said finally. 'This is Dixon Street. The people 'ere are nice and friendly, you shouldn't get too much trouble from any other costers or traders to start you off, but where I take you to later, you'll have to be on yer toes! I'll be in the next street over should you have any trouble.'

'But how much should I charge for the apples?' Ada wanted to know.

'For the good 'uns it's six for a penny or three for a ha'penny. If they just want one, it's a farthing! Yer'll have to mix the fruit up a little mind as some of it is bruised. And the big baking apples, they're four for a penny.'

Ada nodded and smiled but she didn't like the thought that some of the fruit she was going to sell might be bruised in case people complained to her.

'Well, go on then, gal!' Danny said shooing her away. 'I'll only be on the next street over if you have any problems.'

Seeing the look on her face, he pushed his barrow towards her, stopping it to cock a cheeky grin at her. 'I'll tell you what, I'll come with you to start you off until you make a few sales, then I have to get off as my best customers come out early. They're expecting me, see. It's me regular patch to work on.'

She nodded. What must he think of her? That she was a big baby that was what.

They found a pitch at the end of the road and then Danny began yelling out. 'Get yer fresh apples here this morning! Nice eating apples and bakers too!' He also rapped on a few knockers and Ada watched in awe as heads appeared behind doors and at windows, and then, ladies made their way over to them with coins and purses in hand. Pretty soon she was rushed off her feet as people collected their apples in wicker baskets and bowls, clutching their prized possessions to their chests to make an apple pie for their husband's next meal or to hand their kids a fresh apple as a treat.

'See, it's not that difficult, is it?' He cocked her a grin. 'I'm off to Queen Street. See you soon! Just watch you keep your takings safe like I showed you to!'

For a moment she felt her heart slump but then another customer came along, distracting her, and she discovered she could manage without him. All the money she took, she placed in a leather wallet that was attached to a belt strapped to her waist, hidden beneath her shawl. Danny had advised her to hide it there and she had tied the shawl around her waist instead of around her shoulders so it wasn't visible to anyone.

The early morning sun had risen and was now high in the sky, so when she turned to face a customer, she was almost blinded by it. She brought her hand to her eyes to shield them. A large form stood before her, now blocking the sun completely. She swallowed hard as she gazed at the man in front of her. He was tall and broad shouldered. He wore a long black shabby coat and his wideawake hat, which was slightly askew on his head, was slightly battered. His face was stubbled as if he hadn't shaved for a couple of days and his dark hair, which was overly long, clung to his forehead. His eyes though, were sharp and green and his lips curved into a wicked smile.

'Well, hello, what do we 'ave 'ere then, missy?'

Ada was too petrified to reply and she looked around anxiously for any sign of Danny's return or any approaching customers, but unfortunately, the last of the stragglers had returned indoors.

She swallowed hard as he said, 'Well?'

It was then she noticed the donkey in the man's wake with a cart hitched to him.

'I'm Ada Cooper,' she said.

'And I'm Frank Malone,' he said. 'Who sent you here?'

Ada frowned and shook her head. 'Sorry, I don't understand?'

He let out an exasperated sounding sigh. 'Who are you working for, girl?'

'For meself, sir.'

He threw back his head and laughed uproariously, the alcohol from his breath causing her to gag. 'Don't try it on with me, missy. Yer must be working for someone and yer on me patch!'

It was then she noticed there were wooden tubs and crates of all manner of fruit and vegetables on the back of his cart. Ada swallowed hard. 'I'm sorry, sir. It's me first morning. A friend brought me here. He's working on another street.'

'Well, yer seems to have sold a lot of stuff very quickly. People are suckers for a pretty young face.' He smiled salaciously at her as if mulling something over in his mind. 'How'd you like to come to work for me?'

There was just something about the man that chilled her to the bone. She couldn't say what it was. Not his appearance as such, more the look behind his eyes that warned her to be wary as he'd been drinking.

'I really have to find me friend now, Sir,' she said beginning to get worried as he closed the space between them, and then, to her horror, he brought his grimy hand to her face. For a moment, she feared he was about to strike her but instead, he lifted her chin between his thumb and forefinger.

'Open yer mouth!' he commanded. 'I want to see your teeth!'

What on earth did he want to see her teeth for? She did as she was told, though she wasn't happy about it. 'Hmmm, pretty face, good teeth, looks a picture of health. If I started you off now at a young age, I could make a mint from you, darlin'.'

'Hey, leave her alone!' shouted a voice, Ada recognised all too well. Relief flooded through her as Danny abandoned his barrow to come racing towards her.

Frank Malone stepped backwards, taken by surprise but once he saw that Danny wasn't much older than the girl he was accosting, he began to laugh. 'Leave it out, sonny! I'm only perusing the goods to see how fresh they are. I'll take 'er orf your hands for a sovereign!' He rattled some coins in his pocket. 'She can come and work for me!'

'Never!' Danny said firmly. 'Ada is now living with us, she's one of the family. Leave 'er alone or I'll go and fetch a bobby on you!'

'And tell them what exactly? That I was offering the little miss the chance to work for me instead? They'd think you was insane. Right benevolent sort, I is!'

As if Danny realised it would be the man's word against his, he stood beside Ada and began to move her barrow towards his. 'Come on, Ada!' he shouted, the whites of his eyes on show as if fearful himself.

Ada did as instructed, and walked behind Danny as she pushed her barrow away. By the time the pair had reached Danny's barrow and turned around, the man was back on his cart and headed off in the distance as his donkey plodded along. Danny breathed out a loud sigh. 'Look Ada,' he said firmly, 'whatever you do you need to keep away from someone like Malone. I know his sort and what he's capable of.'

'And what is that?' she asked with hands on her hips.

'I reckon he lures young girls like you for immoral purposes. He's associated with a house on Cresswell Terrace, where women sell their wares to men. All sorts of ages they are and I bet he makes them drink alcohol too. Some of them think they are off to a better life but I reckon they've gone to a living hell. Gawd only knows what goes on in that place he seems in cahoots with the madame there!'

A shiver coursed Ada's spine as if someone had just walked over her grave.

***

That evening, Ada stood in awe outside the theatre as she watched the crowds spilling in through the double doors as they rushed towards the foyer. Posh carriages and hansom and hackney cabs were drawing up outside. Men in shiny top hats, wearing white silk cravats and scarves were taking the arms of elegant ladies in glistening gowns adorned with smart capes and fanciful hats. Oh, it was exciting and all.

'Watch what I do,' said Danny. 'Then have a go yerself.'

She nodded at him. 'Is it hard to do?'

He shook his head and cocked her a cheeky grin. 'Not really once yer gets the 'ang of it.' Then he turned away from her to shout, 'Get yer fresh oranges and bags o' shelled nuts here, folks! Two a penny! Gents, don't be mean, don't be shy, step right up and buy, buy, buy!'

As he did so, people began to flock around him, gentlemen digging into their pockets to locate their bursting leather wallets.

He sure has the gift of the gab. I've never seen anything like it in me life! Ada smiled at his street patter and polite manner with the nobs. The lad was a natural.

Within a short space of time, Danny had sold everything in the wooden tray that was suspended around his neck by a piece of cord. It reminded Ada of the trays that the matchgirls and boys used to sell their wares from around the streets of Whitechapel.

'Try shouting this,' he advised. 'Sweet blooms for your sweetheart for a penny!'

Ada swallowed hard, taking his advice, but no one seemed to hear her as people barged past.

'Try again, only louder this time,' he persisted.

'Sweet blooms for your sweetheart for a penny!' she shouted. This time heads turned and before she knew it, a gentleman was fumbling in his jacket pocket for some coins. He bought a pretty corsage for his companion who fluttered her long eyelashes in appreciation, and he purchased a matching buttonhole for himself. He even dropped an extra penny in Ada's hand as a tip.

'See, what did I tell you?' said Danny. 'It's not difficult and people will take to you if you keep coming out with me on me pitches. Yer've got a sweet little face like an angel, you're a cherub, me love! People will love you for it!'

Ada felt herself blush. Then she suddenly remembered something she wanted to ask him, but he'd been too busy selling his wares up until now. 'I'm looking for my older sister, Connie,' she told him. 'One of the matchgirls told me she'd seen her last night in a pub and she ain't come home since. I wondered if when we've finished, you'd help me to look for her?'

He tipped back the brim of his flat cap with his hand as if to study her face. 'That's rough,' he said. 'So that's why you've come to live with us for time being, is it?'

She nodded and realised she would be near to tears if he asked too much, so instead she said, 'The name of the pub was The Duke of Wellington.'

'That might prove difficult. There's a few pubs with that Duke name or similar around. Any idea where it is exactly?'

She shrugged her shoulders. 'No. And I didn't think our Connie would go into such places, either!'

'Well, don't worry yourself none. I'll ask me brothers if we can't find it ourselves. They love their ale and their bleedin' gambling but me Ma, well she don't hold with that kind of thing.'

Ada nodded. 'So, which Duke public house do you know of?'

'There's one on the corner there, see, but I think that's The Duke of Buckingham.' He sniffed loudly then proceeded to rub his nose as if in contemplation. 'And there's another a couple of streets over, or is that one The Lord something? Can't rightly remember, but when we've finished off 'ere, I'll take you there. Don't you go in any of them, mind. They're not places for ladies. There's one on the corner back near home which is a well-known coster pub, loads of people I know in there. Our Billy and Davy goes in there sometimes, but they fell out with someone once over an illegal dog fight and ain't been back for a few weeks.'

'What happened, then?'

He shook his head. 'Some geezer in there was a bit cruel to his old dog and allowing other men's dogs to fight it to make money. Billy knocked the man flat to the floor and Davy tucked the little thing under his jacket and ran off with it!'

Ada's mouth popped open in surprise. 'Where is it now, is the dog all right?'

'Aye, he is and we're taking care of him now. Jasper his name is. He was probably in his kennel at the bottom of the garden when you arrived. Ma always brings him into the scullery at night to keep him warm in his basket under the sink.'

Ada nodded approvingly, realising that Maggie was a kind-hearted sort.

'I got to warn you,' he glanced up and down the street. 'Some of the flower girls you might encounter are rum sorts.'

'Rum sorts?' she quirked a curious brow as she glanced around them, furtively.

'What I mean is, they ain't just selling flowers if you get my meaning!' He tapped a grubby index finger to the side of his nose.

Still none the wiser, she asked, 'What other stuff are they selling then?'

He drew in a breath and let it out again. 'Themselves. They follow some of the city gents who buy their blooms from them and pester them half to death sometimes, until they succumb to their particular charms.' He looked at her and chuckled. 'Yer still don't get it, do you?'

She shook her head. 'Nope!'

'They offer their bodies in return for a few pennies or let the gents have a quick fumble up a dark alleyway, or sometimes…even inside the gentlemen's coaches.'

Ada felt herself grow hot. 'I…I didn't know they did things like that!'

'Well, they do. You'll be able to recognise them as they are the ones reeking of strong perfume!' He pinched the end of his nose with his thumb and forefinger which caused Ada to giggle. 'And they wear bright coloured dresses and bonnets so as they'll get noticed—they're easy to pick out from the rest of the flower girls. If they think you're after their patch they'll try to scalp you, they will.' Ada shivered, she didn't much like the sound of that. 'But don't worry I'll protect you—as long as you stick with me, you'll be fine. It's at night time you need to take care really.'

Danny led her to another place which he explained as a variety music hall. The sorts going in there were different to the theatre crowd. Not a toff in sight here but lots of uproarious sorts she noticed, but trade was brisk, and she noticed how Danny would drop his prices here and there if he felt sorry for someone, yet with the theatre crowd of nobs he was happy to accept over the odds for his produce. Ada thought she could learn a valuable lesson from watching him.

When they had sold up for the evening, he led her to The Duke of Wellington pub nearer home and told her to wait outside while he slipped inside as he assured her it was no place for a lady like herself.

Then what on earth did our Connie go into a place like that for? It puzzled her.

The stench of beer fumes mingling with tobacco smoke caused her to gag and she wished Danny would hurry up. It seemed an age since he'd entered via two half glazed swing doors. Every time someone exited or entered the premises that smell would hit her full force. She heard clinks of glasses, loud voices, laughs and cheers and every so often, the sound of someone playing some sort of jolly song on the piano as the pianist tinkled the ivories.

Someone was now singing along too, *'The boy I love is up in the gallery!'* Whoever she was she she had the most beautiful singing voice. It was a song that Ada recognised as her sister sang it a lot. Surely that wasn't Connie singing in there? Without giving it much thought, she dashed in through the door, but she couldn't see who was singing as there were so many men stood in the way. With determination, she nudged past various elbows, almost knocking the silver tankard out of one young man's hand. Their heads were all turned towards the woman in front of them and to her dismay, Danny was stood there open-mouthed as if spellbound by the young woman who most certainly was not her sister Connie. His head whipped around when he saw her approach.

'I thought we were supposed to be looking for my sister not that lady!' she said with her head held high.

'Sorry, Ada. She does look nice though, don't she?'

Ada had to admit that she did indeed look rather lovely in her low-cut amethyst dress edged with black lace. The young woman's raven black hair was pinned up and she wore a flowered comb to secure it in place. Her eyes were dark and shining, reminding Ada of a Spanish lady she'd once encountered in the marketplace. The woman had been selling some exquisite materials: silks, satins, and cottons edged with threads of silver and gold. Connie had been keen to purchase some from her, but the materials were a little too expensive. That woman did look a mysterious creature indeed.

'Come on, Queenie!' a man from the crowd yelled behind cupped hands as others clapped and cheered.

Much to Ada's disgust, several men were now shouting, and one even wolf-whistled. 'Let's get out of here sharpish!' She nudged Danny's elbow.

'Don't be too hasty, me love,' he consoled. 'You wanna find your sister, don't ya?' She nodded. 'Then trust me, darlin'. I know what I'm doing.'

Ada felt it total humiliation as she stood there as the woman lifted the skirts of her dress to reveal her slender ankles in her high heeled leather ankle boots. You could even see the frills of her petticoats. Ma would have called her a trollop even though she was pretty to the eye.

When the performance had ended and Queenie made her way from the makeshift stage, Danny yelled, ''Oi Queenie, you got time for a word with me friend by 'ere?'

Queenie nodded and smiled, then she sauntered towards them lifting the hem of her dress to ensure she didn't trip over it as she approached. It was obvious to Ada that Danny had encountered the young woman before as they seemed familiar with one another.

'This 'ere is Queenie!' Danny introduced. 'She's a flame of me brother, Billy.'

Ada nodded, totally awestruck.

'And who might we have here then?' Queenie raised an inquisitive brow.

'My name's Ada Cooper,' Ada began, 'pleased to meet you, Miss.'

'Cor, ain't you a sweet one. Good manners and all. I like that!'

Ada blushed but she began to warm to the woman. 'I'm looking for me sister, she was in here last night someone said.'

'Who's yer sister then, ducks?'

'Connie. Connie Cooper, she works at the match factory.'

For a few seconds, Ada thought she detected a flicker of recognition in the woman's eyes but then the shutters came down as she said, 'Don't know her, luv. Now you both better be getting along as children ain't allowed in here.'

Danny smirked at her and tipping his cap in a theatrical way as he bowed said, 'Yer'll never keep me away from this place, Queenie. I loves coming in 'ere, I do.'

She smiled broadly. 'I know you do but you can't bring a young lady in a place like this.' She began to playfully shoo them away.

Ada turned and said, 'Please, Miss. If my sister does show up here, I'm staying with Danny's mother, Maggie, in the house beneath the arches…'

Queenie nodded as if in sympathy for her plight, but Ada couldn't help sensing that maybe the young woman knew more than she was letting on.

***

'You're quiet, gal!' Danny said, draping his arm protectively around Ada's shoulder. He'd already warned her that the area they were now in was quite dangerous, especially for young women like herself. She'd blushed when he'd referred to her as "a young woman" as mostly she was referred to as a "kid", "child" or "little girl". It made her feel very grown up indeed.

She drew in a deep breath and let it out again. 'I don't believe that Queenie one!' She said quite suddenly, causing him to whip his head around and look her in the face.

He frowned and cocked his head in a quizzical fashion as he removed his arm so he could stand before her and challenge what she'd just said. 'But why not? I really like Queenie, she would never lie, not in front of me!'

'Got it bad, 'ave you?' Ada tapped her foot as she stood with the wicker basket over her arm.

'No, I ain't, but I know she's not that sort. What would make you say such a thing?'

'I could see it in her eyes. She knows something about Connie but she's not going to tell us for some reason.' Ada felt her bottom lip quiver and noticing her distress, Danny pulled her towards him and hugged her.

'Now, listen to me,' he said firmly, as he wiped away her tears with the pads of his dirty looking thumbs. 'If Queenie knows something then I'm going to find out for you. It might be that she couldn't say anything to us there and then as there were others around.' He sighed. 'She's got another boyfriend now. She doesn't see our Billy anymore. He treated her well, but they fell out over his gambling, but the new beau, well he's a rum sort. Nasty bit of work. It's possible she fears him and maybe that's why she said nothing tonight.'

Ada nodded, then sniffed, 'Please can we go back there and ask her again?'

Danny shook his head. 'No, time is getting on and Ma will worry if we're late. I'll be back this way in the morning, and I'll ask her then. She helps clean the pub as well, see.'

Long shadows had fallen across the cobbled street and now archways and alleys seemed threatening to Ada beneath the dim glow of the gaslights. She wasn't used to being out this late and not being familiar with the area, a shiver coursed her spine. Was Connie here last night, like that woman from the match factory claimed? And if she was, what on earth had happened to her since?

They walked in companionable silence back to Danny's house. Every so often, Ada'd notice something that was unusual for her to see, like a couple spooning against a lamp post or a couple of ladies hanging around outside various public houses attracting attention from certain men folk.

'There's another reason I don't want you to stay out here too late,' Danny said.

'What's that?'

As he said that a chill wind whipped up sending a sheet of newspaper drifting across the road. 'There have been reports of a man watching the women folk around here—bad girls like those what hang around these parts at night.'

'A bit like those flower girls you told me about?'

Danny nodded. 'It's not safe around here for a female on her own.'

'Y…you don't think the man people are talking about caught our Connie and killed her?' she asked, with terror in her voice.

'No. Your sister's a good gal by the sound of it, ain't she?'

Ada nodded, but now she wasn't at all convinced that Connie was as good as all that. No decent young woman would be seen dead in a pub, well that's what her parents had always instilled into their daughters, so why was Connie seen in one last night? That match woman with the red hair that she'd seen in the queue outside the factory, she could believe it of as she seemed common as muck, but her sister, Connie? No. Never in a million years.

'Then she should be all right as he doesn't follow good girls from the pubs!' Danny reassured, patting her on the back.

She blew out a breath of relief. Surely, he'd realise she wasn't that sort? But then again, Connie had looked a little dressed up last night when she left home and she was wearing scent too! Trying to push her concerns to the back of her mind she tried to focus on what Danny was now saying to her.

'Me ma always says, "As home-life vanishes, the public 'ouse appears!"'

Ada frowned. What on earth did Maggie mean by that? 'You see,' Danny continued, 'the folk around these parts they crave alcohol. They're exhausted and overworked and fed up to the back teeth of their poor lives…'

'I think I understand,' she said meekly.

'So, sometimes when a large family lives in one room and has to struggle to get the rent money together and to put food on the table, their home life proves impossible. Some are even worse off than that, they live hand to mouth.'

She stopped for a moment. 'What does that mean?'

'What it means, my dear Ada, is that they live day to day. Some work hard to get a few pennies to stop at a doss house overnight, and when they can't, well they have to seek desperate measures like those unfortunates—those women who ply their trade outside pubs. Sometimes it's the only way to get some food in their bellies.'

'That's so sad.' Maybe that's what had happened to Connie last night as she'd been fearful about the rent money.

'Do you know, me ma knew a family living close by. Twelve of them they were all living in two small rooms, rented they were. One of their kiddies passed away and they had to keep that poor child laid out in the same room they ate and slept in for days on end until they could afford to bury him. Even then it was classed as a pauper's grave. Sad that was.'

'So, you knew the family?'

He nodded. 'Aye, they used to call around to see me ma.'

'What became of them?'

'Think a couple more of the kids died and then eventually so did the father, and once he'd gone, they all ended up in the workhouse as there was no head of the house to look after them anymore.'

Ada shivered as the memory of how Winterbourne wanted to throw her to the mercy of the workhouse, washed over her.

'Never mind, gal,' said Danny as if trying to cheer her up. 'Me ma always makes me a nice cup of cocoa and some thick toast with strawberry jam on top of it when I get home after a theatre trip. Fancy some?'

'Yes, please.' She was feeling rather hungry now as they'd been on their feet the best part of a couple of hours to catch the theatre crowds.

When they arrived home, Sam was already tucked up in bed by the window.

Maggie looked at her. 'Yer brother will have to bunk up with Danny for tonight as I just noticed he soaked through that mattress pallet last night…' Ada felt a sliver of guilt for not warning the woman. 'I've got an old piece of rubber sheeting to go under the main sheet. Once the pallet is dried out he can go back to that with the rubber sheet of course and Danny can have his own bed to himself once more…' Maggie added. Danny frowned. 'It's only for one night, son.' She shook her head. 'Can't expect the lad to sleep on a wet mattress, can we?'

Danny forced a smile. 'Suppose not.'

Ada sighed. 'Sorry, Mrs Donovan. I should have told you about Sam's bed wetting. He doesn't do it much now but I think he was petrified after the night we had last night.'

Maggie smiled. 'I quite understand, love. Think no more of it. We'll manage. I might start rousing him at night so he can have a little tinkle in the chamber pot, until he grows out of it.' She angled her head at Ada. 'Anyhow, how'd you do tonight, Ada?'

Danny grinned and answered for her. 'Ada did very well, Ma. I think the theatre goers really took to her selling those buttonhole flowers and the small corsages too. She's a natural now with all the patter! Some of the city gents dropped a little extra into her hand too as she looks like a little angel—so pretty and sweet!'

Ada blushed at Danny's kind words about her.

'That's the spirit!' Maggie said rolling up her sleeves. 'Now strawberry jam on toast and a cup of cocoa for the both of you it is!'

Ada nodded and smiled, they'd certainly fallen in lucky to have met Maggie and her family. If they hadn't, by now she and Sam might be separated, he'd be living in a big house with a posh lady and she residing at the workhouse, just another inmate lost in the crowd of vacant faces as they eventually gave up hope of ever getting out of there. It didn't bear thinking about as if that had occurred then maybe with time, and Sam's young age, he'd have forgotten about her and Connie as he became a young gentleman with a future ahead of him. Was she selfish for not allowing him to go off with that lady? But then again, if he had gone how could she be certain that he would be treated well? To Ada, it was family that mattered and good old love and loyalty, not money. Money was necessary, yes, of course it was, but if they could be happy and healthy on very little then that was all that mattered in the end.

Chapter Five

The following morning passed by without any further problems regarding Frank Malone as this time Danny kept Ada by his side as they both sold their wares on the same streets, then just before midday, Danny suggested they return to the pub to have a word with Queenie. Ada wondered if it would do any good but she went along with him anyway, trailing behind with her barrow as now she ached all over something rotten from pushing that barrow and standing on her feet for hours on end. She could have done with a nice long cool drink too and something to eat. This coster life wasn't as easy as she thought it would be.

'In Dublin's fair city where girls are so pretty…' she heard the most melodious voice singing, surely that wasn't Queenie again? Last night she'd sounded quite coarse in front of the menfolk in the pub but now she sounded like an angel to Ada's ears with her dulcet, soothing tone.

Danny pushed open the pub's double doors to see Queenie bending over some round tables polishing them with a duster. The aroma of lavender and beeswax permeated Ada's senses, reminding her of when her mother had polished their sparse rented furniture. Even though they didn't have a lot Ma had taken pride in their home.

Danny sidled up behind Queenie as she continued to sing, *'I first set my eyes on sweet Molly Malone as I wheeled out my barrow through streets broad and narrow, singing cockles and muscles alive alive oh!'*

As if sensing someone behind her, and Ada was positive that Danny was up to something, maybe planning on putting his hands over the woman's eyes to ask guess who, Queenie whipped around quickly discarding her soiled duster on the table.

'Well, bless me soul, it's you pair of rascals back again!' she chuckled, this time not at all guarded as she had been the previous night. 'What brings you here? We're not open for another ten minutes.'

Ada eyed the landlord in the background wiping down the bar counter and then there was the chink of beer glasses as a buxom looking barmaid beside him, placed them on the shelf behind her.

'We want to ask you about Connie again…' Danny began.

Queenie removed his cap and ruffled his hair, then replaced it on his head. 'Look, I told you last night, I don't know nothing.'

'Please,' said Ada suddenly, 'me sister was supposed to have been drinking in here the night before last and she never came home. She's still missing.'

Queenie drew near to her. 'What's she look like, yer sister? We get all sorts in here, mind.'

Ada wanted to say how pretty her sister was and that she was one of the best looking girls at the match factory, but instead, she said, 'She's as tall as what you are but thinner, long blonde hair, green eyes and a few freckles like what I have.'

It was as if a light suddenly switched on in Queenie's mind as she gazed up at the ceiling as if trying to think. 'Well now you come to mention it there was a young lady in here that night what fits that description, though her hair wasn't long and loose she had it pinned up. Would that be her?'

Ada struggled to think what Connie's hair had been like that night, and then she remembered, she had pinned it up. 'Yes, that sounds like her. She was wearing a floral dress.'

'Sounds like the same young woman then. Well…' she said lowering her voice to barely a whisper so that Ada had to lean in to listen carefully. 'I'd not seen her before, she did look a little out of place and was in the company of a much older, well-dressed man. Never seen him in here before but then I noticed suddenly he was alone as if she'd left in a rush, he bolted out of the door as if in pursuit of her, and didn't return after that. I thought it a bit strange meself at first but then thought no more of it as we often get men from up West looking for girls around these parts, particularly those of easy virtue, if you get me drift?'

Ada bit her bottom lip. 'Our Connie isn't of easy virtue!' she said as she stamped her foot.

Queenie smiled. 'I'm sorry darlin' was only trying to tell you how it is around these parts. I don't know anything about your sister but young women around Whitechapel don't go off with smartly dressed gents unless they get paid for it.'

Ada felt like punching Queenie in the face for saying that. Danny appeared to sense how Ada felt, so he placed a reassuring arm around her shoulder. 'I don't think Queenie means any harm by what she said, Ada,' he said softly. 'It's true what she says though, I know that meself. Might there be any reason she was trying to earn some extra money?'

'Yes,' said Ada, sobbing now as reality hit, 'we needed the rent money badly. I wish she had told me what she was up to.'

'Happen she couldn't, darlin',' Queenie reassured. 'Maybe she was going to go off with him just the once to straighten out her finances. That happens sometimes around here, seamstresses or factory workers who have fallen on hard times, will often go off with fellas to earn a few shillings. Some may never, ever do it again, but for others it becomes a way of life. Trouble is they put themselves at risk as there have been one or two murders that I know of working girls!' she said, her eyes enlarging as if she were fearful of the situation.

'Anything of late?' Danny asked.

'None that I've heard of for a while but that don't mean *he* ain't about—that geezer what's been watching women and following them home. It's just not safe for young women in this area.'

'I do hope that gent me sister was with wasn't him!' Ada felt panicked and for a moment felt as though she was struggling to catch her breath. Aware of this, Queenie insisted she sit down for a minute while she returned with a glass of water for her.

Noticing what was going on, the landlord looked on and shining a silver tankard with a cloth, said in a loud tone of voice, 'Yer talkin' about that prowler?'

Queenie nodded at him. 'Yes, Fred.'

He placed the tankard down and ran his index finger across his throat, causing Ada to shiver from top to toe. 'One of the working girls in here the other evening reckons she was followed home by some bloke with a knife, she managed to run away from him but not before he'd tried it on with her and slashed her cheek with his knife—she's petrified half to death, she is! Kept off the streets for a couple of night but now back out working again as she needs the dough!'

Ada noticed Queenie casting a hard glance at Fred. 'Please, Fred.'

Looking at Ada and now aware of her tender age, he sniffed loudly. 'Sorry 'bout that, young lady. I get carried away sometimes as one of me girls working here was also attacked once but not as bad as that. Not sure if it were him, the bleedin' butcher!'

Queenie drew near to him. ''ere, Fred…' she said as if about to ask the man a favour. 'Did you see a young lady in here night before last? She was in the company of an older smartly dressed gent? Left before him she did…'

Fred nodded. 'Aye, I noticed that. He weren't around from these parts.' He glanced at Ada, 'is she belonging to you, lass?'

'Yes. She's me sister Connie. She never came home.'

Fred slowly shook his head and tutted. 'Oh, dear…'

'Think, Fred, please…' Queenie pleaded. 'Did you notice anything about the man? Or anything he said?'

He frowned and looking up at the ceiling as if trying to think said, 'Well now you come to mention it, he mentioned something about going up West…'

'Did you manage to catch sight of them leaving, Fred?' Queenie pursed her lips and tilted her head on one side.

'No, saw the young lady go as if in a rush but didn't notice him leave here. About the same time one of the customers told me there were a posh coach parked up outside.'

'Posh in what sort of way?' Danny intervened.

Fred grinned. 'Posh as in the way what it was monogrammed with some sort of crest.'

'Cor!' Danny's eyes lit up like a pair of flaming beacons. 'You mean like a king or something?'

'More like a prince,' Fred nodded.

'Hey, you don't reckon that might have been Prince Albert, do you?' Queenie stood with hands on hips, but Fred vigorously shook his head.

'No, I do not. That guy was posh, granted, but noble, definitely not and he were too old to be him. Tis a coincidence with the name, that's all. Anyhow, think that gentleman was on foot and it weren't his coach.'

Ada's thoughts were swimming in her head, whirling around and around. Nothing made sense. Why would Connie go off with some kind of gent like that after promising to come home to her and Sam?

'Are you all right, darlin'?' Queenie asked as she turned her attention back to Ada.

'It's 'orright,' Danny intervened, laying a hand on Ada's shoulder to show his support. 'I'll get her back home for a rest.'

Queenie nodded. 'I think you'd better had.'

***

As they arrived back at Danny's house, Ada could sense something was amiss as Maggie rushed out to greet them. 'Oh, I'm so glad you're both back. I have to get the doctor out to your Sam, Ada…' Maggie said breathlessly.

Ada let go of her barrow as it veered off on its own towards the garden wall, finally coming to rest against the low, white fence of Maggie's prized flower garden. Ada was no longer even aware of it, nor did she care, as she looked at Maggie and asked, 'Is it his chest?'

Maggie nodded holding the palm of her hand against her bosom as she panted out the words. 'I'm. Afraid. So. He's been struggling for breath since he woke up this morning. I've dosed him with that medicine you gave me but it's not doing anything. We need to get the doctor.' She turned towards her son. 'Danny, can you run over to Charlton Terrace and ask Dr Scott to come as quick as possible?' Danny nodded and was about to leave when Maggie reached into her apron pocket and handed him a few coins. ''Ere take this. He'll need paying. Go as quickly as you can.'

It was just a few seconds as he absorbed his mother's words and then he was off as quick as a whippet chasing a hare.

Maggie draped her arm around Ada's shoulders and led her into the house to the living room where Sam was sitting propped up in the bed near the window. His little face looked tinged blue and his eyes were sad, large and doe-like, but he didn't even force a smile when he saw his sister had returned.

'Hello, Sam,' she said softly as she approached and wrapped her arm around his thin wiry frame and she cuddled him towards her as she sat on the bed beside him. Fat tears slipped down her cheeks, but Sam couldn't see she was crying and neither did she want him to.

'I tried him with the cough medicine like what I told you and some nourishing soup, but he has hardly taken a thing, bless him, as he's finding it difficult to swallow. Hopefully, the doctor can spot what's wrong with him,' Maggie suggested, but by the look on her face, Ada could see the woman didn't look all that hopeful herself.

Ada nursed her brother, constantly telling him all would be all right as she rocked him against her chest and sang softly to him, but she feared he was going the way of their parents as he gasped to take even a breath and as the clocked ticked away, Ada urged the doctor in her mind to get there as quickly as he could but it was almost an hour later that he turned up with Danny in tow, with his black leather Gladstone bag in his hand.

By now Sam's nose, mouth and fingernails looked tinged blue. Drool was running down the sides of his mouth and he was making a high-pitched noise.

Doctor Scott smiled as he entered and turning to Maggie asked, 'How long has the boy been like this?'

'Since early this morning, Doctor. From around seven o'clock when he first rose. I tried to get him to eat and drink but he's been having trouble swallowing and his breathing has got considerably worse ever since. That's why I decided to call you out.'

'You did right,' the doctor reassured. 'Go and boil a kettle on that stove there,' he commanded.

Ada thought it was very inappropriate of the doctor to want a cup of tea at a time like this. Couldn't he see how sick her brother was? As if reading her mind, he said, 'Now if it's what I suspect it is then it won't be as bad as all that. I want a bit of steam released into the room from the kettle, that's all.'

Sam coughed making a barking sound like a seal which Ada had once seen at the zoo, which caused the doctor to smile. 'Yes, I think my diagnosis is correct. I'll just examine his chest though.' Ada got off the bed and stood by the window to allow the doctor access. He leaned over to open his leather bag which was resting on a chair by the side of the bed and removed his stethoscope plugging it into his ears, so he could listen to Sam's chest. Ada had seen one of those before when her parents were ill and they'd scraped some pennies together to fetch the doctor but it had been to no avail as their parents had passed away anyhow.

Holding her breath while the doctor palpated her brother's chest with his fingers, she watched as he listened intently through the stethoscope. Ada let out a long sigh of relief as he finally announced. 'It's as I suspected, croupous cough, more commonly known as "croop", Ma'am. Has the boy had any sort of fever or cold symptoms before today?' He looked at Maggie.

Maggie stood before them opened mouthed as she obviously wasn't all that sure, she exchanged glances with Ada. 'Well has he, Ada?'

Ada nodded slowly. 'Yes, sir. He had some sort of cold and Mrs Adler gave us some medicine for him.'

'Fetch it to me,' said the doctor.

'Don't fret none, darlin'' Maggie reassured. 'I got the bottle safe in me cupboard.' She walked off to fetch it as the doctor replaced his stethoscope inside his open bag.

'Here it is, Doctor. What do you reckon might be in it?' Maggie handed the bottle over to him for inspection.

There was no label, so he removed the stopper and sniffed. 'Smells like some sort of onion water to me, homemade. Some folk swear by the stuff, at any rate it won't harm him but I think I'll give you some cough mixture instead. He's got the remnants of a cold complicated by croup. Just keep boiling kettles for a few hours to keep the air in here moist, keep him sitting in an upright position well propped up with pillows and give the lad plenty of fluids and peace too!' He winked at Ada, who smiled at the medic. Initially, she'd been fearful of him as he had quite a sharp tone but now he didn't seem too bad. He reached into his bag and handed Maggie a brown bottle with a rubber stopper in it. 'Give the lad one spoonful three times a day,' then he glanced at Sam. 'It won't taste very nice, but it will do you the power of good, young man, and I'm sure Mrs Donovan will give you something afterwards to take the taste away if you're a good lad.' He patted Sam affectionately on the head.

For the first time Sam nodded and smiled, which gladdened Ada's heart. She felt so full of happiness and relief now that Sam was not going the way of their parents that she forgot all about her earlier tiredness. Though, she had not forgotten about Connie and the fact she was still missing and maybe with some toffed up gent and all.

Chapter Six

Ada had the idea to return to the tenement to speak to Mrs Adler and Jakob in case her sister had shown up in their absence and was seeking her and Sam. She pushed her barrow there after selling up her produce the following day. The apples had all sold out apart from two which were badly bruised, but she and Danny polished those off for their dinner.

As she gazed up at the red dilapidated brick building before her with its rotting window frames, this time she felt no fear as her protector, Danny, was by her side. He'd promised he wouldn't let anyone take her away from him. Besides, as his elder brothers had warned Mr Winterbourne off with the promise of the pasting of his life, it was now doubtful he'd even approach her.

The battered looking green front door to the property with its peeling paint, was ajar when they approached, which was most unusual as tenants were warned they were to keep it shut apart from when they were entering or leaving the property. Besides which, most felt safer keeping it locked as who knew who could just walk in off the street otherwise. And as many owed money to various lenders in the area, that suited them just fine.

'This is strange,' said Ada frowning, 'the main door is never left open like this.' She glanced up and down the street before gingerly pushing it a little.

'Maybe someone's moving in or out and it has to be left open for ease of use, like,' Danny said.

'Ah, maybe.' That would make sense and Ada felt herself relaxing as she huffed out a breath of relief. But as soon as Danny pushed the door wide open to allow them access to the building as it creaked loudly, it was evident something was wrong.

'You stay here,' he advised. 'Keep an eye on our barrows.'

'Please, Danny. Be careful.' She chewed her bottom lip as she nervously glanced up and down the street, still convinced Winterbourne was out there somewhere.

Her earlier relief now turned to anxiety as Danny stepped into the property over the threshold of the doorstep. A strong smell wafted out to meet her, which reminded her of sooty smoke when there was a blow back down the chimney.

Danny turned behind to look at her. 'There's been a fire here at some time or another,' he said, his voice echoing down the long passageway. 'All the doors to the rooms are wide open. Doesn't look like there's anybody here.'

'Please, let me come inside, I have to check up on Mrs Adler and Jakob, they're our friends.'

He nodded, then turned, watching her as she nervously stepped inside. 'It's all right, there ain't much left on the barrows to steal but I don't want to leave them unguarded for too long. I'll come with you in case this place is in a dangerous state.'

As she stood in the passageway, apart from the strong acrid smell of smoke which caused her to choke, she noticed the soot-blackened walls. It no longer looked like their home. It had been shabby to begin with but now it looked like something else entirely.

'Where do your friends live?' Danny wanted to know.

'Upstairs in the rooms opposite ours.'

He glanced at the staircase, 'We'll have to take care climbing that wooden staircase as it could give way after that fire.' He frowned.

She nodded as gingerly they made their way up the stairs, one careful footstep at a time, as the wooden staircase creaked beneath them. This felt unreal to Ada as if she were in some sort of dream. 'Mrs Adler!' she called out as she approached the front door of the apartment, but there was no reply only her own voice echoing back at her.

The doors to all the rooms were wide open just as they had been downstairs. Ada could have cried when she stepped inside Mrs Adler's place as her beautiful flocked wallpaper was all soot stained and ruined, and some pieces of furniture Ada had admired, had now mysteriously vanished. Where was the walnut dresser that the woman had taken such pride in polishing?

'Maybe the Adlers returned and took some of their things with them?' She looked at Danny with hope.

He shrugged. 'More likely after there was a fire here, people came in and looted the place. Sorry, darlin' but that's what folk are like around 'ere, they see an opportunity and grab it with both hands. Seen it happen afore now.' He sniffed loudly as he dug his hands deep into the pockets of his corduroy trousers.

Oh no! This was too much for Ada to bear as her shoulders wracked and she began to sob bitterly, which caused Danny to place a reassuring arm around her shoulders. 'Don't take on so, Ada. The

Adlers might have escaped and might now be staying somewhere else.'

She nodded, hoping he was right. Something else just occurred to her. 'We better check my old place opposite,' she said, 'in case there are any signs our Connie had returned home.'

Reaching out, Danny held hold of her hand. 'Don't be too hasty, Ada. Are you sure you want to check the room out, it might upset you, love…'

Oh, no, was Danny thinking that her sister may have perished in the fire?

She looked up at him through glazed eyes. There was a lump in her throat that was refusing to go away, so she just nodded. He released her hand and she made her way tentatively across the landing, hesitating as she stood outside the door which was partly ajar. She lifted her hand and pushed it as her heart pounded beneath her dress. What she saw there caused her to gasp with surprise. 'Oh!'

***

'What is it, Ada?' Danny came rushing up behind her so she could feel the warmth of his breath on her cheek as he spoke. 'What's bothering you, love?'

'It's our rooms, they look untouched by the fire,' she said, hardly believing her eyes as she blinked in complete disbelief. 'The room looks exactly the same as we left it except the fire in the grate has gone out now.'

Both children stood in the room, looking around them. 'So, there's no sign your sister has returned?'

She rushed to pull open a couple of cupboards and drawers and checked their contents before saying, 'No, she's not been here, all her things are still in the drawer. Jakob had said he'd keep them safe for us so I wonder what happened.'

Danny shrugged his shoulders. 'Maybe the fire started not long after you left here and the Adlers had no choice but to get out as soon as they could.'

'Maybe…' she stood staring at the room not quite understanding what had occurred until Danny gently tapped her on the shoulder.

'We need to get out of here, fast,' he said. 'We could get into all kinds of trouble otherwise.'

She nodded, realising he had a point, especially if Winterbourne discovered them, she figured he'd be angry as hell as the Donovan brothers had laid into him and snatched Sam. 'I'll just take our Connie's stuff,' she said.

'Hurry then,' he urged now as his eyes darted back and forth as if he were suddenly spooked by something but now, strangely enough, Ada no longer felt that way at all. She was perfectly at peace. This was an omen. No bad thing would happen to her sister. Even her clothes had somehow survived a raging fire.

She quickly bundled them up and threw them into an old wooden crate they'd previously kept for firewood, which Danny carried down the stairs for her. Someone must have been looking out for them as even their barrows were still outside where they'd left them, but Danny thought maybe someone had nicked some onions off his, although Ada reckoned it looked the same amount as there had been when they'd entered the property. She guessed though he was used to being suspicious being in his line of work as there was a lot of competition not just from other vendors but from people thieving from his barrow as well if he was distracted. He loaded the crate onto his rather larger barrow and pushed it towards home as Ada followed behind in his wake as she pushed hers.

Although she felt remorse about the fire, her spirits soared now that she had retrieved some belongings of Connie's. As well as a couple of dresses, skirts, and blouses, she'd even managed to locate her sister's tortoise shell hairbrush that Ma had bought her for her birthday one year—it was a cherished and much loved possession of Connie's.

***

When they arrived back home, Ada was relieved to see that Sam was now up and about. He was seated at the table as Maggie placed a bowl of soup in front of him. 'It's chicken,' she proudly announced. 'A friend of mine from the Ukraine used to swear by it, not a lot of meat in it mind you, but I boiled some bones with bits o'chicken still on them and added some tatas, onions, herbs from me garden, and a bit of salt and pepper.' She ruffled Sam's hair and he looked up at the woman and smiled.

'How are you feeling, Sam?' Ada asked.

He nodded at her and said, 'I'm all better now thank you, Ada.' Then he carried on eating.

'There don't seem to be all that much wrong with him now since he's had a couple of doses of that medicine, and I kept boiling the kettle to keep the air moist here. Suppose I could have saved meself a few pennies if I'd realised croup is all it was…'

Ada, feeling embarrassed, unclipped the leather money belt from around her waist and was about to hand it over to Maggie. 'Sorry about that,' she said.

Maggie held up her vertical palm. 'Now I'm not wanting any money off you at all, 'cept maybe occasionally to help buy a bit of food if we run out. We're all right for time being and I don't begrudge paying the doctor for his diagnosis of Sam's ailment. What I meant was, I should have realised that it was croup in the first place. I thought it was something more serious than it really was.'

Danny shook his head and placed the wooden crate he'd just hefted from his barrow, onto the table. 'You did the right thing though Ma as it might have been more serious.'

'What's in that crate?' Maggie raised an inquisitive brow.

'It's their Connie's belongings from their old digs. We went over there to see if we could speak to Ada's friends, but the place looks like it's had some sort of fire and all the tenants have left. Ada found these bits and pieces, so we brought them back here.'

'Most curious,' said Maggie, rubbing her chin.

Sam looked up from his soup. 'You saw our Connie then, Ada?' he asked hopefully.

'No, I didn't,' said Ada. 'But our old digs has been untouched by the fire and I've saved all Connie's stuff so when we find her someday, we can return them to her.' That answer seemed to satisfy her brother for now though but Ada could tell by the look on Maggie's face that the woman doubted the pair would ever set eyes on their Connie again.

***

That evening it was time to work the theatres again but Ada was dismayed to discover a few other flower girls had set up their pitches in that area, they seemed confident too as some of them cried out to appeal to the crowds flocking in. Some were younger than her and barefooted and those girls seemed to do best as they cried out, 'Please, sir, do buy me flowers fer yer lovely lady! I'm only a poor little girl, I am!' or 'Please kind lady, buy me violets. O, do! Please! I'm a poor little girl, I am! Do buy a bunch, please, kind lady, kind gent!' But there were other older girls around who seemed more dressed up, their faces powdered and rouged who were obviously plying their wares in favour of the unaccompanied gentlemen who passed them by.

Ada watched in horror as one, who appeared even younger than Connie, maybe she was around fourteen or fifteen, disappeared around the corner with a furtive looking gentleman, who kept glancing around himself. She now had a fair idea what that flower girl would be getting up to and that maybe that man who had just arrived in a shiny coach had no intention of going to the theatre at all, or of purchasing any flowers for that matter. He'd just arrived to take her off somewhere for some other reason that had nothing at all to do with flowers or theatre performances.

'Don't be put off by that Covent Garden lot, Ada, love,' Danny soothed. 'I think they've flooded over here from their usual pitch as I hear the theatre they favour is shut this evening. Most nights they're not here, just now and again, like. They can earn more at the other theatre as it's a lot bigger than this one so they get more custom.'

Ada opened her mouth and closed it again. 'I just couldn't believe how that young flower girl just went off with a man who looked almost old enough to be her father.'

Danny shook his head. 'It happens, I'm afraid. Maybe that gal will earn enough tonight for her family to eat for the rest of the week. That's how it works. She might earn more from going off with one or two gents in one night than she would selling her moss roses for a full fortnight!'

'But me Ma and Pa would never 'ave allowed me or Connie to do something like that. Do you think her parents know what she's up to?'

He dug his hands into his trouser pockets and absently kicked the kerb with his boot. 'I expect so.'

Ada shivered. She still had a basket of flowers to sell—how could she compete with this lot? Noticing her distress, Danny guided her out of the way until they stood in another place where carriages were now drawing up. 'We'll work together tonight if you like?' he asked.

She nodded, pleased that he would be by her side throughout the evening. As it happened, Danny had chosen a perfect pitch and soon people were queueing to buy buttonholes and small sprays, bags of nuts and small oranges. Ada had been too busy to notice anymore of the flower girls' antics though she had still heard them calling out as she served her own customers, and hoped she'd remember what they'd shouted, so she could use those words herself in the future. As they were packing up to leave, the last of the theatre goers entering the foyer and the final flower girls leaving the scene, she noticed a young woman in the distance.

No, it couldn't be, could it? *Connie!*

Ada swallowed and was about to call out her sister's name to see if it really was her when she noticed a man in a top hat and long frock coat, appearing on the scene as he ushered the young woman by her elbow into an awaiting coach.

I need to call out to her to see if it is Connie before it's too late! Try as she might, the words just wouldn't come as they caught in her throat but then, the young woman turned and faced her. She was near enough so Ada could see her face but if it was her sister then she wasn't showing any recognition, she appeared to be looking through Ada and not at her. Then in an instant, she turned her head and got inside the coach, closely followed by the gentleman. Ada watched wordlessly as it made off in the direction of Adam and Eve Court.

'What 'appened there, Ada me love?' Danny asked, pushing back the peak of his cap as if to get a better view of Ada's face.

'I…I really don't know,' Ada frowned, still feeling mystified. 'I just thought I saw our Connie there getting into a coach with a gentleman I didn't recognise, but I'm not too sure it really was her as she was a fair distance away for me to be certain and well toffed up.'

'Huh?' Danny quirked a puzzled brow. 'I don't think I quite get yer, love.'

'I mean the girl looked like my sister but she looked posh somehow, all dressed up like in a lovely gown and a fashionable looking hat, but when she turned her head and I caught her eye it was almost as though she didn't see me as if I was invisible or didn't exist.'

Danny draped a reassuring arm around Ada's shoulder. 'That does sound most odd, Ada. Maybe yer wanted to see yer sister so much that you imagined that young woman was her. I mean I saw her and all and she looked very posh to me not someone like us.'

Ada nodded and then she sniffed. Oh no, she didn't want to cry and not in front of Danny again.

'Look, I'll tell you what, we'll go and ask Queenie what the young woman she saw that night in the pub that might have been yer sister, was wearing? See if it sounds like the same person. Did you notice anything about the gent?'

Ada fought to think as she hadn't paid so much attention to the toff as to the young woman as of course she'd thought she was Connie. 'All I remember was he wore a shiny top hat and a long black coat with a velvet collar, oh and there was something else…'

'What? Danny blinked.

'He had a thin black moustache.'

'Cheer up. That might help a bit.'

Add forced a smile but she realised in her heart that there were a lot of gentlemen who fitted that description in London.

***

'That coach went in the direction of Adam and Eve Court you say?' Queenie was in the middle of setting out chairs around the small tables in the pub.

'Yes,' said Ada. 'Where do you think they might have been off to?'

Queenie stopped what she was doing to look her in the eye before saying, 'Well, I don't like to tell you this but there are several houses of ill repute in that area, ducks. And a posh gent only tends to go over that way for one thing and one thing only, if yer get me drift.' She tapped the side of her nose with her index finger.

Ada wasn't quite sure she understood so she looked at Danny for some assistance.

'What Queenie means,' said Danny, 'is that the toff was going off to do the business by the look of it, a bit like the flower girl did, Ada. Only not up some stinking back alleyway but in a house where such business is conducted for money.'

Ada felt sad to think that if it were her Connie that her sister had resorted to that kind of behaviour.

'Don't take on so,' Queenie comforted. 'It's the way of the world, ain't it? It's how people survive when they 'as to.'

'B…but I know my sister and she'd never do such a thing unless she was forced into it!'

Danny and Queenie exchanged glances before Queenie said in a soft tone of voice, 'Then maybe that's what happened, Ada. Sometimes girls and young women get abducted from the streets and…now I don't want to frighten you but you have to know the truth of it, they get held against their will and forced to work for someone. Perhaps that's what happened to yer sister, but if it is her and she's wearing such nice clothes then it might be she's involved in that kind of thing up West not in the East End. So maybe she

68

wasn't working out of a whore house in these parts, but they were calling to one for some other reason.'

Ada scowled, she didn't understand the world of grownups at all. She realised that the flower girl earlier had enticed a man around the corner but what exactly for she wasn't quite sure. It might involve a kiss and a cuddle she thought but what else?

'What's the matter now, Ada?' Danny asked.

Ada folded her arms, her chin jutting out. 'I don't follow what these girls are doing and why. Why would that flower girl go off to kiss a man around the corner? Doesn't she want to sell her flowers, then?'

'Aw, you're young and innocent, Ada love,' Queenie said sagely, 'and maybe you're better off not knowing for time being what goes on. Suffice to say, it's more than a kiss, the girls let the men take advantage of them and sometimes, if they're lucky, they get paid handsomely for it an' all. That flower girl you refer to has more than likely to have risen at the crack of dawn to spend her pennies at Covent Garden to secure some blooms, maybe moss roses and the like. She'll need to buy paper and twine to make them into little bouquets and then stand in all sorts of weather to sell her wares, come rain or come shine. Now, if she gets the chance to go off with a handsome gentleman for a bit of a fumble around the corner and maybe earn thrice as much as she would selling those blooms, who could blame her? For ten minutes work she could earn three night's pay as a flower seller, or if the gent is generous, rather more. And she still has her blooms to sell as well, she's quids in. The ironic thing is that she has deflowered herself in the process, I suppose.'

What on earth did Queenie mean by "deflowered"? Though, she thought she did now understand why the girls did what they did. So was Connie trying to earn money for their rent by doing the same thing? But of course, even if she returned home soon, now there would be no home to return to and she would probably have lost her job at the match factory too.

***

On their way back to Maggie's house, Ada said nothing, just pushed her barrow in front of her. She hardly took in her surroundings as she was getting to know these streets so well. Her heart felt like it was going to break and she fought to hold back the tears that were threatening to form.

'You're quiet, gal?' Danny said sombrely.

'I was just thinking that's all,' she said with a trembling voice.

'A penny for them, then?'

'I don't know if me thoughts are worth that much but I was just thinking if that was Connie why would she ignore me? Isn't she concerned about me and Sam and how we're surviving?'

Danny rested his barrow for a moment. 'I'm sure she is, and if it was her, which does seem likely, then there was a good reason for her not showing the gentlemen she was with that she knew you for some reason.'

She swallowed a sob. 'So, she'd disown me because she's ashamed of me, the way I'm dressed when I'm in the street in rags and tatters and she's in all her finery?'

'Come 'ere, you silly sausage,' he said as he embraced her.

It felt good having a hug and soon he had her smiling again. 'Now listen to me,' he said, 'don't be taking on so. There'll be a good reason why she can't show you are her sister I'm sure.' He paused for a moment to hold her at arms' length, and said what she'd known all along, 'You know deep down it was really her, don't you, love?'

She nodded and swallowed a lump. 'Yes. I was trying to convince myself that maybe it wasn't our Connie after all as I've never seen her dress in a fancy gown like that, nor be escorted by a posh gent into his coach. But deep down, I would swear it on me life that the young woman I saw was me sister.'

'Then it's good news really, ain't it?'

She blinked several times, not really understanding what he was getting at. 'How so?'

'Because that means for one thing we know she's still in the area and she was probably the young woman that Queenie saw the other night, and most importantly of all, she's still alive. Yer must 'ave wondered, love, after what the landlord said about that stalker man in the area and what I told you.'

She had to admit, she had. Ada turned away to reflect for a moment, lost in her thoughts. Her head whipped around suddenly as she turned back towards Danny. 'W…what if that gent I saw me sister with is that same man?'

Chapter Seven
August, 1888

Days settled down into a pattern of early risings for Ada as she accompanied Danny to the marketplace, selling her wares from the barrow around earmarked streets during the daytime and at nighttime, stood outside the theatre with her flower basket hooked over the crook of her arm. Fortunately for her, the other flower girls hadn't been outside her preferred theatre for some days so she was free to perfect her sales pitch. She decided not to use the "I'm only a poor little girl," like some of those did, but instead to use their cries of, "Please, sir, do buy me flowers fer yer lovely lady!" and her own, "Fresh flowers for sale, the finest in these parts!" and Danny's suggestion of, "Sweet blooms for your sweetheart for a penny!"

So, for time being she was happy enough at her work while Sam stopped at home with Maggie, helping the woman to sort out rags for her trolley or taking refreshments to the down and outs beneath the arches. Things could be a lot worse she realised but it still didn't stop her from looking out for Connie at any available moment. How she'd love it if a coach drew up and she saw her sister step out of it onto the pavement and into the theatre foyer in a fine gown. Even if she didn't get to speak to her, she'd love to see her again.

'Cor look at that newspaper headline!' Danny suddenly shouted, breaking Ada out of her reverie. He pointed to a newspaper placard that had just been set up by a paper lad on the opposite side of the street which read:

"HORRIBLE MURDER IN EAST LONDON!"

'Oh, no! Surely not!' said Ada, wide eyed with horror.

Danny headed off to where the paper lad was stood beside the placard with a bundle of newspapers in his hand and he slipped a couple of coins into the lad's filthy looking hand in exchange for a copy. By the time he'd returned to Ada's side, the paper lad was shouting behind cupped hands: 'Whitechapel murder! Read all about it!'

Ada noticed how the lad had now grabbed the attention of the theatre goers as several gentlemen headed towards him to purchase a copy.

Danny glanced at Ada. 'Me brothers would like to see this!' he said as he scanned the front page and read out:

'"Scarcely has the horror and sensation caused by the discovery of the murdered woman in Whitechapel some short time ago had time to abate, when another discovery is made, which, for the brutality exercised on the victim, is even more shocking, and will no doubt create as great a sensation in the vicinity as its predecessor. The affair up to the present is enveloped in complete mystery, and the police have as yet no evidence to trace the perpetrators of the horrible deed. The facts are that as Constable John Neil was walking down Bucks-row, Thomas-street, Whitechapel, about a quarter to four o'clock this morning, he discovered a woman between thirty-five and forty years of age lying at the side of the street…"' he paused for a moment, 'are you sure you want me to carry on with this, Ada?'

She nodded and then listened intently. *'"…with her throat cut right open from ear to ear, the instrument with which the deed was done tracing the throat from left to right. The wound was an inch wide, and blood was flowing profusely. She was immediately conveyed to the Whitechapel Mortuary, when it was found that besides the wound in the throat the lower part of the abdomen was completely ripped open…"* I better not read anymore but needless to say the victim was between thirty five and forty…'

Ada breathed out a sigh of relief. Definitely not Connie then.

'It goes on to say here that she was wearing a brown dress and petticoat with the Lambeth Workhouse on it and taken to the mortuary at half past four in the morning…'

Ada turned her face away at the mere thought of it, relieved that Danny hadn't read out the full details to her.

He folded the newspaper and slid it into his jacket pocket with a sombre expression on his face. 'Those Convent Garden flower girls ought to take care,' he added.

Ada had to admit she agreed with him. It seemed that no woman or young girl was safe in Whitechapel these days.

***

When Ada and Danny returned home, Ada was in for a surprise because there sitting at Maggie's table, getting along famously with the woman, was Rose from the match factory.

'Yer sister's friend arrived 'ere not a half hour since!' declared Maggie with a big smile on her face. Ada though, was not so sure this was going to be good news for her. Rose had promised she'd call if she found out anything at all about Connie so she wasn't certain whether it was good or bad news.

Rose looked up from the cup of tea she'd been in the midst of sipping to meet with Ada's piercing gaze. 'Come and sit down a while, love,' Rose said in barely a whisper as Ada's stomach flipped over. She had some information that much was for certain otherwise, why else would she call by?

'I'll go and brew up another pot,' said Maggie kindly rising from her seat and taking the brown earthenware pot with her. 'You two 'ave been on yer feet all day, so I daresay you need one.' She turned to Rose. 'Another cuppa, dear?'

Rose smiled. 'I don't mind if I do. I get parched working at that factory all day long though conditions are starting to improve since that Annie Besant has been helping to fight for our cause.'

Maggie nodded and smiled. 'It's great news you won your campaign after that strike yer all had! Those fat cat bosses needed pulling down a peg or two!'

Ada had heard about all the unrest at the factory from her sister before she disappeared but Connie hadn't returned to take part in any of the campaigning. Wouldn't she have loved to have been a part of all that unrest! The workers going on strike for better pay and conditions, challenging the management at Bryant and May and then marching on Parliament!

Ada took a seat beside Rose. 'It's not good news I'm afraid, Ada. So please prepare yerself.' She reached out and touched Ada's hand which caused her to tremble in anticipation.

'She's dead, isn't she? Me sister's dead!' Ada shouted in an hysterical fashion.

Rose shook her head. 'No, it's nothing like that, honestly it ain't, love.' Rose met her gaze. 'It's just I was speaking with one of the factory girls earlier, not a woman I normally bother with but she was sent to work on one of the match cutting machines today beside me, and I had to show her the ropes, like, so naturally we had to converse. Well, I happened to mention yer Connie to her and her face took on a strange expression, like.'

'A strange expression?'

'Yes, all sort of guarded and she stiffened up like as if she knew something. Anyhow, after a bit of persuasion I managed to get out of her what she knew.' Rose drew in a deep breath and let it out again. 'Yer sister Connie's been working up West for the past couple of months, love. Not every night but now and again. She was probably sneaking out during the night while yer were sleeping. Now I come to think of it there were one or two occasions when she must have been awake all night long and then come into work next day as she was hanging all the way through her shift. What I mean is she could hardly do her job as she seemed so weary and I thought it might be dangerous with her using the match cutting machine. I did ask her what was going on but she told me she thought she was sickening for something.'

Ada thought back and realised that once she and Sam slept during the night, they rarely awoke until Connie rose for work the following morning, so it might have happened without their knowledge. 'But what was she doing up West?'

'Escorting gentlemen.'

'So, it's true then!' Ada said sharply. 'Queenie at the pub implied that my sister was going off with a toff from the pub where she works at but I didn't want to believe it. I thought I saw her meself the other evening getting into a fine looking coach with a man. Didn't want to believe it was her and tried to convince meself it weren't really her, but it was her all right—

toffed up to the eyeballs in fine togs, like a lady, but from what Queenie implied she's no more than a trollop!' Ada's bottom lip began to quiver and she had shocked even herself saying that word.

'Oh, Ada, love,' Maggie said rushing over to the table, 'you must never say that about yer sister, she must have her reasons for doing what she's doing. Please don't judge her, love...'

Ada vigorously shook her head. 'I can't help it! I can't believe she'd abandon me and Sam like she has!'

Rose looked at her with a great deal of sympathy in her eyes. 'It happens to the best of us, darlin'. To tell you the truth, me older sister did something similar herself like that when times were hard and it were with a toff an' all what approached her at a local pub— you see, they come looking for working class girls as they think we're easy meat for them and they know how desperate we can get to survive an' all. It were only the once mind you and she did it to put food on the table and pay the rent and ever since, she's not had the need to do it again. But don't tell anyone, will yer? She's courting a nice young man these days and he'd be mortified if he ever found out she'd done something as dirty as that. I think he wants to marry her, so she will have a good life from here on in as he's in regular employment.'

Ada nodded. 'I won't say anything to anyone,' she said not exactly certain what Rose meant by it all, but she guessed it was something like what that flower girl had been up to the other evening. The only difference between Connie and that girl though was that her sister didn't need to go around dingy corners, she was obviously well kept by someone.

She turned to Rose after giving it some thought. 'Me sister is somehow being cared for by the sound of it if she's dressed in expensive looking clothes, so I suppose she is all right?'

Rose nodded. 'That's the way to look at it, gal. She's not having to risk her life at that horrible match factory working with the risk of getting phossy jaw at least, even though changes are being made, it's taking a time for the management to enforce them. And at least you know she's alive. My guess is that once the time is right she'll try to find you. Maybe she's trying to save up her earnings to get you nice digs somewhere.'

'But she won't know where to find us!' sighed Ada.

'No, that's as maybe,' Maggie shook her head, 'but she knows Rose, and when she fails to find you at your old place, she might well head off to the factory and Rose can tell her where you are— staying with me in the house beneath the arches—she'll easily find you and Sam then!' Maggie said cheerfully.

Ada nodded, feeling only marginally better now.

Before Rose left, Ada heard her discussing matters in the passageway with Maggie. Their voices were low and mumbling but she managed to pick up the odd phrase here and there. Rose was saying something about how she'd try to find out more from the woman who had given her the information in the first place and Maggie was agreeing with her.

'Ada, what's going on?' Sam wanted to know. He began to tug on her dress as she laid her ear against the closed door.

'Ssssh, Sam!' she said, pushing him away but then she felt sorry for seeing the hurt look on his little face so she lifted him up into her arms, drew him towards her and hugged him tight. 'Sorry, sunshine. I just got to hear what they're saying, that's all.'

He nodded and smiled as if he'd forgiven her. Then he laid his head on her shoulder for a while until she set him back down on the floor. Then he left her alone as she listened further. Something was being said about Connie being a "lady of the night" and "good money being earned up West". What on earth was a "lady of the night"? That would make sense though if Connie had been out all night. Then Ada caught something that almost bowled her over when she heard Maggie saying, "That's the sort The Whitechapel Murderer goes after!" and Rose was agreeing with her. So Connie wasn't as safe as she thought she was.

Chapter Eight

Ada found the Covent Garden flower girls cunning and conniving. Some of them were now trying to elbow her out of her regular pitch outside the theatre.

'Buzz off, you little tyke!' Ada yelled as one of the smaller girls collided with her almost knocking the wicker basket of flowers she was carrying from her arms. The girl could have been no more than seven years old and she was about to push her out of the way when an older girl of maybe around fourteen years old, showed up causing Ada to take a step back.

The girl had long auburn hair which she wore loose on her shoulders and she had a smattering of freckles dotted across her face; she was very pretty though, but the look now upon her face wasn't.

'You keep out of our way!' she said, jabbing her index finger in Ada's chest.

'I…w…wasn't in yer way,' Ada protested. 'That young girl there was in me way if anything.'

'That's me sister,' said the girl sharply, 'and we use this pitch regular! It's ours!'

'Liar!' said Ada as her chin jutted out in defiance. If there was one thing she couldn't stand it was someone who told untruths. 'I've been coming here for weeks and I ain't seen hide nor hair of either of you before.'

The girl scowled and then her face took on a sad expression, her dark brown eyes brimming with unshed tears. 'Our Ma passed away, so we ain't had the heart to go out for a while,' she said sadly. Ada knew all too well what that felt like.

'I'm sorry to hear that,' she said. 'Me parents died as well a few months back. And I'm sorry if I'm standing in your spot, I didn't know. Me friend, Danny, see him over there selling the nuts and oranges?' The girl nodded. 'He told me it would be all right.'

To Ada's surprise the girl suddenly beamed. 'Aw, I know Danny. I haven't seen him in ever such a long time. It's all right, you can stay where you are, we'll go the other side of the foyer entrance. There aren't usually too many flower girls on this site unless one of the other theatres is closed. What's yer name, anyhow? I'm Frannie and that's me little sister, Molly.'

'I'm Ada and I have a brother called Sam who is a bit younger than your sister. We're staying at Danny's house for time being as we were turfed out of our digs by our landlord the other week.'

'That's rough,' said Frannie.

Ada nodded. 'Where do you both live?'

'Well now we're on our own, we look for digs when we can get them. Usually if we make enough money selling our flowers we lodges with a kindly lady in her house where we get a shared bed for the night, breakfast and an evening meal, but when we can't make enough money we go to the Hanbury Salvation Army Women's refuge where we get a mug of tea and a piece of bread and dripping and a bed for the night. Beds there ain't so great as they're a bit like coffins, like wooden boxes all lined up in a row, but it's better than nothing. 'Course, we have to be out first thing in the morning after breakfast but it suits us as we go off to market early anyhow to buy the best blooms if we have enough money for 'em. Other times, we ain't so lucky…'

'How'd yer mean?'

Frannie nodded. 'Some nights we don't make enough money for a bed for the night so we end up sleeping rough. It only costs us a penny a night at the mission but sometimes we ain't even got that much, particularly if it's a bad day weather wise and there's no one wants to hang around to buy any flowers from us.'

Ada glanced at Molly's bare feet. 'Don't yer sister have any shoes to put on?' she asked.

'No. She used to have a pair of leather boots but they were stolen when we slept in an alleyway one night.'

'That'd awful.' Ada suddenly had an idea. 'Danny's mother collects all sorts, clothing and the like which she sells on. I know sometimes she buys old boots and shoes, I could ask her if she has a pair for yer sister.'

'Oh would you?' Frannie was now smiling with gratitude as Ada hoped Maggie could find the girl something for her bare feet.

***

Later back home when Ada recounted what had happened to Danny, he shrugged and said, 'Goes to show you must never judge a book by its cover. Yer thought that girl was out to cause yer harm when she's only trying to eke out a living fer herself and yer've learned that she and her little sister are in worse trouble than you and yer Sam.'

That was true. Ada looked at him in earnest. 'Yer Ma collects all sorts for her rag trolley, do yer think she'd do a kindness for the little 'un, Molly?'

'I should expect so as me Ma has a heart of gold. What's it yer wanting for her?'

'Well, Frannie told me that Molly had her boots nicked off her feet when they were sleeping rough one night. She has nothing on her feet now, they're bare.'

'Gosh, that's rough. I'll ask her fer yer later when she comes back.'

Ada frowned. 'Where is she? I thought she was feeding the down and outs again?'

'Naw, she's already done that, she's gone to church. She's very devout these days. Hasn't been for a while since yer've been here and Sam has been ill an' all but now yer've both settled down here, I think she feels it safe to leave you alone.'

Ada nodded. 'I see.'

'What's the matter, yer don't look very happy, Ada?'

'I just feel maybe me and my brother 'ave put your ma to a lot of trouble with us arriving so unexpectedly.'

'Now don't you go worrying about that at all,' he said, placing a firm hand on her shoulder. 'She loves it. She often takes in waifs and strays whether they're the animal or the human variety!' he chuckled and shot her a cheeky grin which made her laugh.

'Where's Sam though?' she asked suddenly.

'Don't you concern yerself, he's gorn off with me brothers. Ma left a note.'

'Oh dear. Will they be dragging him around the pubs with them?'

'Nah, they also do some handiwork for folk, I expect they got him helping them now that he's fully recovered. Be handy for them as people take note of a young child with them on their rounds. They used to take me along and people would give them extra money as they felt sorry for me, or they'd make us all something to eat. He'll love it.'

***

When Billy and Davy returned with a smiling Sam, Ada could see that Danny was right, Sam had enjoyed every moment and he couldn't wait to tell her about how he helped them clean folks' windows and one woman had given him a slice of bread that was fresh from the oven with thick salted butter smeared over it.

'He's a natural,' said Davy. 'Ma not back from church yet?'

Ada shook her head. 'Is she usually gone this long?' It had been a good two hours since she and Danny had returned themselves and it was most unusual for Maggie not to be at the heart of the house cooking something on the hob or stoking up the fire as she recounted tales of what had gone on that day and listening to what had occurred for them also.

Billy frowned. 'She's never usually this long, I think I'll take a walk to see if I can find her. I know the route she usually takes, but with that murderer out there, no woman is safe, no matter what her age.'

'I'll come with you,' Davy said, frowning.

Now Ada felt concerned. Maggie had been expected home in daylight but now it was dark outside. 'Has your Ma ever been gone this long before?'

'No, but she might have bumped into someone as she don't half talk when she gets started!' Danny reassured.

Ada hoped that was the case but a hour and a half later when Maggie and her sons still hadn't returned, she couldn't help thinking for sure that something was definitely up.

They got ready for bed in silence both unsure now what to say to the other, Ada noticing that Danny's usual happy-go-lucky manner was now absent as she guessed he was more worried than he was letting on. She was about to suggest she make them a cup of cocoa before going to bed when she heard the front room door burst open and there was the sound of Billy and Davy's voices speaking to one another.

'Quick get her in here to lie on the bed!' one of them was saying, by the tone of his voice, Ada knew something was up and that they'd found their mother. Danny rushed to the living room door and opened it for them. And there, staggered the brothers with their mother between them, appearing to be holding on to them for support. Her right eye was swollen and black, her hair messy, her clothing torn and Ada noticed there was a cut on her chin surrounded by what appeared to be, dried blood.

Ada asked Sam to get out of the bed and she drew back the counterpane and puffed up the pillows for Maggie to lie down.

'Aw, Ma!' Danny groaned and then he was on his knees beside her as she lay prone in the bed. It was a minute or so before he looked up at his brothers with tears in his eyes. 'W...what happened?'

'We don't rightly know,' said Davy as he rubbed his chin. 'We found her not far away under the bridge of her usual route home from church. We think someone attacked her, maybe tried to rob her but there was nothing for them to take...'

'No...' groaned Maggie. 'I was followed by a man but he weren't after any money...'

Davy and Billy exchanged curious glances with one another. 'Then what were he after, Ma?' Billy asked.

'Me life, I think...'

***

Ada helped Maggie up into a sitting position on the bed so she could speak properly. The woman's breaths seemed fast and shallow as though she were still spooked by her ordeal.

'Take your time, Ma,' advised Davy.

Maggie nodded and drew in a composing breath, leaving it out again as she began. 'I'd left the church and was on me way home...' Her face began to change as she related the tale, almost as though she were reliving the experience. 'It was a nice night and I wasn't paying much attention to anything at all, just comfortable with me own thoughts. Then as the crowds outside the pubs ebbed away and I walked through a couple of different courts, I turned down this alleyway and it was while I walked through it, I became aware of me footsteps echoing back at me. At first I thought it were me imagination but then I realised that it were another set of steps as well as if someone was following me. I'd stop and then the footsteps would stop. I was beginning to think it was my imagination but the next street I turned into was deserted, unfortunately. I didn't dare look around and the faster I walked, the faster those footsteps came echoing after me. Then I felt a hand clamp down on me shoulder and an arm came around me neck holding me in a vice like grip so I could scarcely breathe...' Maggie's eyes were now wide with horror and Ada startled as she waited to hear what the woman had to say next.

'Then I saw it!' Maggie shuddered as both of her hands flew to her neck almost as though she were being strangled.

'What, Ma?' Davy urged.

'The steel from a blade, he had a knife in his hand. I almost fainted there and then on the spot. I tussled with him and caught sight of his profile from the light of the moon, then he slapped me hard across the face. Something must have disturbed him at that point as he muttered something and ran off in the direction of Fournier Street…'

'Aw, Ma,' said Billy. 'I'm so glad we found you when we did in case he returned.'

'I must have collapsed then as next thing I know I'm lying on the cold pavement and I feel something hot and sticky running down my chin and I realise I'm bleeding, he must have just nicked me with the blade of the knife when he pulled away. Somehow, I get the strength to drag meself up onto me feet and stagger off but I've lost me bearings and that's when I heard you two calling out me name. I don't know what would 'ave happened to me otherwise…'

Then to Ada's horror, the woman began to sob profusely.

***

Commercial Street was a wide, busy street linking Whitechapel to Shoreditch, slicing its way through the dilapidated slums of the rookeries. Riots, protests and strikes had recently broken out in the area, and so, the overcrowding of the area only added to the problem as people from everywhere descended on the place. Despite this, people were sleeping on the streets in increasing numbers and it wasn't getting any better. Now Maggie had been attacked, Ada and Danny saw it as their duty to take over where she'd left off as the down and outs needed her more than ever as their numbers had swollen. So before heading off for market in the mornings, they brewed up for 'The Archies' as they were known, supplying them with a crust to eat, and late at night returned to do the same thing, often offering any leftovers from their barrows. The Archies didn't mind if the fruit were bruised or not or whether they were served soup made from potatoes that had started to sprout nor would they have noticed such things as they were just glad to be fed and watered.

All of this going on, and now Maggie was acting as if she didn't care for anything or anyone anymore, not even her beloved rough sleepers: Sally, Wilf and the rest of them. She no longer rose at the crack of dawn to help Danny and Ada get off to work nor did she even ask about the Archies which was most unlike her. She no longer cared to get out of bed at a reasonable time in the morning or to get herself washed and dressed for the day ahead either, preferring to wear the same old clothing for days on end and it was an age since she'd even dragged a comb through her hair. The middle aged woman had lost pride in herself and appeared to be slipping away before the children's very eyes.

A few days later, another murder occurred and according to local gossip, that woman was known as "Dark Annie" or Annie Chapman. She was discovered in the backyard at 29 Hanbury Street her body all bloodied and mutilated. This was all getting too close to home for Ada. What if the man who had attacked Maggie was the murderer himself?

The police in the area had begun to question the neighbourhood's prostitutes and discovered there was a character who the women nicknamed "Leather Apron" who had been extorting money from them for the past twelve months. There was a lot of speculation as to who this character really was, some thought he was a butcher and others that he was some sort of person who worked with his tools of his trade in some way.

The Star newspaper ran an article with a headline naming him as the man linked with the Whitechapel Murders. He was described as a strange character who stalked the area after midnight and put fear into women as he prowled around in slippered feet carrying a sharp leather knife.

It was after reading the article that the brothers really thought the man who had attacked their mother was the same man. Yet, no matter how much they tried to persuade her to report the incident, she just wouldn't. 'What's the use?' she said one day, burying her head in her hands. 'I didn't even get to see who he was only that he was carrying some sort of knife. In any case, from his silhouette, he appeared to be some sort of toff in a cape and a top hat not a man wearing a leather apron!'

'No, Ma,' said Billy gently as he laid a hand of reassurance on his mother's shoulder. 'Even if he is some sort of craftsman it doesn't mean that he can't dress up or nothing.'

Ada realised that Billy was right and she so wished she could do something to help the woman to repay her for her kindness towards herself and Sam. That evening, Ada informed Danny that she wouldn't be working on the streets with her barrow the following day, instead, she was going to stay behind and gee Maggie along. Something had to be done for the woman but heavens knew what.
***

The following morning when Danny had left for the early morning market place, taking Sam with him, and Billy and Davy were out selling from their cart for the day, Ada took a cup of tea to Maggie. The woman was awake but lying very still beneath the covers of her bed, staring at the ceiling as if deep in thought.

'Mrs Donovan,' Ada spoke quietly not to upset the woman, 'I've brought you a nice cup of tea and I've put some porridge on the hob.' Ada watched tears course down Maggie's cheeks. It took some persuading to get the woman to sit up in bed to drink her tea and Ada propped her back up with pillows.

It can't go on like this, Ada thought to herself. Maggie's appearance had got no better and Ada thought she could whiff a scent of perspiration and it wasn't fresh either. The past couple of days, the weather had been extremely hot which didn't help the situation.

Maggie took a long time to sip her tea and refused the porridge prompting Ada to announce finally, 'Well, I think it's come to the point that I shall have to go and fetch Doctor Scott,' she said sharply, causing Maggie's head to whip around and the woman to stare at her.

'No, please. No doctor,' she said as she began to sob into her hands.

'Look,' said Ada kindly, 'let's try it like this then…' Maggie dropped her hands to her sides to watch Ada's face as she spoke. 'You finish off your tea and at least eat some of the porridge, then I'll fill the tin bath with hot water while the boys are out and you can have a nice long soak in the bath. I'll even help to wash yer hair like I used to for our Connie. How does that sound?'

For the first time in ages, the woman smiled through her tears. 'There's good you are to me, gal,' she said.

It took some time for Maggie to spoon the porridge into her mouth, but finally she finished every last bit. Next, Ada assisted her to remove her filthy clothes and she helped her into the tin bath, handed her a fresh flannel and soap and went off to scrub the dirty clothes clean in a tin bowl, eventually rinsing them as best as she could by twisting the items between her hands. She'd seen Connie and her own mother doing it often enough out by the pump in the back yard. Ada then hung Maggie's clothing on the rope line in the back garden.

When she returned indoors, she was pleased to see that Maggie had soaped herself up well and was lying back in the bath now with her eyes closed with a damp flannel across her forehead. Not wishing to disturb the woman for now as she seemed to be enjoying the water, Ada went through Maggie's wardrobe and located a pretty floral dress, some clean bloomers, a corset and a lightweight shawl and a large towel.

Maggie's eyes opened wide when she saw the clothing Ada brought with her. 'Cor blimey!' she said, 'I ain't worn that dress in years. I don't know if it will still fit me, can't you find something else?'

Ada laughed. 'You've got a bit thinner this past week or so as you ain't been eating, try it on.'

Maggie nodded and Ada washed the woman's hair using a jug of clean warm water and soap, rinsing it well, then helped her out of the bath and handed her the rough towel so she could dry herself off.

To Maggie's surprise, the dress fitted, only just, but it was enough to raise the woman's spirits as she smiled like a young girl, which made Ada realise that in her youth she had been an attractive young lady. Ada draped the shawl around Maggie's shoulders to keep her warm and went in search of a hair brush to sort the woman's hair out. It had got a little matted in places as she hadn't kept it combed, so when after several attempts the knots failed to comb out, she gave Ada permission to trim the matted bits with a sharp scissors.

Ada was pleased with the end result. Although Maggie's hair was a lot shorter now, it did much for her appearance. 'That hair cut has taken years off you, Mrs Donovan,' she said as she passed a hand mirror to the woman so she might examine her reflection.

Maggie beamed when she saw the end result but even though she was smiling, Ada detected a sadness still behind her eyes which her shaky voice betrayed. Ada was pleased she'd made some progress with the woman's physical appearance and that she'd actually managed to persuade her to eat breakfast. The next hurdle was to get the woman involved in her normal daily duties, people relied on her for sustenance and her rag trolley now lay idle too.

'Now then,' Ada said firmly, 'I want you to help me, if you will?'

Maggie wiped away a tear with the back of her hand. 'I'll do me best...' she said and then she sniffed loudly. 'What is it you want?'

'There are two young flower girls, sisters they are. One is a couple of years older than me and she can fend for herself, the other one is near Sam's age. The poor girl had her boots stolen off her feet while they slept in an alleyway one night.'

'But how are they sleeping rough at their ages?' Maggie wanted to know and it was almost as if something had been turned on inside her at that point as she was that kind hearted.

'Their mother recently passed away so now they're orphans like me and Sam…' she said sadly. 'Sometimes they're fortunate to get digs with a nice lady if they earn enough money that is, other times they can get shelter at the Salvation Army Woman's Refuge in Hanbury Street…'

Maggie nodded. 'Aye, I know it. Good the staff are an' all, very helpful to womenfolk in the area.'

'Trouble is, if they don't get that penny to stop there overnight then they have to sleep rough on the streets.'

Maggie shook her head. 'Those poor girls.'

Ada had no intention of making the woman sadder than she already was but desperate times sought desperate measures. 'So, you think you might be able to give the youngest, Molly, a pair of boots from your trolley?'

'I daresay I'll find something to fit her,' she said, then crossing her hands one over the other she added, 'but I can do better than that. We'll bring the girls here to stay with us.'

Ada's jaw dropped open, incredulous at the woman's suggestion. 'But how will you cope? You were hardly able to get out of your bed this morning?'

'Aye, well I'm done now with my feeling sorry for myself bit, what happened to me was awful but I was lucky to get away, those two young girls are at risk being on the street like that. Do you know where they are right now?'

Ada shook her head. 'Danny might have some idea of their whereabouts as he seems to know the eldest, Frannie.'

'Frannie, did you say?' said Maggie raising a brow. 'Got a sister called Molly?'

'Yes. Do you know them?'

'Aye, I should say I do. They're Martha Conhurst's girls. I didn't even know she'd passed away, poor soul. She was a sickly woman anyhow. Never the same after her husband, who was a cokum chap, ran off with a barmaid from The Feathers public house. He left her with those young girls to bring up all on her own. Hit the bottle she did. Those girls 'ave been working the streets as flower girls for some time, they learned their trade from their mother but I fear much of their time working was to keep their mother well supplied with gin.' She shook her head and sucked in a breath between her missing teeth. 'Sad state of affairs it were.'

'I see,' said Ada, beginning to understand now why the girls were in the predicament they were in. 'In any case, if Danny doesn't know where they are, they'll be selling flowers outside the theatre tonight. That's how I encountered them, see.'

'Well,' said Maggie rising out of her armchair, 'I better see what I got on me trolley for them. Might have some clothing as well. In any case, we need to warn them gals to keep away from Flower and Dean Street and Dorset Street an' all as those are dangerous places. You too, Ada. Don't go walking around those parts unless you 'ave an adult with you. You hear?'

Ada nodded, secretly pleased that Maggie had sprung to life again.

Chapter Nine

The brothers and Sam were astonished to see their mother was up and about when they returned home all spruced up and well dressed. Danny's eyes widened with astonishment.

Billy took Ada to one side to speak with her in confidence. 'What's happened to Ma?' he asked with a big smile of surprise on his face.

'I just encouraged your mother to have a bit of breakfast and helped her have a bath and get dressed, that's all,' Ada said modestly.

'Aw, it's more than that though, sweetheart. You've worked wonders. Me and Davy have been trying for days to get her going again, you've bucked her up no end! Thank you so much!' He cupped her face in his hands and laid a kiss of appreciation on her forehead. 'We won't forget this,' he said releasing her.

Ada beamed. 'I also told her about a couple of flower girls what I know who need a bit of help and she's agreed to sort them out.'

'That's good, we need to keep her active and interested. Anyhow, if you can just carry on with what you've been doing for a few days at least so we can see she really is back to her old self for good, we'd be eternally grateful. That's if yer don't mind abandoning your barrow work for a few days?'

'No, not at all. I'd do anything for Maggie after the way she's helped me and our Sam.'

Billy nodded. 'Now, I'd better go and make something to eat for us all as I can't expect Ma to do that as well as she's still recovering. I imagine she's still a bit sore after the assault after being pushed to the ground like that.'

'I can do it if yer like?' Ada offered. 'There are plenty of veggies in the cupboard and bit of scrag end of lamb. If yer don't mind waiting for it?'

'Smashing,' he said as his eyes lit up.

'Meanwhile I'll make you all a cup of tea.'

And so, Ada managed to cook a lamb stew for them all and even coped with slicing a cob loaf of bread that Danny had brought home with him. She realised her stew wasn't a patch on Maggie's but they all ate it up without complaint. She'd watched her mother and sister cook often enough to know what to do and had, on occasion, helped them out.

'I can teach you to cook properly if you like,' Maggie offered when the meal was over. 'We can make a start tomorrow.'

Ada nodded enthusiastically. 'Thank you. I'd like that. It'd be my dream to cook like you do, Mrs Donovan. Your meals are ever so tasty!'

'Now,' said Maggie nodding, 'how about we go to look for those sisters you told me about?'

Ada beamed. She asked Danny if he had any ideas where they might be but he thought it best to stick to the theatres and he offered to go back out with Ada in place of his mother but Maggie was having none of it. 'I can't become a prisoner in me own home,' she said firmly. 'I have to reclaim those streets for meself instead of fearing them like what I 'ave been doing of late.'

Ada thought it was very wise of the woman to push herself to go out once again.

**

The area outside the theatre was busy that night as coaches and carriages drew up outside and people swarmed towards the foyer, so much so that two smartly dressed doormen had to keep warning people to step back. There seemed to be an air of excitement around which Ada was picking up on. Crowds were beginning to line the street as well, ordinary folk who didn't appear to be going into the theatre itself which puzzled her.

'What's going on here?' she glanced at Maggie.

'I've no idea,' she said as her eyes scanned the crowd around her. 'The only time I seen something like this afore now was when someone famous was about to arrive for a special performance. Go and ask someone, Ada.'

Ada found a beshawled young woman who was stood beside two children teetering on the edge of the pavement. The crowd was four deep behind them as they stared at the foyer entrance as if expecting something to happen. 'Excuse me,' she said, 'but why are all these people here?'

The woman looked at her and smiled. 'Ain't you heard? Her Majesty herself is inside there, she's due to leave at any moment, there was a special performance put on for her. I think Prince Eddy is with her an' all.'

'Prince Eddy?' Ada wondered who he was.

'He's the Queen's grandson otherwise known as Prince Albert Victor,' explained the woman.

'Oh, I see.' Ada had never heard him referred to as Prince Eddy before. She thanked the woman and returned to Maggie's side as she didn't want to leave her alone longer than was necessary in case she felt uncomfortable, but she was cheered to discover that Maggie was chatting amicably to a lady of a similar age who was stood beside her. When she turned her attention towards her, Ada said, 'It's the Queen herself and her grandson what's in that theatre. A special performance was put on for them today.'

'Aye, I just was told the same thing by that lady. I'd love to stay around and see them but we need to find those friends of yours.'

'They're not really my fr—' Ada had been about to explain that she didn't know the girls all that well but what did it matter? The important thing was to find them. Maggie was already elbowing her way through the crowd and checking out the various flower girls, who for once, seemed more interested in watching for any sign of the Queen and her grandson than they were for selling any of their flowers.

'It's no use,' Ada said after a while, 'I can't see them anywhere there are just too many people around.'

Maggie nodded. 'Don't worry, ducks. We'll return again tomorrow—it'll be quieter then.'

Suddenly, a huge cheer rose up from the crowd, prompting Ada and Maggie to take a peek just in time to see Her Majesty and her grandson leaving from the theatre's entrance as she waved her white gloved hand with a flourish and disappeared into her very fine looking coach with Prince Eddy in tow.

Ada had never seen the queen in person before and she felt as though her heart ceased beating for a moment, but it was all over before it had time to begin which made her disappointed. 'What was the point in all those people waiting here just for a few seconds glimpse?' Ada looked at Maggie.

'Yer missing the point, gal. That was the most exciting thing those folk have had happen to them in a long time. The thrill of the expectation of waiting and knowing that Her Majesty herself might catch a glimpse of them is what excites them so much!'

'I suppose so,' said Ada, but as she had more pressing matters on her mind she found it all a bit of a waste of time and was rather annoyed that the crowd had made their search for Frannie and Molly less fruitful.

***

They did not manage to locate the sisters for another two days and when Ada finally found them they were not outside the theatre selling their wares as expected.

From a labyrinth of courts and alleys, she discovered the pair sheltering in a stone passageway which was a couple of streets from the theatre itself as it pelted down with rain outside. At first, Ada had mistakenly thought they were a bundle of dirty rags that someone had tossed on the ground, but on closer inspection, she'd noticed "the rags" begin to move as Molly tried to get herself comfortable. The dresses they wore were now filthy and torn, which told Ada that the girls hadn't been at a lodging house nor at the woman's mission for a long while. They appeared so thin, gaunt and pitiful that it was a sad sight to see.

'Aw, what's happened to you pair?' Ada asked gently as she drew nearer.

Frannie looked up at her with doleful eyes. 'Hello, Ada. We can't go on anymore, all our money has run out. I can't even go to Covent Garden to buy some blooms to sell and without selling those, I can't make any money for us to live on. It'll be the workhouse for us next…'

Tears streaked down the girl's grimy face as Ada's heart went out to her. 'We tried to sell some blooms here the other night when the Queen made a visit and we sold some which would have given us enough coppers to get a bed and something to eat that night, but our earnings were stolen from us by two lads who had followed us and made their escape through the crowd. People tried to help but it was easy for the boys to escape as there were so many people on the street that evening. I managed to sell some blooms that had fallen from a coster cart the other evening so we could 'ave a bite to eat but since then, nothing…' The girl's voice portrayed her utter despair with life—it was as if she had given up on everything and everybody.

'That's dreadful,' said Ada, chewing on her bottom lip. 'But I've got good news for you both!'

On hearing this, Molly, who up until now had been huddled up, head down, beside her sister, almost as though she were asleep, perked up as she raised her head and looked at Ada in expectation.

'What is it?' Frannie wanted to know.

'Mrs Donovan, who I'm staying with, is a kind hearted woman and so good to me and Sam. Anyhow, I asked her if she had any boots for Molly and explained your predicament, and she said she could do better than that and would take you both in!'

'B….but we can't afford to pay her for our lodgings,' Frannie said desperately.

'You won't have to neither. As long as you don't mind sharing a bed. She don't charge me or Sam. She has said if she ever runs short that we can pay her some of our earnings but so far, she hasn't asked for anything. You see, she has three working sons and she works herself buying and selling old clothes, so there's plenty of money going in the house and a good supply of food too as they're a costermonger family. Don't get me wrong, they ain't rich or nothing but they don't go short either. Come with me and we'll feed you up!'

Frannie's face lit up. 'That's so kind of you to come looking for us, Ada. We're competition for you with us selling flowers an' all. I can't say I would have been so charitable if the shoe were on the other foot.'

'Aw, don't be daft.' Ada stretched out her hand to help Frannie to her feet as Molly hauled herself up beside her. 'I think you would be just as kind to me.'

Both girls looked at one another and hugged. 'From now on,' said Ada, 'all your troubles will be over.'

***

While Ada hoped that the sisters' troubles would all be over that wasn't exactly true. They still had to go out at night to peddle their wares and kept late hours selling to the theatre crowds, it was a fair walk home as well and who knew who lay in wait in a dark alleyway or along an unlit back lane. Maggie insisted that Danny was always around in the background to keep an eye not just on those pair, but Ada too, as she insisted that no female was safe in the area with that maniac around. But at least now the sisters, thanks to Maggie and her clothing trolley, now had clean duds to wear even if they were second hand. She also provided them with a new pair of leather boots each to wear which were a Godsend for them, particularly in bad weather. Good food and plenty of rest, put a bit of colour back into their cheeks and a sparkle into their eyes, so that they looked far healthier than when Ada had first encountered them a couple of weeks previously.

Maggie, too, was starting to look a lot better. Her bruises faded from purple to yellow and finally disappeared altogether, though she was still sore for some time where she'd been pushed to the ground by the assailant, though luckily, no bones appeared to have been broken. Finally, the brothers summoned Doctor Scott to the house who gave Maggie a clean bill of health.

'Yes, Mrs Donovan,' he said as he closed his leather medical bag, 'you had a lucky escape there.' He handed Maggie a brown medicine bottle with a cork stopper. 'This is a tonic for your nerves, take a large spoonful morning and night, until you feel thoroughly back to normal.'

She nodded her thanks at him. 'I've 'eard all sorts about the beast though,' said Maggie as she puffed out her cheeks as if in indignation, 'some say he's a butcher, others that he's some sort of craftsman such as a cobbler, someone else even accused Prince Eddy! Now I ask you! Why on earth would Prince Albert Victor stalk those streets when he can live comfortably in the lap of luxury?'

Ada thought back to what Queenie had told her and Danny about a gentleman who had accompanied her sister that evening and the monogrammed coach parked outside the pub which might have belonged to him. Maybe there was something in it? But she said nothing. But surely if that had been Prince Eddy someone at the pub would have recognised him? She quickly dismissed that thought.

'Yes, I've heard rumours myself, Mrs Donovan.' The doctor said as he fitted his top hat back on his head at a jaunty angle and smiled at her. 'And some say he might even be a doctor like myself!'

Maggie began to chuckle. 'Oh, you are funny, Doctor!' she said.

Ada thought it no laughing matter though but it was good to hear the woman laugh once again, nevertheless.

Doctor Scott bade them a good day and left the house swinging his bag and whistling a tune as he made his way to his coach which was parked outside Maggie's garden gate—Ada marvelled that the man even had his driver park up there when there were supposedly so many dubious sorts in the area, but all she'd encountered so far were salt of the earth types at No Man's Land.

'Now there's a thought,' said Maggie. 'Can't imagine our Doctor Scott stalking nymphs of the pave around Whitechapel, but I can't say the same for all doctors, mind you. There are some right quacks out there, I seriously question their training. Some can't be trusted whatsoever!' And with that she sniffed very loudly with disgust which caused Ada to chuckle herself.

**

When Ada was out with the barrow selling veg one morning, she spotted a young lad selling newspapers on the corner of the street. 'A double murder overnight!' he shouted. 'Police search for a killer carries on!' People were crowding around him to purchase newspapers, elbowing one another out of the way to snatch one from the lad's hand before they all sold out. Ada looked on aghast.

A cold shiver coursed her spine. If The Whitechapel Murderer wasn't caught soon, who knew how many more women would be bludgeoned and butchered.

An ice-cold fear gripped her heart. Later when she arrived home and Billy was reading a newspaper at the table, he told them all what had happened. On September the 30th the unidentified serial killer that the press was now dubbing "Jack the Ripper" had killed his third and fourth victims, Elizabeth Stride and Catherine Eddowes. The newspapers were now referring to it as the "double event" as the maniac had committed two murders on the same night.

'Oh, my word!' said Maggie, 'he's really going at it now, ain't he? Upping his game an' all—two for the price of one!'

Ada worried that this would bring it all back to the woman as Maggie was around the same age as the murdered women. The first being forty four and the second being forty six years of age.

One woman had been discovered outside some sort of socialist club in the yard and the other discovered by a policeman on his beat, just three quarters of a mile away at Mitre Square.

'When will this ever end?' said Billy as he shook his head.

'Not until someone puts a stop to it!' Davy banged his fist down on the table. 'I've heard talk of another vigilance committee being set up. Want to go to a meeting tonight?' He asked his brother.

Billy nodded. 'I'm in!'

Danny looked at both brothers. 'Me too!'

Maggie threw up her hands in horror. 'You're far too young!' she said.

'No Ma,' Davy laid a hand of reassurance on his mother's shoulder, 'he's almost a man now. He can come along. We won't let anything happen to him, honest.'

Maggie nodded, but Ada could tell that nothing would make her happy about her younger son's involvement in seeking The Ripper, and to be truthful, Ada herself would rather have him home as she felt protected when he was around. Now all the women of the house wouldn't have a man around while the brothers were out.

'What about our flower selling tonight though?' Ada asked as Frannie and Molly looked on in her wake.

'What do you mean?' Davy glared at the girls.

'Danny usually accompanies us to watch out for us while we work and he sees us safely home afterwards.'

Noting their distress, Danny looked at his brothers and said, 'I'll stay home to protect them all and go out on the flower round with the girls as usual.' He glanced at his mother. 'But Ma, I don't want you staying here alone. You either come with us or get someone in to keep you company.'

Maggie caught Ada's eye and smiled as if she thanked her for what she'd just said. 'I'll come along with you girls, then,' she said.

When the two brothers had departed, Ada asked Danny what a vigilance committee was.

'I don't know too much about them,' he said, 'but from my understanding, the original one was set up by some local tradesmen to hunt the killer down as the police ain't got a grasp on the situation. Various men patrol the streets at night and watch out for the unfortunates too. The police don't seem to mind too much that they help out as long as they don't interfere with their duties.'

'But what will the men do if they catch the killer?'

'Skin him alive, I expect!' Danny grinned.

The only thing that concerned Ada was what if they captured the wrong man?

***

The girls had a very successful evening selling flowers outside the theatre and arrived home safely, they were surprised to see Davy and Billy back home with cuts and bruises on their faces but the young men appeared to be in a joyous mood, nevertheless. Almost celebratory in fact.

''Ere what's bleedin' going on?' Maggie wanted to know as she stood there staring at her sons.

'We got him, Ma. We found The Ripper and we carted him off to the police station. The coppers are questioning him right now as we speak!' Davy grinned.

'I hope they hang, draw and quarter the bleeder!' Billy said with a glint in his eye. 'He was strong and he was fleet of foot but we caught him, we tracked him down. He put up a good fight mind you—I'll give the blighter that!'

'Until we gave him a hiding he'll never forget!' yelled Davy.

'Well, I never!' said Maggie as she stood there in astonishment.

'But where did you find him?' Danny wanted to know.

'He was stalking around the back alleyways just off Mitre Square, and told us he was looking for a particular woman. I know his sort!' Boasted Davy. 'A good hammering he wants. He's after those ladies of the night when he probably has a wife and a houseful of kids back home.'

'Should be in all the newspapers tomorrow then,' Maggie said, and she let out a long sigh. 'I won't believe the police have him in custody though until I read he's safely behind bars and someone has thrown away the key!'

'Or else someone hangs him!' Danny added, which caused his brothers to nod vigorously in agreement.

The following day, the case did make the headlines but it wasn't the headline the brothers were expecting to read:

MAN WRONGLY ACCUSED OF BEING "JACK THE RIPPER" IS SAVAGELY BEATEN AND CARTED OFF TO POLICE STATION BY BARBARIC DUO

A thirty-year-old man was savagely beaten up after being hunted down by members of an unofficial vigilance committee that was recently set up in Whitechapel. This is not the official committee set up by local businessmen that the police are aware of but it appears to be an offshoot of it. Their behaviour has been widely condemned by a spokesperson of the original committee. The young man in question said he was innocently minding his own business when he was approached from behind by two men who interrogated him, chased him and hunted him down like a fox being hounded by a pack of hunting dogs. They savagely beat him, raining blow upon blow on his body and then, dragged him off to the police station. If anyone knows the whereabouts of these two men who are believed to be in their late twenties, heavy set, and possibly brothers, please contact the police immediately.

Maggie stared in stunned belief at her sons. 'What 'ave yer gorn and done?'

'Sorry, Ma,' Davy shook his head while Billy had his lowered almost as though he were a naughty schoolboy being told off. 'We thought we had the right bloke, 'onest we did. What was he doing looking for a woman anyhow?'

'Don't you see though?' Maggie wrang her hands in despair. 'What you both did to that young man is as bad or even worse than what that attacker did to me a couple of weeks ago? He was innocent! I can't imagine what that poor man is going through. I think we need to find out who he is and make amends to him.'

Davy shook his head as if the horror of what they had done was finally sinking in. For the rest of the day the brothers were unusually quiet and didn't even go out to the pub at the end of their working day as they usually did.

Finally, Billy approached his mother. 'Ma, we've been discussing this and we've decided to give ourselves up to the police,' he said stoically.

'Good lads,' she said. 'You're doing the right thing.'

In silence, both donned their jackets and flat caps which were hanging on hooks behind the back door and went to turn themselves in. Meanwhile the rest of them waited near the fireplace as the hours ticked away on the clock. Several times Maggie closed her eyes as if in silent prayer and Ada noticed her cross herself as she'd have done at the church. Then just as the hands of the clock approached five minutes to midnight, the living room door burst open and both brothers stood there.

'Well they didn't keep you in then,' said Maggie smiling. 'So, what happened?' Then she lowered her eyelids as if in suspicion. 'Hey, you did go to the police station and not to *The Bull's Head* as usual?' She drew up close to them and sniffed loudly as if to check they hadn't been drinking alcohol.

'Of course we did, Ma!' Davy replied huffily. 'We turned ourselves in and the police sergeant on the desk said as long as we make some sort of amends to the young man in question as we had suggested, then no further action would be necessary. He was on our side really as he said he'd seen it happen several times of late where men had frogmarched suspicious characters into the station, though none had been as badly beaten up as our man was, mind.'

'So, then,' said Maggie, as she folded her arms and stood as if she meant business, 'how do we go about finding this fellow to apologise and help him and his family as best as we can?'

'The sergeant said he won't give us the man's address, and understandably so, but he's going to bring the man back into the police station tomorrow midday to speak with us. A police officer will need to be present and a record made of it in his notebook I expect. He suggested we offer him some financial recompense for the injuries caused too.'

'Can we afford it?' Danny asked.

'Aye,' Billy said. 'I dare say we can.'

'Yes, it's the least we can do,' Maggie said sombrely. 'That poor fellow will probably lose work because of it.'

And so that night, the family slept more soundly knowing that they were going to make it up to a man who had been unjustly accused of being a serial killer. But the concern was that Jack the Ripper was still out there somewhere and when would he strike again?

Chapter Ten
October

The costermonger and his donkey and cart was the first sight Ada set her eyes on when she wheeled her barrow into Hawthorn Street. She gulped hard. *Frank Malone!* It had been weeks since her first encounter with the man and then he'd warned her to keep off his patch so she'd assumed she was safe selling her wares in her old neighbourhood. Hawthorn Street was the next street over from Sycamore Street. After all, she'd never noticed him peddling his wares when she'd lived in that the area. She was about to turn her barrow around and go off in the opposite direction to avoid possible conflict, when he walked briskly towards her leaving his donkey and cart behind.

'Well, what do we 'ave 'ere then?' he appeared to sneer at her.

'Look, I took your warning last time,' she said with her chin held high. 'I thought I was safe to sell on this street as I used to live around these parts and I ain't ever seen you here before.'

He threw back his head and chuckled. 'Now hang on a mo, little missy. I didn't say I was complaining, did I? In fact, I've only been working this patch fer a couple of days, so you weren't wrong in your assumption. Now how about we share this patch? You can do one side of the street and I'll do the other? Can't say fairer than that, can I?'

She wasn't quite sure whether to trust the man or not, so feeling tired as she had been out all morning, she nodded her thanks at him and wheeled her barrow to the other side of the street. It was a long, double-sided street of houses anyhow, so there was plenty for everyone and to her amazement, she sold very well there over the next hour. Some old neighbours recognised her so that might have prompted them to buy off her. Meanwhile, Frank seemed to be doing equally as well on the other side of the street and she noticed that from time-to-time he was even sending customers to her if he didn't have the items they required. Maybe she had got him all wrong?

When she'd finally sold out of her stock, he crossed the road and digging his hands deep into his trouser pockets while jangling some coins, asked, 'I expect yer hungry and thirsty by now?'

The sun was high in the sky which told her it was around midday and her legs were aching so badly that she needed a break. She shrugged her shoulders and forced a smile.

'How about I take you for a bite to eat, little lady?'

She shivered. What was he after? 'I…I don't know…' she said. Danny should have met up with her by now to walk her home as he'd been working in neighbouring streets but there was no sign of him.

Malone shook his head. 'Look, I ain't after anything. I just know of a little pie shop a few streets away. An elderly lady called Florrie runs it. I daresay she'll make us a cup of tea and all to go with one of her steaming pies. They're the best around these parts, not all fat and gristle like yer get in some pie shops.' He gazed at her intently and spoke softly towards her. 'Look, I am sorry that day I first encountered you. I was sharp and I regret that. I was in a bad mood as someone who'd borrowed money off me—well, he was giving me the runaround—

it was quite a lot of money an' all what he owed me. And I'm ashamed to say…' he shook his head sadly, 'I'd hit the bottle that day an' all. That's why I wasn't very nice to you and I should've been. It wasn't your fault I was owed money…'

Ada shielded her eyes from the glare of the sun by using her hand. 'Did he pay you back in the end?'

'Unfortunately not!' He huffed out a breath. 'He's moved out of his digs his landlady told me. Did a moonlit flit. Didn't pay her either. I'll not see the colour of his money again and neither will she.' He paused and smiled and when he did that, Ada could see that beneath his scruffy looking veneer, he was quite a handsome chap and was probably younger than she'd first imagined. 'So, what do you say? A pie and a cuppa? Best pies around they are! I kid you not!'

Ada nodded and smiled. 'Thank you, Mr Malone,' she said. 'I'd like that.'

'You may call me Frank!' he said and he patted her on the shoulder.

'And I'm Ada Cooper!' she proudly announced.

He even allowed her to ride on his cart with him as he managed to heft her small barrow onto the back of it.

Sitting on the top of the cart with him, she smiled to herself, reflecting on the current situation. *Who'd have thought when I got out of bed this morning I'd be riding like a queen on Frank Malone's cart?* She chuckled inwardly to herself.

***

The pie shop was situated on the corner of Inkerman Street where it intersected with Dane Street, almost as though it were the pinnacle of produce for the masses in the area. The peeling blue and white sign above its large bay window read: Florrie's Pies and Pastries: Purveyor of Fresh Food.

Ada clambered down from the cart with a little help from Frank as he lifted her beneath her arms and swung her onto the pavement, settling her down safely on terra firma. Shyly, she followed him inside the shop. Its interior was small and steamy, but the aroma of meat and pastry was mouth-watering to her senses. There were just three pine tables with four chairs to a table, and behind the counter was a small lady with the most wrinkled face Ada'd ever seen in her life. She had the clearest cornflower blue eyes which belied her many years on this earth. The woman smiled when she spied them both approaching. 'Glad you arrived early, Frank,' she said 'as these tables soon fill up and then you can only have pies to take with you.' She glanced at Ada. 'And who do we have here then?

'This,' said Frank, 'is Miss Ada Cooper. She's a rival costermonger!' he chuckled, which caused Ada to smile.

'Pleased ter meet you,' said the woman. 'I'm Florrie Foster. I owns this place. Now then, whatcha both be having?'

Ada glanced at Frank as if seeking some clue what to order.

'The meat and potato pie is good,' he said. 'I usually 'ave it with peas and gravy. Would you like the same, Ada?'

Ada's stomach growled with hunger. She'd not eaten since before 6 o'clock that morning when she'd set off for market with Danny so she nodded. 'Yes, please, Mr Malone.'

'Two meat and potato pies with peas and gravy it is then, Florrie, me darlin',' he said, 'and two mugs of tea with plenty o' sugar in them as we need to keep our energy levels up!'

Frank led her to a table near the window so he could keep an eye on his donkey and cart as there was still produce on it. As they patiently sat waiting for their meals to arrive, the shop began to fill up with eager customers as the tables became occupied as other people queued at the counter for pies and pastries to take away with them.

'See, I told you,' Frank said, 'this is the best pie shop around these parts. Very popular it is an' all.'

Soon Florrie had placed two steaming plates of food before them with a tin mug each of tea, well sugared, while her young assistant dealt with customers at the counter. Ada had to admit that Florrie's pies were every bit as good as Maggie's and probably even better as she put a lot of meat in hers, whereas Maggie added more veg to eke them out so she could give some to the down and outs.

When Ada had eaten her fill she thanked Frank for his kindness.

'That's all right, me darlin',' he said. 'It was a pleasure to have your company. Us costermongers 'ave to look out fer one another!'

He helped to retrieve her empty barrow from the back of his cart and returned to the pie shop for another cup of tea, waving from the door at her while she marched off with her barrow in search of Danny—fully sated by her very filling meal. Frank explained the route she needed to take to get back to Hawthorn Street. It was quite straightforward really.

When she located Danny, her excitement turned to confusion as he was annoyed that she hadn't waited for him.

'Yer did what?' he asked as he looked at her as if she had lost her mind. 'Yer went off with Malone for something to eat in a pie shop? Have you lost yer senses, gal? Yer don't really know the fella. I've had some run ins with him afore. I wouldn't trust him as far as I could throw him!'

Ada shook her head and defiantly stuck out her chin. 'Well, all I know is he was nice to me, he allowed me to work on his new patch and he took me out for food afterwards.'

'Yer'll be tellin' me next he's yer friend!' Danny mocked.

'He might be. I like him.'

Danny abandoned his barrow to draw closer to her. Then he spoke softly. 'Don't be an idiot, Ada. He's not to be trusted with young girls, honestly. I knew of this girl who worked selling off a barrow like you. She ended up working for him, going out with him on his rounds. The rumour was that he sold her on to a house of ill repute and she ain't been seen since!'

'I don't believe you!' Ada put her hands on her hips and tossed her dark hair.

'Believe what yer like, Ada. There's no smoke without fire though…'

They walked back home in silence and for time being, Ada felt there was now a rift between them and that made her so sad.

***

Back at the house, Ada was amazed when Billy told her that they'd invited the man around that he and Davy had beaten up, for supper that evening. 'It was Ma's idea really but I have to agree with her it was the least we could do. I feel so bad about it now, but we really thought we had The Ripper in our clutches as he kept on about looking for a woman. Turns out though, according to the sergeant at the police station, the young woman he was searching for was a tidy young woman.'

Ada didn't much fancy having the man around for supper at the house. She found the whole debacle truly embarrassing but she could well imagine Maggie bending over backwards to make amends for her sons' bad behaviour.

'Well, you can count me out! I have other things I need to be doing!' said Danny, as he left the room, almost taking the door off its hinges as it slammed shut behind him.

'What's got into him?' Davy frowned. 'Haven't seen him in such a temper for a long time.'

Ada face grew hot. 'I…I think it might be something to do with me…'

Billy and Davy exchanged glances with one another. 'You, sweet, young Ada?' Davy said. 'How come?'

She took a deep breath in and let it in again as she explained her encounter with Frank Malone and waited for their response, then to her astonishment both brothers began to laugh wholeheartedly, which made her confused.

'I really don't think it a laughing matter,' she protested.

'It's not that,' said Billy, 'but Danny has got the wrong end of the stick about the man. He's a good man. He was widowed young. He went a bit to seed after his wife died during childbirth and so did the baby leaving just him and his twelve year old daughter to cope alone. He's not some sort of whoremaster as Danny is making out. He's just friendly with a lady who runs such an establishment. In fact, I've heard that he tries to help those girls by getting them into the Salvation Army Woman's Mission as they save fallen women.'

'I wish they'd save one for me!' Davy chuckled, but Billy, seeing Ada's crestfallen face, chose not to join in with the merriment.

'You can trust him, Ada,' Billy said. 'I think Danny doesn't like him as he had a falling out with him once over a particular pitch, so he's happy to believe any old gossip about the man put his way. Speak as I find, but Frank Malone has always been fair with me and Davy.'

Davy nodded. 'Yes, he's never done us any harm and Queenie at the pub speaks highly of him too.'

'Whew! That's a relief,' Ada said. She had taken Danny at his word, but of course, having had a previous falling out with the fellow, it had coloured his view and he was keen to accept any gossip about the man as fact.

About an hour later there was a knock at the front door and Maggie sprang to her feet to open it. Ada heard voices out in the passageway as Davy and Billy exchanged nervous glances with one another.

It was the visitor they'd been expecting and Ada wondered how the young men would handle it.

As soon as Maggie escorted the man into the room, Ada realised there was something familiar about him. His face was badly swollen from the unwarranted hammering the brothers had given him. Bruises of varying shades of purple and green graced his face, with the odd graze here and there. She winced as she saw there was one eye he could hardly open as it was swollen so much. The brothers appeared shocked by his appearance.

'We are so sorry,' Davy said, swallowing hard and stepping forward to greet the man.

The man took a step back as if in fear he might be struck again but he needn't have worried as it was evident both brothers were profusely apologetic towards him, and it was obvious they intended making amends. The man spoke almost in a mumble as if he'd hurt his jaw, it was then his blue eyes were drawn towards Ada.

'Ada!' he said. But how did he know her name? Was he a customer of hers?

She frowned. 'Sorry, do I know you?'

'You should do. I'm sorry you probably don't recognise me as my face is so swollen and I'm finding it hard to speak properly.' He winced as he massaged his swollen jaw. He removed his hat and began to smile although it obviously caused him pain to do so. It was then she recognised him as she ran towards him as the others looked on in surprise.

'Oh Jakob! Jakob!' she cried as she ran into his open arms and he leaned forward to embrace her. 'I never thought I'd see you again, particularly after I went back to look and I could see you'd moved out of Harlington House. I only recognised you when you took off your hat as your voice sounds strange.'

'Yes,' he nodded vigorously. 'My jaw is still swollen. We had to get out of our old place as there was a fire. In fact it happened the following night after you left. No one was injured, thankfully. But I reckon old Winterbourne might have paid someone to light it so he could get his hands on the insurance money. Can't prove it though.'

Ada opened her mouth, dumbfounded that maybe the man had done that, risking everyone's lives in that building. 'B…but your mother? Where is she now?'

'She's fine, honestly. We've got rooms now in a new place which is so much better than our old one. Wait until I tell her I've seen you, she will be so pleased.' His eyes scanned the room. 'But where is Sam?'

'He's all right, he's gone outside with Danny.'

'That's our youngest brother,' Davy explained.

Ada glanced nervously at Davy and Billy, feeling as though she ought to explain something to Jakob. 'It was Davy and Billy here who helped rescue Sam.'

Jakob drew in a shuddering breath and let it out again. 'Really?'

'Yes,' said Maggie. 'I found Ada in a terrible state after that landlord tried to capture them. She told me he was trying to sell him on to a rich lady. I got my sons to find him and bring him here to safety.'

'Yes,' said Billy. 'That twerp was trying to push him into the lady's coach but we caught him and threatened him and brought the boy safely home with us.

'Well done!' Jakob said grinning now as if oblivious to his earlier pain. 'Anyone who tangles with you two is a mug as I discovered to my cost.'

'We are sorry,' said Billy. 'It's because you said you were seeking a woman that night. We misunderstood your intention as we were looking for The Ripper.'

Jakob nodded then looking directly at Ada explained, 'It was your Connie I was looking for that night, Ada.'

'Jakob, I saw her one night getting into a gentleman's coach!' Ada said excitedly.

Jakob's jaw dropped. 'And where was that?'

'Near one of the theatres where I sell me flowers. She were looking right grand, not like our Connie at all. Dressed in finery and being accompanied into a coach by a gentleman…' There was a catch in her voice and tears sprang to her eyes as she carried on with all eyes upon her, 'but…but..'

'There, there, don't upset yerself, gal,' Maggie said kindly, placing a hand of reassurance on Ada's shoulder.

'No, Mrs Donovan…I need to tell Jakob what I saw that evening,' she inhaled a shuddering breath. 'Connie turned her head and she looked at me but it was like she was looking through me and not at me. It was awful. For a while, I tried to pretend it was another young lady who looked right like me sister, but I knew in me heart it was her.'

Suddenly, she was in Jakob's arms as he cuddled her towards his warm body. 'Aw, Ada, that must have been truly dreadful for you.' He held her at arms' length so he could look into her eyes. 'One thing I do know about your Connie though is that she's a caring person and no way would she want to upset you or Sam. It's my guess when she saw you right at that particular moment, there was a good reason for her not revealing she recognised you in front of the gentleman in question.'

There were murmurs of agreement in the room and Frannie stood beside Ada and took her hand to comfort her. 'He's probably right, Ada,' she said softly. 'No one would want to ignore a lovely, caring sister like you unless there was a good reason to do so.'

Hearing that from Frannie gladdened Ada's heart and she realised the girl had become like another sister to her and was speaking from experience.

There was a long silence and then Maggie suddenly banged a wooden spoon on the side of a saucepan announcing, 'Come along, everyone, I think it's time we ate!'

There was still no sign of Danny and Sam, so Ada ran to the window to see them both outside in the back garden playing with Jasper, who was enjoying all the attention. It was good to see the dog was now having a happy life here instead of being pitted against other dogs for cruel entertainment and illegal betting at dog fighting venues in the area. The brothers and Maggie had done that dog a great kindness in rescuing and caring for him.

Ada banged on the window to the lads who both looked up and smiled at her. A rush of relief washed over her, Danny was obviously no longer annoyed with her and wasn't bearing a grudge.

As the boys washed their hands before the meal, splashing around in a bowl of warm water Frannie provided for them, Ada helped Maggie to dish up the meat and veg stew onto the awaiting plates—it did smell good and all. Maggie had baked some soda bread to go with it and slathered with salted butter, it all went down a treat. By the time the apple pie with custard arrived, Ada felt fit to burst. She glanced at Jakob who was seated beside her looking nicely sated.

'My, my, you've fallen in lucky here with all this fine food and generous hospitality,' he said smiling at her.

She returned the smile. 'I think I have. Maggie is so kind to us all, she even helps the down and outs beneath the arches.'

'I can see she's a benevolent sort, and with those three strapping sons she has, you know you'll always be protected. I wish I could protect your Connie, though.'

She nodded. 'Me too.'

Suddenly he brightened up. 'You said you'd spotted her when you were selling your flowers outside the theatre recently?'

'Yes.'

'Are you going there tonight?'

'Yes, I always go there in the evenings along with Frannie and Molly. Danny usually accompanies us but he can't tonight as he has to walk Maggie to church…' her voice petered away.

'What's wrong, Ada?' He leaned in closer towards her to hear what she was saying.

'Maggie was attacked recently,' she whispered as the others chatted amicably amongst themselves.

'Attacked?'

'Yes, by a man with a knife who threw her to the floor. That's why Billy and Davy joined that vigilance committee.'

'Oh, I see. Now I get why they gave me such a hard time as they thought I'd attacked their mother?'

She nodded. 'Anyhow, it's only now she's coming back to her normal self…'

'That's understandable. What I was about to say was, how about I accompany you girls to your pitch tonight and I can watch out for you? I'll also keep an eye out for the carriages that may arrive in case Connie is in one of them.'

Ada's eyes lit up. 'That's so kind of you Jakob. I'm so glad to have found you again.'

Jakob nodded. 'Me too. Though I don't think your Sam was too sure of me when he came in from the garden,' he chuckled.

'He was probably scared that's all. I didn't recognise you meself.'

'I suppose I do look a little grim at the moment.' He lightly touched his jaw and winced. 'Give it a few days and all the swelling will have gone right down. It'll take a bit longer for the bruises to go away though.'

'What did your mother say about it all?' Ada wanted to know.

'Not a lot. She was upset at first, of course she was, but then when I explained that Billy and Davy got the wrong end of the stick as they were trying to hunt down a killer, along with others of course, then she understood why it happened. I guess I was in the wrong place at the wrong time, but then again, maybe it was meant to happen.'

'How'd you mean, Jakob?'

'What I mean to say is if I hadn't got connected with Billy and Davy then I might never have found you and Sam again.'

She nodded and smiled, realising that was true enough.

***

The table was cleared away by the girls, and then, Billy and Davy offered to play a few card games with Jakob. Ada suspected they were letting him win their hard earned cash as they felt so guilty about what they'd put him through. Meanwhile, Ada and Frannie washed and dried the dishes while Molly stood on a wooden box and stacked them away on the dresser as Maggie took a well-earned rest in her favourite armchair by the hearth. Ada realised how deadbeat the woman was and guessed quite soon she'd be snoozing away or "catnapping" as she liked to call it. Danny and Sam took Jasper out for his nightly walk while all this was going on inside the house.

***

It was finally time for the girls to leave to sell their flowers outside the theatre, so Jakob donned his tweed jacket to accompany them as Maggie waved them all off. She'd helped them to make some pretty buttonholes before they left and added a couple of touches like small coloured ribbon and sprigs of gypsophila, also known as *baby's breath,* which had been growing in the garden, telling them it would stand them in good stead for the future knowing how to add those little touches to their sprays and buttonholes. Ada couldn't envisage selling flowers on the streets for the rest of her life—she dreamed of owning her own flower shop someday where carriages would draw up outside to purchase her flowers, ordering fancy bouquets for weddings or centrepieces for dinner parties. Of course, she'd serve the poor as well with affordable flowers for the masses. She had developed a good eye for colour and putting floral arrangements together which would stand her in good stead. And so, the girls set off with their flower baskets over the crooks of their arms, well laden with pretty colourful sprays, button holes and even a couple of small bouquets.

Those Covent Garden flower girls are going to be green with envy this evening when they see what we're selling, she thought to herself.

But she needn't have worried about the other flower girls that evening as she was soon to discover that most of them had already drifted away as a famous music hall singer called, Marie Lloyd, was appearing on stage at a rival theatre that evening, such was the young woman's popularity. Ada had never heard her perform, but Connie had one time and she'd often sang one of her songs as she walked around their apartment which was called, *The Boy I Love is Up in the Gallery*. So much so, Ada now knew it off by heart. It was the same song she'd heard Queenie singing in the pub—that's how popular it was. Everyone seemed to know of the song as she often heard someone or other singing or whistling the tune.

A sudden thought struck her!

If Connie knew that Miss Lloyd was performing tonight, wherever she was and whoever she was with, would she try to see her perform? Excitedly, she nudged her way through the passing crowd who were queuing outside the theatre, to inform Jakob of this.

'Which theatre is she performing at?' He raised his brow.

'The Agora Variety Theatre, it's a couple of streets away…she might well try to go there as she was so impressed when she last saw Marie Lloyd on stage. She'd saved up for such a long time for a ticket with some of the other girls from the factory but now money might be no object if she's in the company of one of them nobs!'

Jakob's eyes enlarged. 'Then that is where I shall go. You'll wait here with the girls, won't you, Ada? I don't want you all to walk home unaccompanied?'

She nodded vigorously. 'Yes, we'll wait, don't you worry about that.' She watched as he pushed his way past the throng of people to make his way to the Agora theatre. For now it was the only hope she had of finding her sister. She had considered going with Jakob but Maggie had made so many floral arrangements for her to sell it would be a shame to bring most of them back home again. The competition would now be fierce outside of The Agora and the blooms would be no good to sell tomorrow as they'd have wilted by then.

***

Forty minutes later, Jakob returned to her side to discover she'd sold most of her flowers. By now, there were only one or two people outside the theatre as everyone had gone inside as the performance had already begun. Trade had been brisk and she looked up at the young man in expectation.

'Any luck?'

He shook his head. 'Sadly, no. Connie might have already gone inside though before I got there. I've found out from a poster on the wall that Marie Lloyd's performance ends at 10 o'clock, so I plan to return at half past nine and wait outside the theatre. If Connie is in there, I don't want to miss her. I had thought...' his face reddened slightly as he spoke.

Ada frowned. 'Thought what, Jakob?'

'I had thought that maybe I'd buy a ticket and get in there myself and maybe scout around looking for her during the interval. I asked the girl at the box office if I might purchase a ticket but she informed me the performance is sold out, so no luck there.'

Ada felt touched that Jakob would go to all that trouble for her sister. 'Never mind,' she said lightly touching his forearm, 'maybe you'll have better luck when you return there later.'

'Meanwhile,' he said, glancing at Ada and the other two girls, 'I have just enough time to escort you three ladies safely home and to return here to keep watch.'

Frannie and Molly smiled at him. Molly looked dead beat so Jakob took her little flower basket from her and handed it to Ada, then he gave the little girl a piggyback on the way back to Maggie's. She did enjoy it and all as she squealed with laughter at some of Jakob's antics as sometimes he sped up walking at a brisk pace and then he slowed down like a snail. Ada could see he was playing a little game with Molly and it warmed her heart to see a big smile and whoops of delight coming from the girl as until Maggie had taken the sisters in with her kind benevolence, there hadn't been a lot for either sister to smile about.

'Yer really miss your Connie, don't you?' Frannie said suddenly as they walked in the wake of Jakob and Molly.

Ada swallowed a lump in her throat. 'Yes, I do. I just can't work out why she would have left me and Sam like she did that night. She'd promised she'd be there when we woke up next morning.'

'It must have been something big that happened to her, I reckon...' Frannie's voice trailed off.

'Do you think so?'

'Yes, I do.'

'When me and me sister were staying at the woman's mission at Hanbury Street, there was a pretty young woman what stayed there most nights. One night she never showed up and people were concerned.'

'What happened to her?'

'We found out later on that she'd been abducted by some fellow and taken to a place called Brussels. It's not in this country. She was made to work there "servicing the needs of men".'

'That's truly awful,' Ada said shaking her head. 'How did you find that out?'

'She managed to escape and a kind gentleman brought her back to England. She told us all about it at the mission. She's safe now, thankfully, but I've heard there are people who are objecting to that kind of thing. They call it "The Slave Trade" you know,' she said sounding quite knowledgeable.

Ada caught up with Jakob, 'Remember your mother mentioned something about a gang what took girls to somewhere that sounded like a bell?'

Jakob frowned for a moment and then as if he realised what she meant his features relaxed and he nodded, 'Yes, I do. Belgium the country is called. Why do you ask?'

'Well, Frannie just told me about a girl who was taken to Brussels, where is that?'

'It's the capital of Belgium. Now that is a coincidence.' He quietly set Molly down from his back and onto the pavement, telling her he needed a minute. 'Why did she go there?'

Frannie intervened, 'She disappeared from the Salvation Army woman's mission mysteriously and everyone was concerned about her, even the police were contacted. I remember them turning up and questioning the women who worked there and the people who stayed there, even us pair. Molly couldn't tell them anything and neither could I, 'cos we didn't know what had happened. But she turned up six weeks later and said some fella had abducted her and taken her to Brussels to a house of ill repute where she was forced to work.'

Jakob nodded slowly. 'Yes, I've heard that kind of thing is going on, sadly. The young woman was lucky to have got away. How old was she?'

'Just eighteen I think…'

Ada felt her stomach flip over as she said through trembling lips, 'That's the same age as our Connie.'

'Take a deep breath,' Jakob reassured her, 'and let it out slowly…' Ada did as instructed. 'Now, that girl's case may be different to Connie's—at least you know your sister is still around as you've seen her and so have a couple of others. Hopefully, she has come to no harm.' He stroked his chin as if in contemplation, 'Though it is rather puzzling, I grant you, why she hasn't contacted you by now. Though that might be because she doesn't know where you are.'

'Then how do you explain that time I saw her and she didn't say hello or even smile?' Ada said, holding back a sob.

'That, I can't explain, sorry, but I promise you this, Ada, I shall do everything I can to find your sister. You have my absolute word on that.'

She nodded and smiled but the mood had been broken and they walked back to Maggie's house in silence, Molly no longer caring to have a piggyback, instead preferring to hold her sister's hand as she dragged her feet and yawned loudly.

Chapter Eleven

Jakob failed to locate Connie later that evening but at least he was still in touch with Ada and Sam, his mother had invited them over for tea the following week which excited them so. They had missed the woman who had been almost like another mother to them and couldn't wait for the day to arrive.

Meanwhile, it was early Sunday afternoon and Frannie had persuaded Ada to sell flowers with her in Victoria Park as it was such a lovely day. It was dubbed "The People's Park" as it was the very first park assigned to the people of London. Queen Victoria had come up with the idea to appoint a park for the ordinary folk in the area as there was so much overcrowding and disease. People worked hard and often died young and she felt they needed somewhere special to go as often they had no gardens or even a back yard at home. It was a park for everyone where the wealthy rubbed shoulders with the poor.

As the girls entered via the wrought iron gates of the park, Ada shielded her eyes from the sun. It was now beaming down strongly and she began to think that maybe it wouldn't be such a good idea stood out in the sunshine selling flowers on her day of rest—after all, she worked hard during the week which involved rising early to purchase the best produce and finishing late at night outside the theatre. They were long hours, so Maggie insisted she take a Sunday to herself. She'd much rather enjoy the park instead of trying to persuade people to purchase flowers from her but Frannie insisted it would be a good earner for them both. Molly remained at home with Sam with Maggie keeping an eye on them both. Thankfully, the young children got along famously together, enjoying one another's company.

Ada marvelled at all the greenery in the park: oaks, chestnut and hawthorn trees stood loud and proud, and during the spring, the cherry blossom trees were a sight to behold, then it was as if God had decorated the place especially for the people. The boating lake attracted a lot of interest and she loved the way the weeping willow trees overlooking it, bent and swayed in the breeze. It really was a beautiful place to be on a Sunday afternoon.

Ada glanced around and could see a few couples walking together here and there, some families out for the afternoon, a little boy with a sailing boat tucked under his arm, and a young girl being amused as her father flew a kite high above their heads as she reached up her little arms to the sky, almost as though she could reach it. There were babies in their strollers taking the afternoon air and groups of young women walking arm in arm, giggling together as they had no work to go to today. Ada wondered if they were from the match factory and might know Connie. Two old ladies were feeding the ducks with bits of bread from a basket. It really was an enchanting scene. She breathed in and closed her eyes.

When she opened them, she noticed in the distance, a crowd appeared to have gathered as a gentleman stood on some sort of platform to speak as people crowded around him to listen while another gentleman handed out pamphlets from a wooden cart.

'Who's that?'

'That's William Morris,' Frannie said knowledgeably. 'And where he's standing is speaker's corner.'

'Who is he though?' Ada wrinkled her nose.

Frannie's eyes enlarged. 'Yer don't know who he is? I'll tell yer. He's a socialist, he's bin helping that Annie Besant who's been campaigning to assist the match girls in getting better working conditions...'

On hearing mention of the match girls, Ada's ears pricked up just as she noticed a young woman walking arm-in-arm with a well-dressed gentleman in a top hat. They were heading towards speaker's corner.

It couldn't be, could it? Connie!

'That's my sister!' Ada shouted excitedly as Frannie looked on with her mouth agape. She thrust her flower basket into the girl's hand and made off towards speaker's corner shouting out her sister's name but her cries were soon drowned out by William Morris's booming voice and shouts of agreement from the crowd.

She couldn't lose her now, she simply couldn't, but more people were crowding around the man and now she couldn't see Connie anymore in amongst the bobbing heads, everyone was taller than she was. Of course Connie might come here if this man were helping the match girls then she'd be most interested even if she no longer had a job to go to—she'd be concerned about the welfare of her friends, like Rose. She pushed past a middle aged lady and gentleman, almost receiving a black eye from the gentleman's elbow as she ploughed further forward into the crowd.

People were starting to cheer when William Morris forcefully said, *'There is no square mile of earth's inhabitable surface that is not beautiful in its own way, if we men will only abstain from wilfully destroying that beauty...'* The people seemed to be behind him as he continued, *'this is an industrial capitalist society and the world's natural resources are being drained by it. Those fat cat industrialists sit on their backsides while those beneath them toil for a pittance in poor conditions. Their foremen and managers whip the workers into a frenzy to get what they can out of them. Take for example, what happened recently at the Bryant and May match factory, and why those girls deemed it necessary to strike in the first place and march on Parliament to get those dire conditions changed. We will not sit back and watch the destruction of the environment around us. Join me in...'*

Anxiously, chewing her bottom lip, Ada glanced around for a glimpse of her sister but all she could see now were angry faces as the crowd began to chant, 'Power to the People!' A sliver of fear coursed through her and the crowd surged forward as she got caught up in it. Everyone around her seemed to close in on her as if they weren't even aware of her existence as she became crushed in the crowd. Losing her footing, she tripped and then all went black.

***

Someone was lifting her up and carrying her through the crowd as she heard the words, *"Nothing can argue me out of this feeling...the contrasts of rich and poor are unendurable and ought not to be endured by either rich or poor. Everyone has the right to work and to obtain work that is worth doing and doing so under conditions which do not prove wearisome or anxiety provoking. The price to be paid for making the world happy is revolution!"*

The next thing she knew she was being set down on a grassy verge behind the crowd. 'There you are dear, you fainted there for a moment. It's a bit dangerous as you might get trampled underfoot in amongst that lot.'

She looked up at a middle aged gentleman who was well dressed in a frock coat and top hat. He had kind looking, gentle eyes. 'Connie,' she mumbled.

'Who's Connie?' he asked smiling.

'She's me sister, Connie Cooper. I followed her here but now I've lost her.'

'Don't fret, dear,' he said. 'I'm with William Morris. I'll ask him to address the crowd for your sister to come forward.'

'Oh, would you, sir? That would be ever so helpful if you would.'

'Do you feel all right now?'

She nodded gratefully.

'Then please come with me.' He took her hand, helping her to her feet. She stood shakily for a few moments until she felt able to walk once again. They skirted around the crowd until they had reached the edge of the platform. The gentleman stepped forward and onto the platform to have a word in William Morris's ear. He glanced at her and nodded and smiled before addressing the crowd. 'There's a young lady here who has lost her sister, Connie Cooper? Connie, can you please step forward as your sister is here!'

There was a lot of murmuring in amongst the crowd as Ada noticed a gentleman take a lady roughly by the elbow and march her away from the crowd. Was that Connie? The sun was in her eyes and she just couldn't tell.

No one stepped forward as she waited with a pounding heart.

Had that man just escorted her sister away from the crowd? Or maybe the lady she'd followed hadn't even been Connie in the first place and it was wishful thinking on her part?

It became evident that if her sister was here then she either didn't want to show herself or someone had led her away.

***

Ada returned to the spot where she'd left Frannie and taking her flower basket from the girl's hand, she shook her head. 'It can't have been Connie I saw. I was so sure of it too. That couple I followed disappeared into that crowd who were listening to William Morris but then the people started shoving and moving forward. I tripped and fell over but a kindly gentleman who was with him, picked me up and took me to the side of the platform after I'd explained I'd lost my sister. William Morris even asked if Connie was amongst the crowd for me but no one came forward, though I did see a man roughly push a woman away at the same time as the announcement was made.'

'Couldn't you tell if she was your sister or not?'

Ada shook her head. 'No, there were too many people in the way and the sun was in me eyes, all I saw through the crowd was the lady's pink bonnet. It had been the same woman I'd followed I think but maybe I just wanted her to be my sister.'

To her horror, Ada began to sob as Frannie wrapped a comforting arm around her shoulders to soothe her. 'There, there,' she said softly. 'I'd be exactly the same if I thought I saw me mother in the crowd. Even though I know she's dead, I'd be tempted to follow after her.'

Ada looked up at the girl through glazed eyes and blinked. 'You mean you think Connie might be dead?'

'Aw, I'm not suggesting that at all, Ada. What I mean is it can be easy to convince ourselves that we see someone as we miss them so much, that's all.' She handed Ada a clean handkerchief that Maggie had insisted she take with her that morning and Ada dabbed at her eyes. 'Now, when you feel a little better we'll go and sell some flowers near the refreshment rooms, there's always lots of people back and forth there. I tell you Sunday afternoon is a great time to sell flowers as lots of gentlemen take their beaus out then.'

Ada nodded and smiled. It would keep her mind off things at least.

Frannie was right when she said it was a good little earner selling blooms on a Sunday afternoon. The single roses tied with ribbon sold very well indeed and being at the park seemed to cheer people up so they were more likely to dip into their pockets for some change to purchase the flowers.

Ada glanced inside the refreshment rooms as she noticed a lady and gentleman being served a pot of tea by one maid dressed in black with a white frilled apron and a starched, matching cap, whilst another, who was dressed in an identical fashion, brought a china cake stand that held all manner of neat sandwiches and miniature cakes to the table for their perusal.

Ada's stomach growled as it had been ages since her last meal. 'How the other 'alf live,' she chuckled.

There was a gleam in Frannie's eyes as she said, 'Well we can be the other 'alf just for a while today. I reckon we look presentable enough in our Sunday best to go in there, and we've earned ourselves enough money to purchase a couple of sticky buns and a pot of tea for two.'

Ada could hardly believe her ears. She hadn't set foot in a tea room in such a long while. The last time was over a year ago with the family as a birthday treat for Connie. It was the time her mother had presented her sister with that tortoiseshell hair brush that Ada'd rescued from their apartment. They hadn't been a wealthy family but her parents had done their best to allow them affordable treats from time to time, they might not have had pots of money to play with or valuable things at home, but instead they were rich in love and attention from Ma and Pa.

As the girls entered the refreshment room, Ada gazed around in awe. The tables were adorned with pristine white lace table cloths where people sat amicably chatting away to one another and opposite those, ran a long wooden counter with glass domed covered plates that displayed a variety of sandwiches and cakes. Her mouth watered in expectation.

A waitress smiled and showed them to an awaiting table for two, not batting an eyelid that they weren't wealthy or wearing fancy gowns, after all, they were two young ladies who were clean and presentable and they had the money to pay.

They ordered a plate stand of miniature cucumber sandwiches and fancies and a pot of tea for two. Ada had never eaten a sandwich with the crusts cut off before, this was all new to her and it made her feel very posh indeed.

'Why do you think they allow the likes of us in 'ere?' she asked Frannie.

The girl smiled knowingly. ''Cos it's the People's Park that's why. This area of parkland is for everyone.'

Ada nodded then reached for a cucumber sandwich which to her surprise also contained some sort of cream cheese with chives, and she closed her eyes as she savoured the moment. It also made a change when the waitress poured their tea from a fancy china tea pot into matching cups. At home with her parents, the tea set had mismatched. Her mother had bought all they required cheap at the market place and although, Maggie herself at her place, had a fancy set which adorned her wooden dresser, she chose not to use it as she told everyone she only used it for special occasions—it was for "best". So it was the same there, an old earthenware teapot with mismatched cups, some of which didn't even have any saucers to accompany them, but Ada didn't mind a jot as she was just happy to have a roof over her and Sam's heads for time being and she knew Frannie and Molly felt exactly the same.

Frannie took a sip of her tea and set her teacup back down in its saucer. 'What do you think you'll say to yer sister if yer ever manage to catch up with her and talk to her, Ada?'

Ada shrugged. 'To be 'onest with you I don't know whether I'd be happy, sad or angry with her abandoning us like that.'

Frannie added another sugar lump to her tea with the aid of a silver pair of tongs and Ada watched as the tea in the cup fizzed up and the girl stirred it with a small spoon. They didn't usually drink tea with sugar in at Maggie's as it was expensive, so this was a novelty for them both. Frannie set down her spoon in the saucer and meeting Ada's gaze said, 'Yer sister must have had her reasons though, Ada. From what yer've told me about her, it doesn't sound as if she were the flighty sort. Up until that time she abandoned you it sounds as if she was someone you could count on.'

Ada nodded vigorously. 'Oh, she was and that's what makes it all the more of a puzzle.'

They ate their sandwiches in silence as there was a sudden downpour of rain outside the window which seemed to match Ada's mood perfectly. Where had that come from? It had been warm and sunny a few minutes ago.

***

Out on the street with her barrow the following day, Ada began to tell Frank Malone all about her missing sister. He looked at her curiously, cocking his head on one side as he listened intently to her story.

'What does your sister look like?'

'She's a good couple of inches taller than me with long blonde hair and beautiful green eyes. Very pretty, she is.'

'And how old did you say she is?'

'Eighteen.' She gazed at him as he rubbed his stubbled chin as if in contemplation. 'It's just that there was a new girl taken on at Madame Fontaine's place…'

'Who's she?'

'She's a lady I know what runs a boarding house or should I say bawdy house!' he chuckled, but then seeing the seriousness on Ada's face his demeanour changed as if he didn't wish to upset her.

'Could you take me there, please?' she asked with an urgency to her voice.

'Hey, hang on a mo there, missy,' he said holding up the vertical palm of his hand, 'it's not the kind of place the likes of you and I can just stroll into. Oh no. Madame Fontaine is in charge there and it would be best if I called in the evening time for a few drinks and what nots.'

Ada frowned. 'It's one of them houses of ill repute, Frank. Go on tell me the truth!' she said defiantly as she stood with her hands on her hips as he turned around to pat his donkey, Samba, as if avoiding her gaze through embarrassment.

'Frank?' she blinked.

He turned suddenly to face her, his face pink and flushed. 'Er,' he swallowed. 'I'm afraid it is.'

'Well I don't think me sister would end up in one of those places!' she said angrily.

'Maybe not,' he said gently, 'but it's got to be worth checking out, hasn't it now? 'T'wouldn't hurt, would it?'

She blew out a long breath, maybe it wouldn't. 'All right then, but I bet you won't find her in that place.'

He smiled broadly and pushing back the rim of his wideawake hat said, 'At least I can put the word out for you if I visit.'

She nodded. 'And if you do, then I'm coming with yer, Frank.'

'It's no place for a young lady, mind. You might see sights yer wish yer hadn't.'

'I don't care!' she said defiantly. She now considered herself a woman of the world and if it helped to bring her sister back then what did it matter if she saw some shocking sights, it would be worth it.

Chapter Twelve

Later that evening, Frank met up with Ada. He'd obviously taken the time and trouble to get himself well scrubbed up as his earlier grime had been washed off his skin. Much to her surprise, his face was cleanly shaven which she'd never seen before, and he'd put on some clean togs and wore a top hat instead which made him look more of a gentleman than his usual wideawake one. She guessed he was out to impress as he waved his wooden cane with its gilt-edged top. After finishing his theatrical performance, he lowered his voice and brought his index finger to his lips, and said sombrely, 'Now, we need to be careful as the area we are about to enter is a den of iniquity. It attracts lots of soldiers and sailors who are drawn there by the temptation of their earthly desires, if yer get me drift?' He winked.

She thought she understood. 'Yes, Frank. What do you want me to do?'

'Just leave all the talking to me, young lady. I have an idea to dupe the madame of the house, as in Madame Fontaine, so she should get the impression I might be thinking of selling you on to her.'

Ada stiffened as a chill ran down her spine. What if Danny were right all along and Malone had only befriended her with a view to selling her to such a place in any case and he was doing so right now?'

Noticing her scared stiff demeanour, Frank chuckled. 'Don't be so daft, gal. I ain't got no intention of parting company with you. I just thought as yer want to accompany me anyhow, we could get in the place and while I keep Madame occupied, maybe you could accidentally as it were, get yerself lost and look around for any sign of yer sister. I won't be too far away if yer gets yerself into any bother, shout and I'll come immediately. The walls in that place are so thin, I'd hear if yer were in any trouble.'

Ada frowned, wondering how he knew so much about the place and if maybe he was a regular visitor himself, but then he shot her a cheeky grin and angling his head to one side, said, 'Don't look so worried. I know the joint as Madame Fontaine orders her groceries from me. She has a regular weekly order in place to keep her stable of fillies well fed and the stallions too what visit those stables!'

It took a minute or two for Ada to realise he meant the women of easy virtue and the customers who called there. She was beginning to grow up fast she realised as not so very long ago she didn't even know that such places existed.

As the long street of houses and shops, peppered with advertising for such things as Pear's Soap, Fry's and Nestle Chocolate, Beecham's Pills and Stone's Ginger Wine, gave way to a more grim and grimy looking area, she trembled. There was something mean and menacing about the area, the double doors of a pub on the corner swung open and she heard raucous sounds drifting towards her as she inhaled the alcoholic fumes emitted from within.

Two soldiers in red tunics emerged and began to laugh with one another as they staggered down the street. Then another man with the sleeves of his white shirt rolled up beneath his leather waistcoat shouted after them, 'Now get out and stay out and don't bleedin' bother coming here ever again as you're both barred for good!'

He was evidently the landlord of the pub and Ada wondered what both men had done to warrant a lifetime ban. Catching sight of Ada and Frank, he rolled his eyes and shook his head before entering the pub once again.

As they passed the houses which were three storeys high in what had once probably been a posh area with its wrought iron railings, Ada glanced up at one of the windows to see the sash window upstairs was wide open as a young woman in a red dress sat side saddle on the window sill as she peered down below.

'Is that one of *those ladies*?' Ada pointed out to Frank.

'Sssh,' he warned 'and we don't point as we don't want to draw any attention to ourselves.'

'Sorry, Frank,' she whispered.

When they were out of earshot he replied, 'Yes, that's a lady of the night. Yer'll see plenty of those on this street, either sitting at windows or even on the doorstep trying to attract men inside the houses. Fair play to Madame Fontaine though, she never does that. Her place is a little more upmarket. She makes out it's some sort of bar where drinks are served to gentlemen, she's even got a pianist performing there. It's a front you see…'

'A front for what though?' she wrinkled her nose.

'A front in case the police call. To all intents and purposes if they step foot over the door, they'll find maids downstairs serving the men with beer and spirits and even food so it looks like a sort of gentleman's club. The other women work upstairs, they're very discreet and all, rarely making an appearance downstairs of an evening.'

Ada blinked. 'How do you know this then, Frank?'

His face flushed. 'I…er…just know that's all from when I deliver me goods, the staff talk, like. They often give me a cup of tea and I keeps me ears open and me tongue still. I ain't a customer there, no way!'

'Oh!' That seemed to satisfy her curiosity for time being.

Eventually, they crossed the road and Ada noticed a sign which read "Cresswell Terrace". Frank paused outside a house which stood out from all the others as it was painted a faint shade of lemon with pretty plants and flowers in window boxes outside, it looked too smart for the street, Ada thought. There was a black sign on the wall to the left of the dark blue front door which read, "Exclusive Gentleman's Club: Licensed premises, late night meals available on request." There was no mention of it being some kind of bordello and as Frank had indicated, no women in gaudy dresses hanging out of any windows nor on the doorstep to greet customers here.

They climbed the four steps to the door and Frank raised the brass door knocker and rapped on it three times before taking a step back and standing beside Ada. It was a couple of minutes before anyone answered and then it was a lady in a black dress, white pristine lace trimmed pinafore and mobcap, just like Ada expected to see at a posh house and not at a house of ill repute.

Frank removed his top hat and holding it beneath his arm and his cane in the other hand, put on what Ada thought was a highly affected voice. 'Good evening, miss,' he said as he flashed her his best smile. 'I'm wondering if Madame Fontaine is available this evening? I have a business proposition for her?'

From somewhere inside, Ada could hear the piano softly playing in the background as glasses clinked and the sounds of murmuring men's voices drifting towards them.

'I'll just go and see if she's available. Who shall I say called, sir?' The young maid asked.

'Er…Frank Malone. Mister Frank Malone. She knows who I am.'

'Just a minute, sir.' The maid closed the door behind herself so it was partially ajar as they waited.

Meanwhile, Frank glanced nervously up and down the street.

'What's the matter?' Ada hissed.

'Don't want the police seeing me here,' he said quietly. 'I'm in enough trouble as it is, maybe I should have used the back entrance but it's too late now. Didn't think I'd have to wait on the doorstep as I'm well known here but Madame F. must have taken a new maid on since I was last here, never seen her before.'

She nodded and then a minute later, the front door swung open and a woman stood there staring at them both. The woman was tall, slim and elegant. Her dark hair was swept back from her face. She had attractive features though for someone of her age. Ada estimated that she might be the same age as Maggie but not had such a hard life. Her sapphire blue eyes were her most noticeable feature and her plump magenta lips smiled to reveal a full set of white teeth which were the opposite to Maggie's bad ones. The dress she wore was a shimmering royal blue in colour with a high necked white ruffled collar. Her neat little waist was nipped in with a black belt and she wore a small pink rose on her lapel. Everything about her was pristine, not what Ada had expected at all from someone who ran such an establishment—she'd thought she'd look like one of the women she'd seen sitting at the window on her way here, all gaudy and vulgar, not like the lady of the manor.

'Frank,' Madame Fontaine said warmly as she greeted him. 'Sorry to keep you on the doorstep, the new girl didn't know who you were!'

'And why should she!' said Frank smiling.

The woman stepped back to allow them both over the threshold. Ada was in awe of the black and white checked floor in the hallway with its green leafy aspidistra plants either side beneath the staircase on the left, whilst on the right hand side was an archway which led in the direction of where the piano music was emanating from. She could just make out a long walnut coloured bar where two well-dressed gentlemen were stood drinking glasses of what appeared to be either brandy or whiskey. Dotted around on the plush green and gold carpet were several small tables and chairs. But there were no women whatsoever on view there.

'And what can I do for you, Frank?' Madame Fontaine shot him a salacious smile.

Frank lowered his voice. 'Is there somewhere we might speak in private?'

The woman nodded and then her eyes were drawn to Ada. 'Is what you are about to say suitable for the ears of this young lady?'

'Oh yes,' said Frank, 'it's her I've come about and I'm sure you'll like what I have to say about her.'

The woman's eyes immediately lit up as she seemed to be appraising her appearance. Ada wondered what she was thinking about her. 'Would you both come this way?'

As the woman's skirts of her damask dress swished as she walked along, Ada noticed a silver chain adorning her waist upon which sat several keys clinking as she moved along, and she wondered what they were used for.

Presently, she stopped outside a dark oakwood door and stooping to unlock it with one of her keys, she allowed both to step inside behind her. Ada glanced around herself, it appeared to be some kind of office. There was a large mahogany desk with a leather chair behind it. Several shelves were filled with dark blue ledger style books which she guessed were for some sort of accounts going by all the numbers jotted down on the open one on the desk which the woman immediately snapped shut from prying eyes. On the window sill was an oil lamp and a vase filled with pink peonies. The fire in the grate was unlit, which told Ada the room was only used on occasion. To the corner of the room, she noticed a small table upon which was a crystal cut decanter with several matching glasses on a tray beside it.

'Will you both take a seat.' Madame Fontaine gestured to a couple of chairs with her elegant hand and smiled a smile that Ada thought did not quite reach the woman's eyes. They did as told whilst the woman herself hovered near the decanter on the table. 'Would you like a drink as this is a business proposition?'

Frank nodded eagerly. 'Yes, please.'

Ada felt a little uncomfortable about Frank accepting a drink as she feared it might change his personality like it had on her first memorable encounter with him.

Madame's eyes turned towards Ada. 'And you, dear. Would you like a small tipple as it's a chilly evening?'

Ada could think of nothing worse, she'd much prefer a cool glass of ginger beer or lemonade. She exchanged glances with Frank who nodded at her to accept. She'd once taken a sip of her father's glass of whiskey at Christmas time and thought it a dreadful taste and so strong too.

'Brandy or whiskey, is it?' Frank asked.

'Brandy.' Madame smiled and her eyes locked with his which made Ada wonder if they knew one another better than she first thought. Then she turned her attention back to Ada, 'I'll add a little water to yours, dear, in case it's too strong for you.'

Ada smiled and watched as the woman added water from a little jug nestled behind the decanter.

The woman handed them their drinks, though for time being Ada did not drink hers, she just took one sip and then she nursed the glass between her hands. It tasted better than her father's whiskey but she realised she needed to keep her wits about her.

She listened as the pair chatted about this and that until finally, Madame asked, 'So, what is this business proposition of yours, Frank?'

Frank set his glass down on the desk before him. 'Well, I was wondering if you'd like to take on a new girl here?'

Ada watched the woman's reaction. Her face was a blank canvas, almost as though she were guarded in some sort of way. 'A new girl? Who did you have in mind and how old is the young lady?'

'It's Ada here beside me,' he gesticulated with his hand. 'She's twelve years old, almost thirteen. Not quite a young woman as yet but I do know you've had young 'uns working for you in the past.'

The woman began to look a little flustered in front of her. 'I...I...that is we did employ some young ladies but we weren't that sure of their ages. I think they may have lied to us and pretended to be older than they really were.'

Why was Madame now speaking of "we" instead of "I"? Ada wondered. It felt to her almost as if she was trying to distance herself from employing young girls.

Frank pursed his lips and then let out a breath. 'But as you know, Madame Fontaine, there are some that er...how shall I say...may have a preference for such things.'

Madame's face flushed red. 'I think it might be better if the young lady sat outside while we discuss this. 'Take your drink with you, dear, there's a chair outside in the hallway. Do not speak to anyone, understood?'

Ada nodded, and taking her glass, left the room and found a highbacked chair which was located near the staircase. It was too far away from the office door to eavesdrop, so she placed her glass on the floor and watching that no one was around, put her ear to the door to listen to the conversation inside. Their voices sounded a little muffled but she heard Frank say, 'Come on now, Adeline, think how much money we can make from the lass. You can charge twice, nay three times as much even more and the punters will pay for the privilege.'

Ada gasped. Was Danny correct that Frank could not be trusted? Yet his brothers described him as someone who would do anything for anyone, a salt of the earth character. Had she misjudged him? While she had the opportunity to do so she was going to snoop around and maybe leave before they'd finished their conversation but one thing was certain, she was going to keep her wits about her at all costs. Looking around her to ensure no one was watching, she lifted her glass and poured its contents into the soil of one of the aspidistra plants and set the glass back down beside her chair.

Then, stealthily, she climbed the stairs, all was quiet but she was overcome with the strong smell of roses. It was some sort of perfume permeating the air, powerful and pungent. The patterned stair carpet looked expensive and plush as if newly laid and it would aid her to walk quietly up the stairs without the hobnails on her boots clattering like they did on uncarpeted floors. At the top of the stairs, she glanced both left and right. There appeared to be four bedrooms, each with their doors firmly shut. She listened intently for any sounds from within. Then she heard a couple of feminine voices speaking in a friendly manner to one another.

One was saying, ''ere Freda wish we 'ad a night orf tonight!' A giggle and then a voice replied, 'Never mind, there's always good paying customers at the weekend, luvvie.' Neither girl sounded like her sister. Quite suddenly the bedroom door opened causing Ada to take a step back in fright.

The raven haired woman before her was dressed only in a corset and some sort of underskirt and Ada thought for a moment she was going to get angry and shout at her. She was a very pretty lady—Ada thought the make up on her painted face looked like something an actress would apply for work on the stage. 'What you doing here, ducks?' The woman angled her head with curiosity as she stared at Ada, waiting for a response.

Ada opened her mouth to speak but nothing came out.

'Cat got yer tongue?' said the blonde haired beauty behind the woman.

She had to do this for her sister and now might be her only chance. 'I…I'm looking for my sister…' she said in a whisper.

'Speak up, darlin'!' the dark haired one said, then she said softly, 'Look, my name is Melissa and this is Anna. What did you say?'

This time as she was now feeling more comfortable, Ada said, 'I'm looking for my sister, Connie Cooper. I've heard that a new girl has started work here, what's her name please?'

The women exchanged glances with one another and Melissa said, 'Look, there is a new girl here and I don't know who gave you that information but she ain't called Connie, her name is Arabella or Bella for short.'

'Please take me to her, I just have to make sure she's not my sister.' Her bottom lip quivered. Oh dear, she didn't want to cry at a time like this.

As if noticing her distress she heard Anna say to Melissa, 'Won't do no harm I suppose.'

Melissa nodded and then glancing at Ada, smiled. 'Come with me, young lady, but don't stop long. Yer really shouldn't be up here, how did you get in?'

'Frank Malone, the coster fella, brought me to see Madame.'

Melissa narrowed her gauze. 'I know Frank, but why did he bring you here to see her?'

'He told her he can sell me to her, I think.'

Melissa's mouth popped open and snapped shut again. 'Heavens above! This ain't no place for a young girl. I know it goes on but not at this establishment no more!' She looked at Anna who just shrugged her shoulders. 'Whatever you do don't end up working here, love. I don't know what Frank's up to as I ain't never heard of him doing that before.'

Ada chewed on her bottom lip. 'I think he's only telling her that to get me in here to look for Connie. He told me he's going to keep her talkin' downstairs in her office.'

Melissa's demeanour suddenly changed from being friendly to being slightly hostile by frowning at her. Oh dear, had she done the right thing in telling the women their plans? But then the young woman smiled and said brightly, 'Right, well we won't let on you've been here and I'll check with Bella to see if her real name is Connie. All I know about her is that she's from the East End, she don't talk to us much. Prefers to keep to herself, see.'

Melissa escorted Ada along the corridor with an arm on her shoulder and then knocked on the white door at the end of it. The door swung open and Ada gasped.

***

The young woman who opened the door looked like Connie but it was as if she was wearing a mask. Her face was painted just like Melissa's and Anna's faces were with some sort of light coloured powder, bright lipstick stained lips and charcoal lined eyes, she looked beautiful but somehow grotesque at the same time and there was some sort of sadness behind her eyes.

'Connie!' Ada said rushing forwards towards her sister. It was a moment or two before the young woman could take it all in and then she was hugging Ada to her bosom. Ada inhaled a strong perfume that wasn't like the sweet parma violet aroma she'd inhaled the last time she'd seen her sister when she'd kissed her goodnight with the promise to be back home soon.

Tears were falling from Connie's eyes, mirroring Ada's happiness at seeing her sister again. 'Oh, Ada, love. I've failed you and our Sam. How are you managing and how did you find me here of all places?'

'There's no time for that now,' urged Ada. 'Get out of here quickly. Come with me.' Melissa and Anna were looking on in astonishment so Ada asked, 'How do we get out of here without being seen?'

Melissa exchanged glances with Anna. 'There's another staircase through that door there which will take you out through the side of the building but you'll have to be careful. But I don't think you should both leave right now.'

'Ada, I can't come with you tonight, we'll get caught, the timing ain't right.' Connie sighed.

Melissa nodded. 'You need to come back another time. Tomorrow night would be better as Madame won't be around then, she's going to be out for the evening.'

Ada nodded. 'I'll bring Jakob with me.'

At hearing Jakob's name, Connie's eyes lit up and she nodded through her tears.

'You better get yerself back downstairs before Madame notices you're missing,' said Anna. 'Don't worry about yer sister, just make sure you're here at the back door with Frank or that geezer you mentioned, at eight o'clock tomorrow night as it will be safer then. We'll watch out for your sister till you turn up.'

Ada smiled and nodded. Embracing Connie one last time, she said, 'Don't worry about me and Sam, we're safe and living with

Maggie Donovan and her family in the house 'neath the railway arches…'

'But how come you ended up there?' Connie shook her head in disbelief. 'Ain't you still at our place?'

'No. It was Winterbourne, he threatened to put me in the workhouse and sell Sam to some rich woman as the rent wasn't paid. We managed to escape and Maggie took us in.'

Connie began to sob. 'I failed you so much. Winterbourne shouldn't have done that as I was sorting things out, he promised…'

'Look,' said Melissa firmly, 'you're both in danger if you're found up here, Ada. Get back downstairs to where you were, before Madame notices you're missing.'

Ada nodded and gave them all a silent wave as she headed back down the stairs and in the nick of time too for no sooner than she had settled herself down in the chair again, than the office door opened as Frank emerged and he turned to shake Madame's hand. 'I'm so pleased we can do business together, Madame Fontaine. When will you be ready to receive the girl?'

'Tomorrow evening,' she said smiling broadly. She paused for a moment. 'Oh, no, I shall be out then, I'm going to the theatre. First thing Monday morning should do.'

'That's grand, Madame. We shall see you then. You won't regret this.'

'And I shall have partial payment ready for you for the agreed sum. You shall receive the rest when I can see she is well settled in here. Some of them don't take to it and need to be returned to their parents or guardians.'

He winked at Ada. 'Oh, this girl won't let you down. I'm sure of it.'

Madame looked Ada up and down and approaching her she commanded, 'Open your mouth girl.'

Ada did as instructed but she couldn't for the life of her understand why the woman was peering into her mouth. 'Hmmm a good set of even teeth.' What Madame was doing to her now reminded her of when Frank had done the same thing when she'd first encountered him—she didn't like it then and she didn't like it now. She looked at him and then narrowed her eyes with suspicion.

Then Madame Fontaine began to pull strands of Ada's hair apart as if studying her scalp. Ada felt like kicking the woman in the shin with her boots but she realised she needed to play the game, so she complied.

'No evidence of any lice, thankfully,' she said.

Ada knew there wouldn't be as Maggie washed her hair in vinegar once a week and went through it with a fine tooth comb.

'So, you'll pay me top whack for her?' Frank cocked his head on one side as if expecting a response.

'Yes, gladly. She's in fine fettle.'

What did Madame think she was? A horse? Ada gritted her teeth. No wonder Frank had made that earlier reference to horses and stables.

'Right, we'll be off then, Madame.' He nodded at the woman and then smiled.

Madame nodded back at him but she did not return the smile. 'I'll look forward to seeing you both first thing Monday morning, Frank. Better bring her about 6 o'clock, it will be safer then.'

Ada wondered why? But Frank answered her question for her.

'Yes, less chance of the bobbies being around then.'

Madame summoned the maid who had seen them at the door. 'Nancy, please can you show them out? And next time you see them at the door, please allow them straight in, would you?'

The maid curtseyed. 'Yes, Madame.'

They followed after the maid and soon were back out on the dimly lit street. Ada huffed out a breath. 'I didn't like her one little bit, Frank,' she said. 'She never even once called me by me name.'

He smiled at her. 'Never mind, Ada. We got ourselves a foot in the door.'

She paused beneath the yellow glow of the lamplight to look at Frank. 'We did better than that. I found me sister!' she said unable to contain her excitement.

'Sssh!' he clamped his hand over her mouth, taking her off guard. 'I'm sorry,' he whispered, 'but you never know who's listening. Madame Fontaine may well have sent one of her henchmen to trail us.' He released his hand from her mouth, so she could breathe easily once again.

'Henchmen?' Ada blinked.

'Yes, she has a couple of men who keep a watch over the girls. They must have been busy elsewhere when we arrived. Wait till we get a bit further away from the place and then we'll discuss it but it's good news…'

When they were a couple of streets away, they paused to chat about things as Ada explained how she'd discovered her sister upstairs at the property in a bedroom. 'She's been using the name "Bella",' she explained.

'The girls often use a fancy name, sometimes French. It was probably Madame Fontaine's idea. But what do we do next?'

'The other two women told me to return tomorrow night at eight o'clock as Madame would be out for the evening and they'll let us in the back entrance of the house.'

'That's good then, but we still have to be discreet because of those henchmen.'

Ada nodded. 'We'll just have to take care then,' she said. 'But what sort of deal did you have with Madame about selling me?'

He chuckled. 'Believe me, you don't want to know but she fell for it all right.'

Ada let out a long breath of relief, there was no indication that Frank was up to something and from what she could see, he really wanted to help. Something suddenly occurred to her. 'Have you done this kind of thing before, Frank?'

He nodded. 'It was a while ago, mind. A little coster girl went missing from her round one day, she was only about your age, Ada.' He paused for a moment as if to collect his thoughts and he shook his head. 'Me and her father tracked her down to a house of ill repute but we were too late, sadly. She'd been sold on elsewhere, somewhere overseas. The police did their best to help in the search, but they were up against it as the last trace of her was boarding a ship with a man and woman headed for the port of Calais in France. After that, the police said she could have ended up in any country. Oh, how that father grieved for his daughter as he knows in his heart, he'll never see her again. She might even be dead by now.' He wiped away a tear with the back of his hand as Ada physically felt his pain.

'That father you just told me about, he wasn't your friend, was he, Frank? It was you?'

He nodded. 'Yes, she was my own child and a friend helped me to look for her. Clara never made it back home. That's why I'm trying to help you, Ada love. I can't do no more for my daughter.'

Ada took hold of his large calloused hand, as they walked home in silence. There seemed nothing to say. It was then Ada realised that Frank's daughter must have been the missing girl that Danny had alluded to when he'd warned her off getting involved with the man. The lad hadn't realised she was Frank's own child who had gone missing in such sad circumstances.

Chapter Thirteen

Later back at Maggie's house, Ada related the tale to them all, including Danny. 'So, you see that's why Frank had been hanging around at those sort of places. He couldn't help his own daughter but he has helped some other young women to escape.'

There was a lot of nodding of heads and murmuring as Danny made eye contact with her and said, 'I suppose I must have been wrong about the man then, but you can see how it might have appeared to folk?' He said with a note of contrition in his voice.

Ada nodded and smiled at him. 'Yes, but Frank has done a lot of good and he's going to help us get Connie out of that house tomorrow evening, if all goes to plan. I'm thinking of asking Jakob to help as well.'

'I reckon you need me and our Billy there too,' suggested Davy. 'I wouldn't ask Jakob to approach the house though as his bruises might put them off.'

Ada nodded. 'I hadn't thought of that. Yes, if you and Billy come along then, but you'll need to be well hidden at the back of the house in case anything goes wrong. My plan is to get Connie out safely through the back door. The two women there, Melissa and Anna, have promised they will help us.'

'I'll fetch the horse and cart,' Davy said. 'Once you've got your Connie safely out of the place, I can hide her under an old tarpaulin so no one sees her and tries to stop us, maybe cover up what we're doing by throwing some baskets of veg on the back. No one will suspect a couple of working coster men of hiding your sister on the back of their cart!'

'That's a great idea!' Ada beamed.

Their plan just had to work.

Everyone nodded and agreed what a great idea it was.

***

The following evening at five minutes to the appointed time, Frank escorted Ada to the back gate of the property at Cresswell Terrace, which was down the far end of a narrow lane, whilst the brothers sat upon the cart which was loaded up with baskets of fruit and veg. Frank knew the back entrance well even in the dark as he delivered there often enough. As both waited outside the back door there was no sign of life inside, so by ten minutes past the hour, Frank became a little tetchy.

'Something feels a bit off,' he said, worriedly glancing at Ada.

'But they said they'd be here waiting for us and would fetch Connie to the door,' Ada insisted.

Suddenly, they noticed a light going on inside the house and the sound of voices headed towards them as there was the click and rattle of someone inserting a key into the lock and the door slowly opened wide.

'See, I told you so!' Ada grinned broadly but soon that grin turned to a grimace as they were faced with Madame Fontaine herself.

She glared at the pair of them. 'Try to make a fool out of me would you, Frank Malone?' Her eyes flashed and her lips were set in a straight line.

'I...I don't know what you mean,' said Frank, obviously trying to rectify the situation. 'I just brought the girl around a little early that's all as I've got a lot on next week. I thought a day or two early was neither here nor there!'

'It is not the girl coming early that I object to, it is who *she* is! I've been informed by my working girls that she was snooping around here yesterday while you diverted my attention downstairs. She was looking for her sister! It's all been a ploy on your part! Well, thankfully, my girls were on the ball and informed me you would be coming here this evening to try to take "Bella" with you.'

'Aw, look, Madame...' said Frank trying to appeal to her better nature. 'All right, you've rumbled us, but Ada and her younger brother need their older sister. They're orphans you see. Please, I'm willing to pay you for her release. You'll have no more trouble from me, I swear!'

'It's too late for that. I've sold your sister on!' Madame Fontaine said gleefully with a glint in her eyes and a smirk on her lips. 'You tried to pull the wool over my eyes! And you'll never find her as she'll be out of the country by now!'

Ada could hardly believe her ears—there was a sinking feeling in her gut. Only a few minutes ago she had been full of hope and expectation at the thought of being reunited with Connie once again but now she felt so deflated.

'Look,' said Frank tactfully, 'we didn't intend to deceive you. The girl just needs her sister right now. Please, at least let us know where she's been taken to. I implore you.'

'Never!' said Madame Fontaine.

Ada glared at the woman as anger surged through her as she ran towards her and kicked her hard in the shin with her hobnail boot. Madame Fontaine reeled backwards but managed to retain her footing but the pain in the woman's eyes was evident. Quick as a flash she slammed the door shut on the pair and they heard her locking it from inside.

'Now yer've gone and done it,' said Frank, with a look of deep concern on his face. 'She'll never let us know now what's happened to yer sister.'

'I don't think the old sow would have anyhow!' Ada said, spitting out the words one by one.

Frank shook his head. 'She's an awkward cuss, I know, but I do have a way of getting around her but I can't see that happening any time soon after what you just did to her! Come on, we'll have to tell the Donovan brothers to stand down and they're no longer needed to lay in wait. They can give us both a lift back home though.' He draped his arm around Ada's shoulder as if he could sense her sadness and they walked back to the cart in silence until he said, 'We'll just have to come up with another plan now, darlin'.'

Ada felt remorse that she had acted in haste in lashing out at the woman but she'd been so frustrated at the time.

'So near so far!' bellowed Frank at the brothers as they sat atop the cart.

'What happened?' Davy frowned.

'The old bird was in and lying in wait, weren't she! I don't reckon the information we had about her being out tonight was correct at all. We were set up. The Madame and her girls laid a trap for us and we got nicely snared. She reckons that Connie was taken away early this morning and is now out of the country. She wouldn't even tell us where she's gone to.'

'That's terrible.' Billy glanced at Ada. 'You all right, ducks?'

Ada nodded though she felt engulfed with grief.

'C'mon, we'll give you both a lift back home.' Davy gesticulated for the pair to climb aboard the back of the cart and Ada was grateful for it too as she felt as though her legs could not carry her any further.

***

When Ada related the tale to Maggie later back home, the woman nodded and sympathised though she didn't seem overly surprised. 'I have to admit I did think it unlikely that you'd return here with your sister, Ada,' she said. 'Those sort of people what keep young women and girls in those houses of ill repute are always one step ahead of the game you see.'

'I suppose we might report the abduction to the police though?' Davy said stoically.

Maggie put her hands on her hips. 'You may do, but I doubt it would do you a lot of a good as sometimes those coppers are in cahoots with those places. The Madames pay them protection money so they can carry on with their racketeering. I'm not saying all police are corrupt like that but they often have friends in very high places. I read in the newspaper of one madame what had a judge as a friend so he was getting all her clientele off any charges and she, herself, got away with murder for years!'

'Aye, he was probably her best customer!' Billy guffawed which prompted Davy to echo his brother's merriment.

Maggie gave them both a stern stare. 'It ain't no laughin' matter, you pair!'

'Sorry, Ma,' they both said in unison.

'We take your point though,' said Davy.

'And not only that,' Maggie looked at both her sons as she wagged a finger at them, 'things can be twisted and it might be made out you were the ones abducting the girl for immoral purposes when your intention was to rescue her.' Maggie had a way of saying things that made complete sense. 'No,' she said, 'leave Madame Fontaine to me. I have an idea that might just work!'

***

Early the following morning, Maggie set off for Creswell Terrace with Ada in tow. Maggie had taken it upon herself to supply Ada with some boy's clothing from her trolley. She scooped Ada's hair up into a ponytail, formed it into a coil and secured it in place with hair grips and then donned Danny's flat cap on her head, so it looked like she had short hair. The little herringbone jacket, shirt, cord trousers and Ada's own hobnail boots, did the trick.

'My, my, you could pass for one of me younger sons,' Maggie proudly announced. 'Just one more thing, I want to get some earth

137

from the garden to smear your face with so it looks as if you're a proper little worker!' she chuckled.

Ada couldn't get over the woman's ingenuity and she wondered if Maggie's plan might work after all.

Maggie, herself, had dressed up in her pretty flowered frock with her best shawl and on her head she wore a mobcap. Ada led the way to the property, but instead of walking towards the front entrance, they chose the back way as that would be the expected entrance for trades people.

'Now remember what I told you, Ada,' Maggie whispered. 'You keep your head down in case anyone recognises you.'

Ada nodded, feeling strange being back at the property once again. All was quiet from the house and the neighbouring properties, all that could be heard was the chirping of the birds as gradually, the night sky faded from an inky darkness to a pearl-grey as day began to break. Maggie had been insistent they knock at first light as that was the time of day when people often sought casual work.

'Why's there nobody around in this street?' whispered Ada. She was well used to being up bright and early herself for work on the barrow and where they were living it was a hive of activity, even at day break. There was the constant sound of the trains rattling overhead as business-suited gentlemen travelled to work in the city. The sounds of cartwheels on the cobbles and people shouting out was common place at the roadside, the clatter of clogs and hobnail boots as the factory workers began their day and even the odd dog or two barking to be allowed back in the house. But here, it was like the cemetery where her Ma and Pa were buried, silent and peaceful.

Maggie smiled. 'There's lots of working girls living on this street. They keep late hours I expect and then spend most of the morning sleeping it all off!' She rapped loudly on the back door and as they waited, Ada felt her heart hammering away beneath her shirt.

Finally, the door swung open and Ada was relieved to see that it wasn't Madame Fontaine who answered this time but the maid that had allowed them access the last time they arrived, she'd only had a brief glimpse of Ada's face and now of course, she looked quite different. Ada was fairly confident that the young woman wouldn't recognise her but she wasn't so sure about Madame Fontaine and her working girls as they'd viewed her at close quarters.

'Can I help you?' asked the maid.

'Aye, maybe you can,' said Maggie. 'I'm seeking work around the neighbourhood. I can do most anything: cook, clean, wash and iron, you name it and I can do most things a woman can.' She placed one hand over the other and pursing her lips said, 'Course I know how difficult it can be getting good domestic help, especially in this sort of establishment. Me son, Tommy, he can help too. He can run errands, chop sticks, light fires.'

The maid looked at them doubtfully. 'To be honest, I've only just bin taken on 'ere meself. I don't think the mistress of the house is looking to take anyone on at this time.'

She was just about to close the door on them when Maggie stuck her hobnail-booted foot in the door, preventing her from doing so. 'Please, would you just ask your mistress though? Me poor husband has just passed away and me and the boy are surviving hand to mouth at the moment. I need to work to put food on the table or otherwise he'll starve…'

The maid stared hard at them for a moment as if mulling things over and then she said, 'I'll ask for you but I can't make no promises. Just stay where you are.' She shut the door firmly behind herself leaving them outside the property.

Ada glanced at Maggie who winked at her. She didn't feel as confident as the woman did about getting a foot in the door with a view to working there, but presently the door opened and it was Madame Fontaine herself who stood there. This time she wore gold framed spectacles and she peered over them curiously at the pair of them.

That's good then, thought Ada. *She weren't wearing no glasses last time I was 'ere so maybe she won't have such a good impression of me in her mind.*

To be on the safe side, Ada kept her head lowered beneath the peak of her cap, so Madame couldn't study her features.

'Hello,' Madame greeted. 'I'm afraid I can't offer you anything permanent but I can offer you a couple of hours domestic work three times a week,' she said with a smile. 'My cleaner has let me down as she's off sick from her duties. I don't know when she'll return but to take the position you'd have to start work right now before I find someone else.'

'That'll suit us!' Maggie said with relish.

Ada felt her spirits soar, they were going to be allowed inside the house!

'But the young lad, I can't possibly have him around here,' Madame Fontaine said in a serious manner as she shook her head. 'It's no place for a young boy.'

'B…but I have to take him with me,' protested Maggie. 'His father 'as recently passed away and there's no one to take care of him.'

'Sorry,' said Madame Fontaine, about to close the door on her offer.

Quick as a flash, Ada whispered in Maggie's ear as she didn't want Madame Fontaine to hear her voice.

Maggie nodded. 'Tommy says he'll go to stay with his uncle while I work here, so it's all right I can work 'ere alone.'

Madame Fontaine beamed. 'Do come in then, Mrs er?'

'Mrs Higgins, Majorie Higgins,' Maggie said, then she glanced over her shoulder at Ada. 'Run along to Uncle Jim's house now then, Tommy. I'll pick yer up later when I've finished me shift 'ere!'

And with that, she stepped inside the house behind Madame Fontaine, leaving Ada stood outside with her mouth wide open with surprise and then she snapped it shut again and her lips curved into a smile. It was a little disappointing not getting inside the house herself after going to the all the bother of disguising herself, but at least now Maggie would be her eyes and ears inside that place.

Ada made her way to leave the property, it was starting to spit with rain, but she didn't give a jot as they would now be that much closer to discovering Connie's whereabouts. Instead of returning home, she decided to see if she could find Frank and tell him the good news.

***

It was some time before Ada discovered Frank's whereabouts, she'd searched his usual haunts at Sycamore Street and Hawthorn Street and she even ventured as far as Dock Street, but in the end she found him at Florrie's pie shop tucking into one of her delicious pies. He eyed her suspiciously as she approached and then she remembered, of course, he wouldn't recognise her in the boy's garb. It was then she realised just how good a disguise this really was.

'Whatcha want, sonny?' Frank asked through mouthfuls of steak and pastry.

Ada, feeling in a devilish mood, decided to play along. She lowered her head so the peak of her cap covered some of her face.

'Got any pennies on yer for a pie please, guv'nor?' she asked in a low, gruff voice, then she stifled a giggle.

He laid down his knife and fork and standing, began to fish about in his trouser pocket for some spare change. 'Here you are, sonny,' he said, handing her a couple of pennies but she stood there and said nothing, then her entire body began to convulse, Ada felt like she might wet herself, as her hands went to her belly as she ached with laughter.

'Hey, what's going on 'ere?' asked Frank, now sounding a little unsure of himself.

Ada whipped off her cap and undid her hair grips so that her hair fell loose upon on her shoulders. 'It's me, Ada!' she beamed.

A huge smile grew across his face. 'But why? How? I thought you were a lad?'

'I'll explain now in a minute,' she said in a whisper.

Frank sat himself down and he invited her to take the chair opposite him and he ordered a pot of tea for two and a pie for Ada. As they waited for their order to arrive, she quietly told him all that had happened that morning.

'Knock me down with a feather!' said Frank, 'that Maggie one has got a lot of guts. Fair play to her.'

'If anyone can find out what's going on, it's her!' Ada said proudly. 'I was a bit disappointed though when Madame Fontaine said she didn't want "Maggie's son" around as it wasn't the place for a young lad to work.'

'Yer mean, Danny?' He quirked a brow.

'No, me,' she giggled.

He nodded and smiled. 'Maybe it's for the best though, Ada, in case anyone recognised you. As it is, no one knows Maggie there as far as we know, so she's our best bet of finding out what happened to yer sister.'

Ada found herself agreeing with Frank and she couldn't wait for Maggie to return home from "work", meanwhile there was a delicious plate of pie and mushy peas headed her way and she was ravenous.

Chapter Fourteen

When Maggie returned home that evening, all eyes were upon her as the family waited to hear how her day had gone working for Madame Fontaine.

'Did you find anything out?' Ada yelled, running to greet the woman.

'Give us a chance to take me shawl off, gal! I need to put me trotters up on a footstool. That Madame Fontaine is a hard taskmaster, I can tell you! I've been run ragged all day, lighting fires, sweeping up, washing and changing bed sheets…' she wrinkled her nose in disgust. 'And you wanna see the state on some of that bedding after what goes on in that place!'

But Ada didn't want to hear any of that, she just wanted news of her sister. Seeing her disappointed expression, Maggie cupped Ada's cheeks good naturedly and planted a kiss on her forehead, then pulling away, plonked herself down in her favourite armchair by the fire with a loud sigh of contentment. 'Yes, I have some news for you, Ada, me love! But first I badly need to remove me boots and have a cup of tea.'

'I'll brew up!' said Frannie tactfully.

'And I'll help you remove yer boots,' Ada offered.

Maggie smiled as she relaxed back into the armchair whilst Ada sat on the footstool to remove the woman's well-worn leather lace up boots. Then she rose from her position and lifted Maggie's legs onto the footstool.

Apart from Frannie going to make the tea for everyone, no one had taken their eyes off Maggie.

Maggie rubbed her tired eyes. 'Well, I've got good news and I've got bad news for you, Ada,' she said. 'Which would yer like first?'

'Oh, the bad, to get it out of the way, please.' Ada's stomach somersaulted as she waited with bated breath for what was to come next.

'Yer sister 'as been removed from the property—that is correct. I overheard those girls called Melissa and Anna speaking on the landing as they were waiting for their clients to arrive. It seems that Madame Fontaine was telling the truth that your Connie was taken away early yesterday morning…'

Ada's bottom lip quivered as she looked at Maggie through glazed eyes. 'And the good news?'

'It's very good, gal. Don't fret, there's nothing to cry over. She's been taken to Dorset Street…'

Ada let out a sigh of relief. 'So, me sister isn't in another country then?'

Maggie shook her head. 'No, not yet. We need to work fast though. Seems the Madame has a close associate who runs a bawdy house in Dorset street which appears to be some sort of holding place. I think the plan is to sell her on to someone else who will transport her to Belgium, probably to Brussels.'

Ada screwed up her face in disgust. 'That's truly awful that someone is treating my sister like some kind of slave. Who is doing this?'

Maggie shook her head. 'I dunno, but whoever is behind it, it ain't Madame Fontaine. I think she was just paid to keep yer sister there as some sort of prisoner. The woman didn't put her to work or nothing, just provided her with bed and board as it were.'

'But how do you know all of this, Ma?' Davy suddenly intervened.

'I know 'cos those two working girls weren't happy at all about it. They saw Connie has having preferential treatment whilst she was there whilst they had to work on their backs for their money. To be truthful, maybe that's why they dobbed you and Frank in, Ada. It was a case of plain old jealousy. But if yer ask me, they're both regretful about it now as they've been told by Madame that soon your sister will end up overseas.'

'Then we have to act as soon as possible,' Billy said.

Davy nodded in agreement. 'Can't we break into that place on Dorset Street, Ma? Do you know which one it is?'

'No, and yes. I mean no you can't do that as there are men on the doors who keep the peace, minders as it were. You'd have to get past them. I know which house it is as Melissa said it was beside The Blue Coat Boy pub. Apparently, she's been there before to deliver a letter from Madame to the proprietor. It's a rough place that Dorset Street and make no mistake…'

Frannie arrived at Maggie's side with a cup of tea for the woman and she set it down on the low table beside her, then she started handing cups of tea to everyone else in the room.

'Rough in what sort of way?' Ada frowned.

'It's one of the worst streets I've ever known…' Maggie shook her head.

'Got to agree with you there, Ma!' Davy colluded as Billy nodded beside his brother, and Danny looked on in an interested fashion. Sam and Molly were taking no notice at all, preferring to play with some dolly pegs of Maggie's in the corner—they'd dressed the pegs up in some old offcut materials the woman had given them and were engaging in some sort of game together.

Maggie continued, 'Dorset Street is a street of thieves, prostitutes and bullies and loads of common lodging houses where nefarious shenanigans abound. Some of those establishments are referred to as "doubles" as they profess to offer double beds for married couples but it's just another name for brothels…' she sucked in a breath which made a curious sound through the gaps in her teeth. 'Dorset Street makes Cresswell Terrace look like the Pall Mall!'

'Don't frighten the girl, Ma!' Billy warned as he glanced at Ada's whitewashed face.

Maggie shook her head, muttering something unintelligible and turned to Ada. 'Well, it might be a terrible place and one of the worst streets in Whitechapel or even the whole of London for that matter, but I promise yer, gal. We'll get yer sister out of there before she gets taken out of the country.'

'But how though, Ma?' Davy urged.

Maggie sniffed loudly. 'I think we should get someone to pose as a punter to get into that house of ill repute!'

Davy raised his eyebrows. 'What? Me or Billy go in there posing as a customer?'

'No, not you pair. Yer too handy with yer fists sometimes and too hot headed to keep cool heads. I was thinking of someone the girl would know and trust. Don't forget you pair are strangers to her…'

'Jakob!' yelled Ada. 'He'd be the perfect choice. Me sister knows him really well and she'd trust him with her life. He's always been sweet on our Connie.'

'But yer said not to send him into the other place as he looked beaten up,' Billy angled his head in confusion at his brother who shrugged his shoulders.

'I know Davy did say that about Madame Fontaine's place which is more upmarket than any of those establishments what is on Dorset Street,' Maggie smiled, 'but in a place like Dorset Street, he'd fit right in with those cuts and bruises! You pair can tag along in case he gets into any trouble, but for heaven's sake watch from a distance, don't let on you're associated with him.'

The brothers both nodded as a plan was hatched.

***

The idea was to rescue Connie from the holding house in Dorset Street as soon as possible as who knew how long she'd be held for otherwise. If there was a delay in reaching her, they might risk losing her overseas forever. Jakob was more than happy to comply with the plan and he set off with the brothers for Dorset Street that very same night.

The street was situated at the heart of the Spitalfields rookery and the locals sometimes dubbed it Dosset Street or Dossen Street because of the large number of doss-houses there were in the area. In earlier years, the once elegant houses had been owned by the silk weavers of the 18th century, but they were now badly dilapidated as plaster crumbled from walls, roofs leaked and even the floorboards in some houses began to fall away, creating hazardous conditions for inhabitants.

The three men approached the area as night fell and the dim lighting cast long shadows across the street, a sense of eeriness took hold beneath the full moon and the men felt something was about to occur. A lot of activity was taking place that night as people of both sexes spilled out onto the pavements from the various lodging houses and pubs, enjoying some flirtation or exchange beneath the golden glow of the lamplights. Although it was autumn, the weather was unseasonably warm. The trio was headed towards the north end of the street where Maggie had explained the establishment was situated. They realised that many of the houses were guarded by doormen who ensured punters paid up and undesirables were chucked out roughly onto the street so they were well aware they needed to tread carefully.

'Even the coppers go around in pairs in this neck of the woods!' chuckled Davy.

His brother concurred. 'Aye, they need to an' all with the amount of murders that have taken place on this street over the years, not to mention all the gambling and prostitution that goes on here! It's like Sodom and Gomorrah!'

Jakob glanced both right and left as if wary of who was around them. 'I've only been here the once in my life,' he spoke in a hushed tone of voice, 'and didn't think I'd be coming back here ever again.'

'Don't worry too much as we won't be far away and shall be keeping an eye on that place when you're inside there,' Davy said, patting him on the shoulder as a sign of reassurance.

Davy and Billy slipped inside The Blue Coat Boy pub which was about half way along the street—it would be the ideal location for them to wait in case there was any trouble with the doormen next door as they'd need to wade in with their muscle power if there was. So, for time being, they decided to go in for a pint of ale and mingle amongst the clientele while an attempt was made to rescue Connie next door. Nervously, Jakob nodded at them and made his way to the house next door.

**

The brothers got chatting with a man called John McCarthy who informed them he was a landlord of several properties in the area. He was a dark haired man with a moustache who seemed to be very business savvy and frank speaking. Billy and Davy warmed to him right away and listened to his tales about the area but they were careful not to give too much away about themselves.

Davy bought him a tankard of ale and then asked, 'The "boarding house" next door, who owns that?'

John had no hesitation in replying, 'There's a fella what runs it called Alf Baker but he doesn't own it. The owner is a gentleman from up West with a French sounding surname. I forget what it is now, begins with De something or other. Don't often see him around these parts and to be truthful, he don't much seem to care what shenanigans go on there as long as he gets his weekly whack from the landlord…'

Davy nodded. 'Yer been in there for a bit of business yerself, John?'

John chuckled. 'Oh, aye, did in the beginning but now I'm a landlord myself I try to conduct a respectable business. Are you both after a good time tonight then, lads?'

The brothers grinned and nodded to put on a good show in front of the man. 'Yes, but we don't want to go somewhere where they'll rob us both blind by morning,' Billy said.

'If that's the case you'd be better off trying elsewhere, somewhere with a little class like Madame Fontaine's in Cresswell Terrace or the one on Charlotte Street.'

'Er, think we'll stay local,' Davy quickly chipped in.

Billy tried to question John further about Madame Fontaine's business but John preferred to talk about his own, telling them both how sometimes he had trouble getting the rent that was due from his tenants, so Billy, not wishing to arouse suspicion, said no more about the matter.

They stayed for a while in John's company, though he seemed to be referred to as "Jack" by the other pub customers.

'He appears to be a decent sort of chap,' said Billy, when John had gone to the bar to order another round of drinks.

Davy sniffed loudly. 'I dunno. I don't trust some of these landlords around these parts—they're unscrupulous sorts with all kinds going on behind the scenes, but I'll give him the benefit of the doubt for time being until I know otherwise.'

Billy nodded. 'Wonder how Jakob is getting on next door?'

'Let's just hope he's got a foot in the door and can get to look around for Connie.'

'And if he can't, then I'm afraid we've run out of ideas.' Billy shrugged.

***

Back at home, Ada nervously twisted her hair ringlet around her index finger. 'I thought they'd be back by now!' she complained.

''Ave a bit o' patience, luvvy!' Maggie smiled. 'They gotta be careful how they handle things. The boys can't go in there with all guns blazing, they 'ave to tread carefully.'

'I suppose so. It's just it feels like me and Sam have been parted from Connie for ever such a long time…'

Maggie laid a hand of reassurance on her shoulder. 'Go and take Jasper for a walk with Danny to take yer mind orf things,' she chided.

Ada nodded and went in search of Danny, who she found kneeling in the back yard, as he repaired one of the wheels on his barrow. He looked up when he saw her approaching. 'Whatcha doing, Ada?' he smiled.

'Yer ma reckoned I should take the dog for a walk to take me mind off things. Want to come with me?'

'I really need to repair this wheel by tomorrow,' he said, but then noticing the look of disappointment on her face, he stood and laid down his spanner on the barrow. 'But I can do that early in the morning. Come on then, you go and fetch the lead and I'll leave Jasper out of his kennel.'

Ada was so pleased they were friends once again, she hadn't wanted to fall out over Frank Malone, but she'd had to set Danny straight about the man.

As they walked along the gas lit street they chatted amicably with one another and even on their return called to see how the Archies were doing.

'What's happened to Wilf?' Danny asked Sally. The woman was sitting around an open fire with four others as they swigged something from some sort of bottle between them.

She pulled herself up onto her feet and brushing down her skirts, eyed the pair. 'He's gorn!' she said.

'Gone!' Ada trembled. 'You mean to say he's passed away?'

Sally chuckled. 'No, darlin', it's much better than that. His daughter came here and took him to her home. So now he's got a good gaff to sleep in and his own bed.'

'B…but how'd did that happen?' Danny wanted to know.

'Well, it were yer ma, weren't it? She got him into that Men's Mission place at Limehouse run by the Sally Army. She heard they'd had some success tracing people's relatives, she had a word with them and they only managed to find Wilf's daughter whilst he was there, didn't they! Apparently, he walked out on his wife when his daughter was only ten years old. He'd tried to find them in later years, seems he had some sort of mental breakdown back then and lost his mind so had no qualms about leaving home, poor thing. Unfortunately, when he was well again, he discovered they'd moved house! But now, both father and daughter are reunited once again. Pity though his wife had passed away in the intervening years, but I guess yer can't win them all!'

'That's fantastic news he's found his daughter!' said Ada.

Danny nodded his head. 'I shall miss the funny old fella though.'

'Aw, don't worry too much about that, he said he will still come back to visit us from time to time. As you can imagine, he's over the bleedin' moon about it all…'

Maggie had been right, taking that walk tonight had done Ada the power of good and by the time she returned home, a surprise awaited her.

***

Davy stood outside the pub while Billy stayed inside chatting to John McCarthy. All of a sudden, there was a calamity as Jakob started rushing down the street with a young woman by his side. He had his arm wrapped around her as if wanting to protect her. Realising it must be Ada's sister, Connie, Davy whistled loudly for his brother which got Billy outside just as the pair turned up.

'We've got to get out of here...' gasped Jakob. 'They'll realise she's gone soon, can you two create some sort of diversion outside?'

Connie looked half asleep, prompting Billy to ask, 'What's the matter with her?'

Jakob looked at him. 'I think she's been given something to sedate her...' He sighed. 'So can you divert the doormen's attention, please?'

Both brothers nodded. 'Quick get out of here and lie low under the tarpaulin on the back of the cart where we left it a couple of streets over!' Davy whispered.

They watched as both departed and then Billy said, 'Those doormen are coming out of the property.'

Davy noticed two well built, shadowy figures, headed towards them.

The brothers began laying into one another outside the premises, blow after blow was executed. The two doormen stood transfixed for a moment as they watched with interest, but then coming to their senses, realising they were searching for a young woman who had escaped the building asked, 'You pair seen a young woman leave here?'

'Do I look like I'm bothered, mate?' Billy growled and as he looked away, Davy punched him on the nose, he retaliated with an upper cut punch to his brother's chin, sending him reeling.

Noticing the pair of doormen were about to head off in the same direction as Connie and Jakob, Davy hissed, 'Now, let's get them!'

Both brothers lunged at the doormen who didn't know what had hit them. Although burly men who were well used to dealing with thugs and drunks themselves, they had been taken by surprise as punch after punch rained down on them. What they failed to realise was that Davy and Billy were bare knuckle boxers who rarely lost a fight in the costermonger community in the pubs around Whitechapel. They'd been accosted by the wrong men.

'I think they've both had enough...for now!' said Billy.

Both men groaned on the floor as blood seeped from their faces. The brothers could be a little heavy handed at times but Billy had seen the sense this time in stopping before the men got badly hurt, allowing Connie and Jakob to get to the cart and hide on the back of it until they reached them.

Both brothers ran down Dorset Street as fast as their legs could carry them before any doormen from neighbouring properties or from the nearby pubs, decided to wade in and help the other two.

'It all went like a dream,' Billy said as they approached the cart.

'Don't say that until we're safely back home…' his brother grimaced. But they needn't have worried as Jakob and Connie were safely under the tarpaulin and ready to head off home.

Chapter Fifteen

Ada blinked in astonishment to see her sister sitting in Maggie's favourite armchair with a cup of tea in her hand. The Donovan brothers and Jakob were stood around as if they'd been listening intently as Maggie sat in the opposite armchair near the hearth.

'Connie!' Ada cried as she rushed towards her, causing her sister's teacup to rattle in its saucer.

Connie smiled up at her through glazed eyes, then she laid her cup and saucer down on the table beside her. Both sisters hugged one another with tears streaming down their cheeks.

Finally, Ada asked, 'How did yer get away in the end?'

'It was all down to Jakob as well as Davy and Billy of course.' Connie swallowed hard at the memory of it all.

'We created a diversion, see,' explained Billy, 'while Jakob got your sister safely away...'

It was then Ada noticed the brothers' torn clothing and grazed cheeks. 'I hope no one got hurt?'

'No one that mattered, at any rate. We had a bit of a scuffle with a couple of heavies on the door, was all,' added Davy.

Ada nodded. Then she stepped away for Connie to carry on with her story as it was evident she had intruded in the midst of it. She stood beside Danny and listened intently.

'So, what happened to you that night you went missing?' Jakob asked.

'It were t...truly awful...' Connie said, head down as she struggled to force out the words that were forming. 'It was an awful night of rain, I'll never forget it. Mr Winterbourne had told me he could no longer wait for the rent as we were overdue once again. It had been a terrible struggle for me—we were living hand to mouth all the time. I was getting desperate as I knew he'd only been benevolent in allowing me time to pay as he was expecting something from me...if yer know what I mean?'

Everyone nodded.

Jakob took the footstool and sat beside her, and taking her hand in his, said gently, 'Yes, we do know what you mean, Connie.'

Ada looked at her sister. 'I know what you mean too, our Connie. He wanted something from yer that nice girl's aren't supposed to give?'

Connie nodded, her eyes watery and slightly puffy, and between sniffs, she dabbed at them with a handkerchief and carried on. 'Anyhow, he told me to meet him at the railway station entrance as he was going to take me out for the night. I thought it was going to be somewhere up West where no one knew me, but he ended up instead taking me to a local pub where one of the women from the match factory spotted me.'

'I heard about that,' Ada said. 'Me and Sam walked to the match factory the next day to ask if anyone had seen you and a woman in the queue of outworkers told me she'd seen you drinking with a gentleman at The Duke of Wellington the night before...'

Jakob glanced at Ada. 'Ada, love, why didn't you tell me of this when we first spoke about Connie's disappearance?'

Ada felt a sudden surge of guilt that she'd deliberately withheld that information from him. Taking a deep composing breath in, she let it out again. 'I didn't want to sully Connie's reputation...' she said, sadly. 'I didn't want her to ruin her chances with you as I knew you were sweet on me sister...'

Both Connie and Jakob smiled which told everyone it was indeed true.

Connie wiped away a tear. 'It's all right, love. It's too late for recriminations anyhow. It wouldn't have made any difference who knew I'd been drinking there as I ended up elsewhere afterwards.'

'But where?' Ada frowned.

'I'll explain what happened now...' Connie took a sip of tea out of her cup and set it down on the table again.

'Would yer rather we all left the room while you explain what happened to yer sister and Jakob?' Maggie asked tactfully, glancing at Connie. 'Frannie, Molly and Sam are safely out of ear shot in the other room...'

Connie sighed in a resigned fashion. 'It's all right. After what I've been through lately, Mrs Donovan, I've lost all me pride. I've seen things and heard things I should'na ought to.'

'But at least yer safe now, darlin'. You can start again.' Maggie said gently, smiling. Then she stood to hand a clean handkerchief across to Connie and settled herself back down in her armchair to listen intently to the young woman's tale.

Connie dabbed at her eyes with the fresh handkerchief. 'Anyhow, I was that ashamed...' she sniffed, 'and I'd already had a couple of port and lemons to work up to what I was about to do, but having second thoughts, I broke free from Winterbourne. I had no idea where I was going, I just had to get away as I felt I wouldn't be able to live with meself afterwards otherwise. I ended running for me life down this alleyway which led to a warren of houses. I had no idea where I were. I heard lots of chatter going on and there was this open door with a light on. I decided there and then I needed to hide as I'd heard footsteps coming after me and feared it was Winterbourne on my trail or even worse, The Whitechapel Murderer! My mind was getting right carried away with itself.'

'So what happened next?' Ada raised an inquisitive brow.

Connie spoke through ragged breaths. 'I fully intended asking the occupants for help to hide for a little while until it was safe to leave and to enquire there how to find my way back home. There was a friendly middle aged woman living there, on her own she told me. She didn't seem all that shocked that I was inside her house now I come to think of it. She led me into her parlour and told me I could sleep on the couch for the night and leave at first light next morning as it would be safer for me then. I figured I could do that and even get back home and out to the factory for me day shift. Only thing was…' Ada's eyes enlarged as Connie carried on with her tale, 'the woman wasn't all she appeared to be. She handed me this cup which she said contained a hot toddy which would give me a good night's sleep and would settle my nerves to help me relax. After that, I hardly remembered what happened that night except that by morning I was ensconced in this bedroom on me own. I thought to meself, "This ain't Sycamore Street and this ain't me bleedin' bedroom!"'

'It were right plush it were. There was a big bed with a fancy carved wooden headboard and a purple bedcover and matching pillows, and the curtains, even they were matching an' all. There was a fancy oil lamp on a table beside the bed and the smell of perfume wafting in the air—I'd never been in a bedroom like that before. I realised then to me horror this wasn't the old woman's house anymore. I discovered afterwards that I'd been taken up West after all that night by a well-dressed man named, Edgar De Courcey. The woman must have got word to him and after she'd drugged me, he'd taken me there in his coach. He seemed nice though and listened to my concerns about Winterbourne, appearing sympathetic to my plight, but he told me that he could solve all my money woes by my working for him at his lovely home. Course I believed him didn't I! He said he needed a hostess to help him when guests arrived and to accompany him to the theatre for evenings out and such like. I thought all my troubles were over and I'd fallen in lucky.'

Jakob looked on with tears in his eyes. 'So, what happened next?'

Connie seemed far away for a moment as if lost in her own thoughts and wondering how to explain what happened after that. 'Well, it was lovely at first as Mr De Courcey got me fitted out with some fanciful gowns and he escorted me to the theatre and told me I was to consider myself his companion. He bought me expensive gifts too and implied that he'd like to marry me...' she glanced at Ada. 'I'm so sorry, Ada. I thought that if I played me cards right I'd end up a wealthy young lady and I could send for you and our Sam to live with us. I would never need to work at that filthy match factory ever again and all our troubles would be over for good. Winterbourne had even convinced me earlier he'd allow us some more time with the rent so I assumed you two would be all right for a little while. I just weren't thinking straight at the time after being sedated that night. Mr De Courcey kept giving me medicine which he said was for my nerves, but now I think he was drugging me so I'd become compliant to his needs and wants. How foolish was I?'

'Foolish?' Jakob echoed the word.

'Yes, bleedin' foolish as after a couple of weeks of me thinking I was to become Edgar's fiancée, things started to change. After a time, I realised where I was living wasn't even his home, it was somewhere he was renting from a friend. He made out I was his special companion but that maybe I could escort other gentlemen too for evenings out or to stay in and listen to them talk instead with a few drinks. He explained them as "lonely men whose wives didn't understand them". It soon became evident what was going on though, he was expecting me to grant them particular favours as I had granted him, believing he was to be my future husband. I refused to do so saying it would make me no better than the whores I encountered on the streets of Whitechapel and he...' she began to sob.

'He what?' asked Jakob.

'He slapped me hard across the face and did other things to me…' She looked at Ada as her entire body shuddered. 'I had little choice but to run away, but he caught me and brought me back, telling me I had been very foolish indeed and now my life of luxury had ended as he'd found somewhere else to offload me. That's how I ended up at Madame Fontaine's going by the name of "Bella". He sold me on!'

Everyone in the room gasped in horror.

'Oh, my darling,' Jakob said, kneeling before her and hugging her tightly to him as Ada watched on, she'd always known he loved her sister. He lifted her chin with his thumb and forefinger to gaze into her eyes. 'You've been treated abysmally. And how were you treated at the other place?'

'A lot better than how Edgar De Courcey had treated me to tell you the truth. I had regular meals and my own room but I didn't want the sort of life where I was kept prisoner. I think the plan was to hold me there though as I wasn't made to "entertain gentlemen" like the other girls were.'

'How'd you mean?' Ada felt puzzled.

'I think the plan all along was to ship me abroad to somewhere in Brussels or maybe Paris for a large sum of money. I know Madame Fontaine lied to you saying I was already out of the country but Melissa informed me that was the plan all along. It wasn't her who ratted on us either that night Frank wanted to help get me out of there, it was Anna. I never did trust that one. So, if Maggie hadn't acted when she did, tomorrow I would be well on my way to Brussels or Paris. The man who runs the house in Dorset Street told me that. He was nice enough to me but told me it was all out of his hands. He didn't get involved in that sort of thing. Only put people up there for payment and his orders were to keep me there until I was picked up early next morning.'

'But he was still holding you as a prisoner!' Jakob shouted. 'I had a hard job getting into that place, had to offer some extra money to get past those two door men and then it was pure chance that I guessed you were behind the door with the bolt on it.'

Connie nodded and bit her bottom lip. 'Yes, if you hadn't broke in, I would still be there now. Apparently, young women get sold to bordellos on the Continent and after that there's little chance of escape unless someone takes pity on them. It would have been even worse than staying in brothels over here.'

'That's preposterous!' Jakob yelled in anger.

'It does go on,' said Connie. 'The working girls at Madame Fontaine's told me a girl was sent to Paris just last month and they ain't seen hide nor hair of her since!'

'It's like the slave trade of young women and their bodies!' Jakob snarled 'And it shouldn't be allowed!' His hands formed fists and he gritted his teeth, Ada had never seen the man so angry. Mild mannered Jakob was seething inside himself.

'There's a man though…' Connie said, now composing herself, 'what is fighting against it. His name is Stead or something like that, Melissa told me about him as he questioned her once by posing as a customer. He's been doing a lot of good work to help rescue young women from those places.'

'Just as Frank has been trying to do,' chipped in Ada. 'But maybe that Stead man has more influence?'

Jakob nodded and turned towards Ada. 'He does. I have heard of him, he rescues girls from the clutches of those people. More people like him are needed to put a stop to this dreadful business. What did you mean about Frank, Ada?'

'That's what Frank Malone's been trying to do for ages,' Ada added. 'Frank's daughter was taken years ago. He thinks she was taken overseas and he's been searching for her all this time. That's why he tried to help me in my search for you, Connie.'

Connie held her hand out to Ada, who took it in her own. 'He's a good man, Ada. Men like Frank and Jakob are hard to find.'

Ada watched Jakob as his face coloured up as if embarrassed that attention was drawn towards him. Changing the subject he said, 'What we need to do now, Connie, is get you well again. There's not a lot of room here so how about you come to stay with me and Ma till you get yourself sorted?'

Connie nodded. 'That's very kind of you. Would you mind, Ada? Until I get back on me feet?'

'Of course not. I'm just glad you've been rescued from that place!' Ada beamed. 'Sam will have such a surprise when he sees you!'

Connie nodded and smiled. 'I've missed you both so much! I intend going over to the factory to see if the foreman will take me back on and then I'll try to find another place for us so we can all be together again, I promise. I have let you down so badly.'

'No, yer 'aven't!' Ada said forcefully, and then in a softer tone added, 'Yer did the best yer could under the circumstances.'

Jakob nodded as he gazed at Connie intently. 'Ada's right. Don't be too hard on yourself. You had little choice because of the pressure you were put under to pay the rent and find food for the table for everyone. Winterbourne has a lot to answer for—I'd like to knock his flamin' block off, I would, and I'd like to pulverise that brute, De Courcey! Taking advantage of you like that!' He fisted his hands and gritted his teeth. It was so unusual to hear Jakob getting angry that Ada realised the intensity of feelings he had for her sister would drive him to do so. She knew he'd die for her if he had to the way he'd been looking at her this evening.

'Any time you want either of them seeing to, we're your men!' grinned Davy.

'Now, there'll be none of that!' said Maggie, sharply. 'If you try knocking a nob around, you'll both get the worst of it all and end up in the slammer. No, there's other ways of dealing with men like that. We need to get hold of that Stead gentleman and allow the courts to deal with the likes of De Corset!'

'Quite right, Ma!' Danny, who up until now had kept quiet, chipped in and then he chuckled. 'But the name is De Courcey not Corset!'

'Maybe I was right the first time as he's a bleedin' corset ripper!' She glanced at Connie. 'Sorry, love, but I speak as I find about blokes like him.'

Connie forced a smile. 'You're right though, Mrs Donovan. Men like him need to be stopped to prevent any other young girls from falling into their clutches.'

'I believe the offices of The Pall Mall Gazette are over on Northumberland Street, Charing Cross way,' Jakob said. 'Stead is the editor there, you could tell him your story when you feel up to it?' He glanced at Connie who nodded at him.

'Why not just go to the police instead?' Danny wanted to know.

His mother harrumphed. 'Some of those policemen are in on stuff like that. Corrupt they are. I've even heard of them charging working girls a fee for plying their wares and even arresting innocent women if they go shopping unaccompanied up West, making out they're on the game! I don't trust some of them an inch. There's always some rotten apple in amongst the barrel somewhere.'

The others nodded in agreement. 'In an ideal world, the police would be the best option, Ma,' said Davy. 'But we'd be taking a chance—it might rebound on poor Connie and she could end up getting arrested herself while that chancer from up West goes scot-free!'

Noticing how exhausted Connie looked, Jakob told her he'd walk her home back to his new place, but first she wanted to see for herself that her little brother was safe. Ada led her to the other room where Sam was tucked up in his pallet beside Molly in hers, while Fran read a book by candlelight in the corner. Connie studied her brother as she watched the rise and fall of his chest and she laid her hand lightly on his forehead, before tiptoeing away.

'I won't disturb him right now,' she whispered. 'I'll be over first thing in the morning when he awakes to see him.'

Ada nodded and smiled and then she planted a kiss on her sister's soft cheek. 'It's so good to see you and know you're safe and well again,' she said.

Connie nodded. 'It's good to see you too, Ada. I'm blessed to have been rescued from it all. We have a lot to thank Jakob and the Donovan family for, don't we?'

With tears in her eyes, Ada smiled as they both left the room.

∗∗∗

The following day, Connie was as good as her word and returned to the house to spend some time with Sam and Ada. Maggie told Ada to leave going to the market place and completing her round later, but instead to spend some "quality time" as she described it with her sister. Sam whooped with joy when he saw his big sister and immediately ran into her arms. When everything had calmed down, Maggie fried them bacon and eggs with plenty of toast and mugs of tea. Jakob had refused to allow Connie out of his sight, so later they took a cab to the offices of the Pall Mall Gazette where there was a long wait until they finally got to see the editor, William T. Stead.

Stead was a formidable man but Connie noticed he had kindly eyes and he was most interested to hear of Connie's case.

Stead cleared his throat as he sat forward in his high backed chair to speak with them as Connie and Jakob sat opposite his desk. 'Three years ago, I published in this very newspaper, an article in instalments that was entitled, "The Maiden Tribute of Modern Babylon". It was a highly controversial expose of child prostitution. I wrote about the entrapment, kidnap and sale of young under-privileged girls to brothels in the London area. These young girls were often under age, some no more than children...'

Connie gasped. In all her time being held captive by De Courcey and at Madame Fontaine's house, she had never encountered anyone that young working in either establishment, though she had heard it went on, but now Stead's words confirmed it for her.

Mr Stead shook his head. 'These offices were under siege for reprints of the article, such was the public interest. Indeed, the whole of London society was thrown into a state of moral panic. As a consequence, an act was passed which raised the age of consent from girls from thirteen to sixteen. I ended up going on trial with several other people who aided me, including Bramwell Booth of the Salvation Army, no less. You see, we ended up getting into trouble due to the methods used for the investigation.' He leaned back in his chair as the palms of his hands dug into the armrests, almost as though he'd been transported back to that very day. 'I ended up spending three months in prison, but of course, I am pleased that the law was changed as a result of my findings. But that wasn't an easy time, I can tell you.' He closed his eyes for a moment as if trying to blot it all out and then they flicked open again.

'Oh, sir,' Connie's face flushed. 'I shouldn't wish to get you into any further trouble on my behalf...'

Stead grinned. 'Now don't you concern yourself, young lady. Lessons have been learned from that time. My article "The Maiden Tribute of Modern Babylon" was controversial yes, but it worked. It's just my methods shall be different this time. I'll get my secretary to take notes while I interview you at length over the following few days and I shall pay your transport fees of course.'

Connie looked at Jakob who was smiling back at her.

'In fact,' Stead continued, 'this newspaper shall pay a fee for your story. I understand that you'd probably prefer anonymity?'

She nodded vigorously. 'Oh, yes, please. I couldn't bear it if everyone knew what had happened to me...'

Jakob patted her hand in reassurance. 'But it wasn't your fault.'

With tears in her eyes, Connie nodded. 'I know it weren't but mud can stick. I'd prefer to keep me name out of it.'

'That's understandable,' Stead agreed. 'I shall use a pseudonym, for you. The name shall be false but the story true and I shall indicate that at the beginning of the article.'

***

A week later, the first instalment of 'Seduction of a Sweet Matchgirl' was published in the Pall Mall Gazette, causing much contention as Stead explained how young, vulnerable women from Whitechapel and beyond, were either still being abducted by nefarious means or seduced into prostitution by big promises made from wealthy men up West. The article went on to explain how once held against their will at local brothels, the young women are shipped over to Brussels and Paris to work at houses of ill repute. The article began:

During the reign of our good Queen Victoria, there are more churches and more brothels in London than ever before. Is it a coincidence that both have grown at the same time? In this article, I shall look at the trade in vulnerable young women that exists between England and the Continent, especially in places like, Belgium and France. There appears to be a huge demand for young English women in the capital cities of Brussels and Paris. Girls and women are kidnapped from the street and held sometimes in a "safe house" until ready for transportation to the Continent where they are forcibly detained in "lock houses" in the Belgian or French capital. The doors of these buildings are to keep the girls and women locked in and well-guarded by the overseer of the establishment.

One such young lady, who is just a tender eighteen years old, but who could pass for younger than her years, is someone whom for the purposes of this story, I shall call "Hannah Smith" – a pseudonym to protect her identity for obvious reason. Her tale is a harrowing but cautionary one, nevertheless, for young women of all ages and their families to read...

The article captured the public's interest so well that the newspapers sold out after the first printing run and more were required for publication to keep up with public demand. A few weeks later, after Connie had been paid the handsome sum of £100.00 for her story, she decided to set up her own business. After she was given a tip off from Frank Malone that Florrie had decided to retire from her pie shop after fifty years, she approached the woman about renting the premises. It would be a risk but at least she wasn't purchasing the property so only needed to find money for the weekly rent and the produce sold within.

Connie called the shop "Connie's Confectionary and Flowers" as she allowed Ada to set up a counter there selling her pretty colourful bouquets, buttonholes and sprays to members of the public. Ada was thrilled with this and vowed to make a success of the opportunity presented to her. It also meant she'd get to spend every day with her sister. Sam helped out too, going to the market place with Ada first thing of a morning and helping to push her barrow there and back. He was turning into a right little costermonger himself of late.

***

It was while Ada was serving at her flower table at the shop one morning and Connie was behind her confectionary counter, that the door to the shop opened and Jakob stood there with a newspaper beneath his arm. 'There's been another dreadful murder!' he announced. 'This time at 13 Miller's Court just off Dorset Street!'

Ada's jaw dropped and Connie looked startled. 'But that was the area I was held at that house! What happened there, Jakob?'

'It appears that the landlord Davy and Billy were chatting to in The Blue Coat Boy pub the evening we rescued you, who was called John McCarthy, discovered his tenant, Mary Jane Kelly, was six weeks behind with her rent. He had allowed the fees to accumulate but yesterday morning, decided that it was time to see if Kelly could pay by sending his assistant Thomas Bowyer there.'

Ada noticed her sister's ashen face. 'What happened then, Jakob?'

'But when Bowyer arrived there, he knocked on the door twice and got no answer. He noticed a couple of glass window panes were broken. He put his arm through the broken window pane and moved the curtain to see whether she was there or not. The first thing he noticed were what looked like two lumps of meat sitting on the bedside table!' Jakob paused for a moment for them to digest the news.

Ada felt quite unsteady on her feet but Connie urged him to carry on.

'The second thing the assistant saw sent him running back to his employers' office. McCarthy returned with him to Miller's Court. What the landlord saw there was a mutilated corpse beyond all recognition. I won't read the rest as it's horrific! Far worse than even the other four murders put together!'

'That's horrendous,' said Connie. 'The poor girl! That could have been me!'

Both sisters exchanged glances with one another.

Jakob softened his voice. 'I want you girls to take even more care now, especially when you lock up here of an evening and it's getting dark. I can't come here every evening due to my work at the tannery, but all three Donovan brothers have said they'll take it in turns to escort you back home.'

That was a consolation at least. What if the madman struck again? No woman seemed safe in the area, after all, even Maggie had been attacked.

Connie came around to Jakob's side from behind the counter and he draped a reassuring arm around her shoulders. 'Now, I've said this before and I'll say it again, Connie. I'd like you to marry me, so we can live together as man and wife. What do you say, love?'

Ada stood there waiting as she held her breath and she had her fingers crossed behind her back.

Chapter Sixteen

'I don't think it's the time to discuss such matters,' Connie said with tears in her eyes.

Ada took it as her cue to leave the room, shaking her head. What was the matter with Connie? Many a young woman would jump at the chance of marrying a smart young man like Jakob but was the real reason because her sister was still getting over what had recently happened to her?

Ada took her time in the background, sorting out confectionary supplies and tidying around the backroom as she heard their muffled voices from the shop. After a few minutes there was the sound of a little bell tinkling, thinking it was a customer arriving, Ada made her way back onto the shop floor to see it was empty, apart from her sister who had her head in her hands, crying.

'What's wrong, Connie?' she asked gently touching her sister's elbow. 'Has Jakob upset you with something he's said?'

Connie shook her head. 'No, far from it. He's saying all the right things, it's just me. I can't wipe some of those images what I endured out of me bloomin' head. Every time Jakob comes near me now, I flinch. So, I don't know how I can marry someone if I can't get close to them?'

Ada wrapped an arm of reassurance around her sister. 'It'll be all right,' she soothed. 'Go and have a chat with Mrs Donovan, she's very understanding.'

Connie sniffed. 'Maybe yer right. I need to talk to someone when everyone else ain't around. There's things I wouldn't like to say in front of yer all.'

Ada quite understood as there were things she wouldn't like to listen to either. She went out to the back room and removing her shawl from the peg on the wall, she wrapped it around her shoulders. Then back on the shop floor, she smiled at her sister. 'I won't be long,' she said.

'Where yer off to?' Connie blinked.

'I'm going to fetch Maggie and bring her back here for a bit. You can have a chat with her in the back room while I keep an eye on the shop.'

Connie looked dubious for a moment and then smiled. 'All right. Thank you,' she said. 'Yer really good to me, our Ada.'

Ada cocked her a cheeky grin. 'And don't you forget it!' She flounced out of the shop and made her way to Maggie's house. The woman often returned home for an hour or two from her rag trolley round around this time of the day. She'd often have a bite to eat and a snooze in her armchair after being up so early attending to The Archies.

Ada found her in the backyard bending over, feeding a juicy looking bone to Jasper. She looked up and straightening herself, when she heard the gate click behind Ada, said, 'What brings you 'ere at this time of the day, gal? Thought you'd be busy on that flower stall of yer's?'

Ada nodded. 'Nah, it's quiet today. Actually, I was wondering if yer could do me a little favour, Mrs Donovan? Well it's for me sister, really.'

Maggie smiled. 'Yer name it, gal!'

'Connie's not right.' Maggie's warm, motherly face was etched with concern as she listened intently. 'She's breaking down in tears a lot of the time. Jakob's asked her to marry him but she just told me that she can't marry someone when she flinches if they come near her. I'm really worried about her.'

Maggie nodded. 'That's understandable, luvvy. After what yer Connie's been through, she ain't going to forget it nor lay it to one side overnight, is she?'

'I thought maybe she'd have felt better after that newspaper article was written about her.'

'Yes, you might think that but the poor girl's been through so much, maybe being interviewed about it all made her relive it again. What can I do for her?'

'I was thinking if yer came back with me to the shop, that's if yer have the time of course, then maybe you could speak to her in the backroom over a cup of tea.'

'Of course I will. Maybe it will help if she can get it all out of her system. After all, I know she told her tale to Stead but he's a man and there's only certain things that another woman can understand about the situation yer sister was forced into. Just lemme get me shawl and I'll come back with yer for a little hour. Gotta get me trolley out after that though.'

Ada understood. Maggie was a busy woman who didn't like letting others down. On the way to the shop, Ada told Maggie all about what had happened to Mary Jane Kelly and the awful circumstances of her death.

Maggie shook her head gravely. 'It weren't that long ago that I were attacked meself. There for by the grace of God, go I.'

***

And so, for the following couple of weeks, Maggie was a regular in the backroom of the shop, listening as Connie spilled out her story which was far more graphic and emotional than she had ever related to anyone before. Sometimes, she'd return to the shop floor wiping tears away with the back of her hand, or other times, she'd just smile and get on with it afterwards, but in all that time, Ada could see her sister was making progress. And then, finally one day, she emerged from the backroom, saw Maggie off from the premises and thanked her profusely in the process. She turned the door sign to "shut" and informed Ada that she felt as though a weight had been lifted from her shoulders and she intended seeing a contact of Ada's at the Salvation Army mission about her recent experience. The idea was to inform the young women and girls there how easy it was to get swept up by a handsome gentleman in the guise of him offering the earth when in reality, he was offering the open gates of hell. It was going to be a risk telling them her story, but Maggie had explained that her contact there said the girls and women were unlikely to judge her as they were in a predicament themselves and may well have already succumbed to the evils of prostitution.

If Connie could prevent just one young girl or woman from ending up being used in such a manner, then she would have done her job. What happened to her, hadn't been her fault to begin with but Winterbourne had started off a chain of events that she hadn't seen fit to get out of at that time. When she'd tried by leaving him at the pub that night, she failed, as in her haste to escape from his clutches, she'd been duped and drugged by an elderly woman and passed on elsewhere.

William Stead was doing his best with his legal team to secure a conviction against Edgar De Courcey for soliciting young women for immoral purposes and for shipping some overseas, but so far, the man had gone to ground and was nowhere to be seen—it was almost as though he hadn't existed in the first place as his peers were giving nothing away and any girls he'd had working for him had seemingly vanished into thin air.

The worse thing of all now for Connie was she no longer knew where she stood with Jakob after turning down his proposal, feeling awkward about the situation with him and Mrs Adler at home, she decided to seize a very good opportunity. Florrie had moved out of the premises above the shop to live with her daughter and offered it to them, so Connie, Ada and Sam moved in there for time being, paying a peppercorn rent for the property.

Ada wondered if Jakob would ever call on her sister again.

**

It was now approaching Christmas and as well as De Courcey going to ground, so had Jack the Ripper. The Autumn of terror was still fresh in folk's minds and an eerie atmosphere descended on Whitechapel as some worried that the murderer would strike again in the East End of London as a way of marking the festive season.

Ada and Connie were rushed off their feet selling Christmas confectionary and festive flowers. People wanted to purchase boxes of chocolates for loved ones and more affordable small pink or white sugar mice and Bentley's Chocolate Drops for children's Christmas stockings. Maggie was taking care of Sam as they had a lot of work ahead of them that day and wouldn't be shutting the shop until late on Christmas Eve. Maggie had invited them over for a Christmas Eve supper that evening and both girls were looking forward to it.

Connie had all but given up on Jakob calling on her again. She figured that by now he'd found someone else. Several times she'd said to Ada, 'He probably got fed up of asking in me in the end! And who could blame him?'

When the final customer had departed, they turned off the shop lights and stood outside as Connie fiddled with her key to lock the door. Twilight had disappeared and now it was dark except for the glow of the gas lights on the street corners. A thick fog had descended giving the street an eerie appearance and Ada didn't much fancy going out in it either.

'It's a pea souper fog tonight!' Connie exclaimed as she linked arms with Ada to walk to Maggie's place. 'We better stick together as we could get lost in this.'

On the way along the street they almost collided with several people, one of whom was a man with some sort of package under his arm.

'Sorry, sir!' said Connie.

The man stopped for a moment. 'Connie? Connie Cooper?'

'Yes, sir. Who is it?'

'I'm Mr Gerald Dunbar of Dunbar, Grimshaw and Associates, a law firm employed by William Stead of the Pall Mall Gazette. We met briefly last month. I was just on my way to see you. Is there somewhere we might speak?'

Ada's stomach lurched, she hoped this wasn't bad news.

'I…I remember now. You can come back to the shop with us,' Connie said with a note of trepidation in her voice.

They retraced their steps and soon were sitting in the living room of the premises above, while Gerald Dunbar explained his presence. 'You see,' he cleared his throat as both girls sat opposite him, 'Edgar De Courcey is a tricky customer. He has many aliases. De Courcey is his real name but he was finally caught trying to board a ship to Calais in France.' He placed the palms of his hands together, almost as if in prayer. Ada marvelled at the fine cloth of his garments and guessed he must be paid handsomely for his profession to afford an astrakhan coat like that.

Ada watched as her sister's mouth popped open with surprise. She closed it again to ask, 'But where is he now, Mr Dunbar?'

Mr Dunbar smiled. 'Currently, he's being interviewed at the Leman Street Police Station…'

Connie frowned. 'What will happen to him, Mr Dunbar?'

'He'll appear before the court on the day after Boxing Day, 27th of December, and charged with the offences of running a house of ill repute and the abduction of females to France and Belgium. Now, I need your help…'

'Anything!' Connie said suddenly. 'I'd do anything to get that man behind bars so he can't hurt anymore innocent young women or girls!'

'Good,' said Dunbar. 'I was hoping you'd say that! I'll be representing you and several other young ladies I've managed to trace who are equally keen to tell their stories to the court on that particular day.'

After the news had sunk in, Connie offered Mr Dunbar some refreshment but he declined telling them he was off to dinner with friends that evening and already running a little late. When hearing he had delayed the two of them from their own Christmas supper at the Donovans, he offered them a lift there in his coach which they gratefully accepted—anything to be out of that thick fog, hopefully it would lift for their return home. In any case, the Donovan brothers would safely escort them back home.

***

Everyone was in fine spirits in the Donovan household when Connie and Ada arrived carrying Christmas packages for the now, extended, family. Frannie couldn't wait to see Ada and took her off for a natter to the bedroom, while Sam ran to Connie asking her what she'd brought for him and Molly from the shop. Both children's eyes lit up like beacons as Connie handed them a white sugared mouse each. Then she turned to Maggie and handed her a beautifully wrapped box of chocolates. 'They're all soft centres,' said Connie, 'as I remember you telling me you avoid the hard ones due to your missing teeth!'

Maggie nodded and embraced her. 'What 'ave I done to deserve this?' she beamed.

'Oh, you've done such a lot for me, I can never repay you.' Connie patted the woman on her shoulder.

'I didn't do much, ducks.'

'Oh, but you did. You wouldn't believe how our little chats and your wise words helped to release the chains that were binding me.'

'That's good, gal. But there's some other reason why yer glowing like that, ain't there?'

'Yes, I have an announcement to make!' she playfully shooed Sam and Molly off to the bedroom with Ada and Frannie. When she'd closed the door behind them, she turned to the rest of them, Maggie and her three sons. 'The reason we're a little late is I just received an unexpected caller, a Mr Gerald Dunbar. He's one of William Stead's legal team…' Everyone looked on with wide eyes. 'And the good news is that De Courcey has been captured!'

Davy and Billy began to whoop with delight and as they'd just entered the house still had their flat caps on their heads, so they tossed them in mid-air, much to Danny's astonishment.

'That's fantastic news!' Maggie beamed.

'That's not all though…I'm going to be asked to give evidence at the police court at Leman Street on the day after Boxing day. The police have found another couple of women who are willing to give evidence…'

'That should carry some weight then, gal!' Maggie hugged her and to Connie's surprise, danced a little jig with her to show how pleased she was. Davy and Billy joined in and finally Danny did the same.

'All we need now is someone on the piano!' Maggie laughed. 'Let's eat! I've prepared enough food for the five thousand!'

It was such a special moment and Christmas Day itself was still to come.

***

Ada woke up in her own bed back at the shop flat the following morning. There was something different, wasn't there? It was Christmas day itself but somehow it seemed quiet outside, too quiet. She rushed to the window and drew back the curtains to see that the whole of the outside street was carpeted with snow and it was still coming down heavily. Thank goodness they'd left Maggie's place when they had last night as they might have ended up stranded there otherwise! Not that Maggie would have minded as she was well used to waifs and strays. Billy and Davy had insisted on seeing them safely back home and were in high spirits after hearing the news about De Courcey's incarceration.

'Sam!' Ada shouted. 'Come and see!'

Sam lay in his single bed, oblivious to the outside world. He was still such a heavy sleeper but she wanted him to see this. 'Whassa want, Ada?' he slurred, opening one eye.

'It's Christmas day and it's snowing!' she yelled.

That was enough to rouse him from his heavy slumber, he pulled himself up on his haunches and got out of bed to stumble towards the window, pressing his nose against the cold glass which steamed up from his breath. He looked up excitedly at his sister. 'Has *he* been?'

'I don't know yet!' she laughed. 'Go and put your dressing gown and slippers on and we'll go to the living room to see.'

'Wheeee!' he shouted. It was lovely to see him so happy after the upset of the past few months.

When they entered the living room, there was a roaring fire in the grate and the table was placed in the centre of the room, laid with a red cloth and set for breakfast. Ada could smell the aroma of bacon frying and hear the sizzle in the pan. Connie had been up early to prepare all of this. She'd even strung some colourful paper chains and lanterns across the fire place and above all the paintings and portraits that hung on the walls were small sprigs of holly and ivy.

'Cor!' said Sam. 'Father Christmas must have done all of this!'

'More like Mother Christmas!' laughed Ada. Then she spoke in hushed tones to him. 'Keep watch and let me know if Connie comes in the room as I want to surprise her.'

His eyebrows lifted with surprise and he nodded.

In her pocket was a small sprig of mistletoe that she'd kept back from her flower stall. She stood on a chair and placed it on top of the door frame, then she replaced the chair back under the table.

'What you doing that for, our Ada?' Sam frowned.

'Ssssh!' she put her index finger to her lips. 'It's a surprise for Connie. Don't say anything.'

Presently, the door attached to the kitchen opened and Connie emerged with a large plate of bacon rashers and another of bread and butter. Sam's eyes lit up.

'There's a jug of fresh orange juice on the table!' Connie announced 'And I've just made a pot of tea and the scrambled eggs are in the covered silver dish, help yourselves. Then you can open your Christmas presents!'

Sam immediately forgot his breakfast. 'Ohh, where are they, Connie? I can't see them?' he asked, baffled.

'They're under the Christmas tree that Father Christmas left in sitting room.' She winked at Ada.

'But please, can I see them now!' He pouted.

Connie smiled. 'No, eat your breakfast first, then you may see them!'

It was hard work for Sam trying to eat his breakfast while having to wait to see what Father Christmas had brought him. Ada didn't mind waiting at all as she was far more excited about something else, if her idea went to plan that was.

Following breakfast, they entered the sitting room which overlooked the street outside to see the small Christmas tree nicely decorated with baubles and candles, which Connie, bless her heart, must have stayed up all night to work on. Beneath it were several gifts, nicely wrapped in boxes and tied with bows.

'Go on then, Sam!' Connie urged wringing her hands. 'The ones with your name on are nearest the fire place and Ada's yours are on the left.'

Sam immediately ran off and threw himself on his knees to tear apart the wrapping paper. His sisters watched his delighted face as there was a wooden train, painted dark blue, with wooden rails; a book about cowboys and Indians; and a sailing boat he could take to the park. His joy was evident as he began to set out the train track and place the train on it.

Ada took her sister's hand and placed something inside of it. 'What's this?' Connie asked as she turned her palm over to see a small box.

'Open it!' Ada urged.

Connie pulled the lid off to see an emerald and gold coloured brooch inside. 'Oh, my, it's beautiful!' she gasped. 'But how could you possibly afford it?'

'It's only glass and paste but it looked so lovely in the window at the dolly shop and I knew it was meant for you as it matches the colour of yer eyes!' she said.

'Oh thank you, Ada!' She hugged her sister to her. 'Now you go and open yer gifts.'

Ada nodded. She knew by now of course that there was no Father Christmas and all the presents beneath the tree had come from Connie. Her confectionary business was doing well and she had become a keen business woman.

Ada smiled when she unwrapped her gifts as there was a new hairbrush for her in amongst them. She had long admired her sister's tortoise shell one which of course the girl wouldn't part with as it had been given by their parents, but Connie had bought Ada a hairbrush and mirror set inside a mother of pearl casing, it was so beautiful. She also received an elaborate leather covered diary and a new fountain pen. Looking up at her sister with tears in her eyes, she said, 'These are the nicest gifts anyone's ever given me…thank you!'

'Sssh!' whispered Connie, 'We still want Sam to believe these have all come from Father Christmas.' She handed both of them a red felt stocking which contained pink and white sugared mice, a small bag of nuts and a tangerine.

Sam couldn't believe his luck as Christmases weren't usually this decadent. 'I must have been a very good boy this year!' he beamed which caused both Ada and Connie to smile with tears in their eyes. It had been an arduous year indeed.

There was one special gift though that Ada knew would make Connie's Christmas for her. She'd looked so sad of late since Jakob no longer called around to see them but Ada had found a way to solve that. Early on Christmas eve morning after calling to the market place for her flowers, she'd taken a detour to see Jakob and explain what had been going on with her sister and how she'd been discussing her feelings with Maggie. She hadn't meant to push him away and now she felt her sister regretted it.

Jakob had listened intently and smiled at her. 'I'm glad you've told me this, Ada,' he said, as his mother beamed behind him. 'Me and Ma were only discussing this yesterday and I was going to call over during the Christmas period anyhow, and now you've confirmed her feelings for me, I shall be over early on Christmas morning, if that's all right with you?'

'Yes, of course it is. We'll keep it a surprise, right?'

He chuckled. 'We will!' Then he'd winked at her.

Christmas morning had now arrived, so she glanced at the clock on the mantelpiece, it was almost a half past ten. Then she went over to the window and lifted the lace curtain to glance outside. There Jakob was walking along the street, it had stopped snowing for time being. When he saw her he looked up and held up his thumb, Ada did the same back at him, then she dropped the curtain to stand at her sister's side.

There was a rap on the shop door downstairs.

'Now who can that be?' said Connie crossly. 'Don't customers realise it's Christmas day?'

'You'd better go down and see!' Ada looked at her sister.

'I suppose so.'

Ada and Sam followed in Connie's footsteps and the shop bell tinkled as Connie drew it open wide. 'I'm sorry,' she said to the male figure in front of her who had his back to her. He was wearing a long black coat and had his collar turned up against the weather. 'We're closed until December the 28th!'

The figure turned around and Connie startled when she saw it was Jakob stood there looking handsome in his new coat. Snowflakes had settled on his cap and on his shoulders. His eyes sparkled with delight to see them all, particularly Connie.

'Come in out of the cold, Jakob,' she greeted as he set foot over the threshold.

He held two gift wrapped boxes and handed one to Sam and the other to Ada. 'Merry Christmas, kids!' he said. 'Those are from myself and my mother.'

Both children nodded their thanks at him.

Ada waited with bated breath. She'd placed another piece of mistletoe on the shop ceiling before going to bed last night. She pointed up to it behind her sister's back. Jakob nodded as he appeared to hold his breath as he moved just beneath it. 'I have this for you, Connie,' he said, offering her a small black velvet box.

She blinked several times as she took it from his hand. 'Oh, what is it?'

'Come and see!'

Ada watched as her sister stepped just beneath the mistletoe.

'Ah, mistletoe!' declared Jakob as Connie looked up and he planted a kiss upon her lips. She closed her eyes and returned the kiss passionately. Then she opened them to gaze at him.

'Merry Christmas, my darling, will you marry me now?'

Connie nodded with tears in her eyes. 'Yes, yes. I'll be your wife, Jakob, and gladly so.' The tears were now streaming down both of her cheeks.

'Then you need to open that box,' he urged.

Connie opened it to see a beautiful ruby ring set with small diamonds, displayed within. 'Do you like it?'

'Like it? I love it!' she said wide eyed with wonder. 'But how did you afford such an expensive looking ring?'

He smiled. 'It was my grandmother's from the old country. When me and Ma were speaking last night, she told me she wanted me to give it to you and I thought that was a wonderful idea.'

'Oh, it is!'

Noticing them embracing once more, Ada turned to Sam and said, 'Come on, let's leave them to it and open our gifts upstairs. They've got a lot to talk about.'

Sam grinned. 'So, Jakob will be living with us soon?'

'I guess he will be and Mrs Adler too, I expect.'

'Oh, good!' said Sam, 'she makes the best crumpets in the whole, wide world!'

Ada chuckled as she closed the door behind them...

Epilogue

It was a glorious spring morning during April of 1889. So far, there was no more news of any further Jack the Ripper murders in the East End of London. Some believed the serial killer may have fled to the Continent or even America. For time being, at least, things felt a little safer in Whitechapel.

Edgar De Courcey had been given a stiff jail sentence of twelve years for his part in importuning young women and keeping them as prisoners against their will. December the 27th of 1888, had felt the day that Connie Cooper could finally move on with her life after giving evidence against the man.

Ada watched as her sister got herself ready for church. She was wearing a beautiful taffeta rose pink gown that Maggie had skilfully sewn for her and she'd even managed to embroider some small seed pearls into the bodice. Frank had delivered the wedding gown the previous evening, both sisters had remarked on how close Maggie and Frank had grown of late.

Ada helped her sister coil her ringleted hair into a very chic looking style so that tendrils of hair framed her elfin shaped face and highlighted her shiny green eyes. 'Yer do look lovely, our Connie!' Ada beamed as she stepped back to admire her handiwork.

'So do you!' Connie smiled. 'Yer look so pretty in that floral dress Maggie made for you. And doesn't Sam look so handsome in his little black waistcoat and white shirt?' Ada had to admit he did. Quite the little gentleman. Sam blushed and he looked away as his sisters spoke about him.

'He does indeed…' Ada chuckled.

'It'll be great to have everyone who means anything to us at the church today!' Connie declared. Apart from the Donovan family, Frannie and Molly, Frank, themselves of course and Mrs Adler, Connie's friend from the match factory, Rose, would be there too.

Sam ran over to the window. 'Billy and Davy are here!' he shouted.

Ada looked down at the street below to see that the brothers had decorated their horse and cart with lots of ribbons and bunting especially for today. Behind them, Frank Malone and his donkey and cart awaited, which was also decorated in a similar fashion.

The idea was for Ada and Sam to travel with Frank and Connie would go with the brothers.

As the horse and cart set off at a brisk trot, followed by the donkey and cart, Ada looked around and smiled. 'It's a lovely day today, Frank!' she said.

'Aye, it is an' all! A grand day for a wedding it is, young Ada!'

People waved at them on the street as they passed by, word had got around that Connie Cooper from the confectionary shop was getting wed today. Ada and Sam waved back enthusiastically.

And as they approached the church and walked beneath the archway, Ada noticed Connie taking a glance at their parents' grave as she dropped a red rose onto it from her bouquet. Then the organist struck up and the strains of Mendelssohn's "The Wedding March" was being played. Ada's tummy flipped over with the excitement of it all as soon heads would turn to focus on her sister as the man she loved stood in the front pew of the church waiting for his bride to be. And Ada knew how Jakob Adler had waited for this special day for such a long time as Connie Cooper was the only woman for him.

Printed in Great Britain
by Amazon